BIT

11/15

UNFORGIVEN

ALSO BY LAUREN KATE

THE FALLEN SERIES

Fallen

Torment

Passion

Rapture

Fallen in Love

THE TEARDROP SERIES

Teardrop

Waterfall

The Betrayal of Natalie Hargrove

LAUREN KATE

UNFORGIVEN

⫷ A FALLEN NOVEL ⫸

DELACORTE PRESS

Text copyright © 2015 by Tinderbox Books, LLC, and Lauren Kate

TINDERBOX

Jacket photograph copyright © 2015 by Carrie Schechter

Epigraph copyright © 2012 Country Ahers Music (BMI) administered by Songs in the House of Hassle (BMI).

All songs © 2015 Amandavid (ASCAP). All rights reserved.

Published in the United States by Delacorte Press, an imprint of Random House Children's Books, a division of Penguin Random House LLC, New York.

Delacorte Press is a registered trademark and the colophon is a trademark of Penguin Random House LLC.

randomhouseteens.com

Educators and librarians, for a variety of teaching tools, visit us at RHTeachersLibrarians.com

Library of Congress Cataloging-in-Publication Data is available upon request. ISBN 978-0-385-74263-4 (hc) — ISBN 978-0-375-99068-7 (lib. bdg.) — ISBN 978-0-307-97630-7 (ebook) — ISBN 978-1-101-93127-1 (intl. tr. pbk.)

The text of this book is set in 12-point Classical Garamond BT.

Printed in the United States of America
10 9 8 7 6 5 4 3 2 1
First Edition

FOR DREAMERS

Serpents in my mind

Trying to forgive your crimes

Everyone changes in time

I hope he changes this time

※

—SHARON VAN ETTEN, *"Serpents"*

PROLOGUE

NEVER TEAR US APART

Cam's boots touched down on the eaves of the old church beneath a cold and starry sky. He drew his wings close and gazed out at the landscape. Spanish moss, white in the moonlight, hung like icicles from antebellum trees. Cinder-block buildings framed a weedy field and a pair of splintery bleachers. Wind rustled in from the sea.

Winter break at Sword & Cross Reform School. Not a soul on campus. What was he doing here?

It was minutes after midnight, and he'd just flown in from Troy. He'd made the journey in a haze, an unknown force guiding his wings. He found himself humming a tune he hadn't let himself remember for several thousand years.

Maybe he'd come back here because this was where the fallen angels had met Luce in her last, cursed life. It had been her three hundred and twenty-fourth incarnation—and the three hundred and twenty-fourth time the fallen angels had flocked together to see how the curse would play out.

The curse was broken now. Luce and Daniel were free.

And dammit if Cam wasn't jealous.

His gaze swept across the cemetery. He would never have guessed he'd feel nostalgic for this junkyard, but there had been something thrilling about those early days at Sword & Cross. Lucinda's spark had been brighter, keeping the angels guessing when they'd once believed they knew what to expect.

For six millennia, each time she turned seventeen, they'd staged a variation of the same performance: the demons—Cam, Roland, and Molly—tried everything to sway Luce's alliances to Lucifer, while the angels—Arriane and Gabbe and sometimes Annabelle—worked to usher Luce back into Heaven's fold. Neither side had ever come close to winning her over.

For every time Luce met Daniel—and she always met Daniel—nothing mattered as much as their love. Time and again, they fell for each other, and time and again, Luce died in a blaze of fire.

Then, one night at Sword & Cross, everything changed. Daniel kissed Lucinda, and she lived. They all knew it then. Luce was finally going to be allowed to choose.

A few weeks later they all flew to the site of their original fall, to Troy, where Lucinda chose her destiny. She and Daniel again refused to side with Heaven or with Hell. Instead, they chose each other. They gave up their immortality to spend one mortal lifetime together.

Luce and Daniel were gone now, but they were still on Cam's mind. Their triumphant love made him yearn for something he dared not put into words.

He was humming again. That song. Even after all this time, he remembered it. . . .

He closed his eyes and saw its singer: the back of her red hair woven loosely in a braid, her long fingers caressing the strings of a lyre as she leaned against a tree.

He hadn't let himself think of her in thousands of years. Why now?

"This can's busted," a familiar voice said. "Toss me another?"

Cam spun around. No one was there.

He noticed a flicker of movement through the shattered stained-glass window on the roof. He edged forward and peered down through it, into the chapel Sophia Bliss had used as her office when she was the Sword & Cross librarian.

Inside the chapel, Arriane's iridescent wings flexed as she shook a can of spray paint and rose off the ground, aiming the nozzle at the wall.

Her mural featured a girl in a glowing blue forest. She wore a tiered black dress and looked up at a blond boy who held out a white peony. *Luce and Daniel 4ever* Arriane sprayed in gothic silver letters over the bell of the girl's skirt.

Behind Arriane, a dark-skinned demon with dreadlocks was lighting a tall glass candle showing Santa Muerte, the goddess of death. Roland was making a shrine at the site where Sophia had murdered Luce's friend Penn.

Fallen angels couldn't enter sanctuaries of God. As soon as they crossed the threshold, the whole place would go up in flames, incinerating every mortal inside. But this chapel had been desanctified when Miss Sophia had moved in.

Cam spread his wings and dropped through the broken window, landing behind Arriane.

"Cam." Roland embraced his friend.

"Take it easy," Cam said, but he didn't pull away.

Roland tilted his head. "Quite a coincidence, finding you here."

"Is it?" Cam asked.

"Not if you like *carnitas*," Arriane said, tossing Cam a small foil-wrapped package. "Remember the taco truck on Lovington? I've been craving these ever since we fled this swamp." She opened her own foil package and devoured her taco in two bites. "Delish."

"What are you doing here?" Roland asked Cam.

Cam leaned against a cold marble pillar and shrugged. "I left my Les Paul in the dorm."

"All this way for a guitar?" Roland nodded. "I suppose we've all got to find new ways to fill our endless days, now that Luce and Daniel are gone."

Cam had always hated the force that pulled the fallen angels to the cursed lovers every seventeen years. He'd left battlefields and coronations. He'd left the arms of exquisite girls. Once he'd walked off a movie set. He'd dropped everything for Luce and Daniel. But now that the irresistible pull was gone, he missed it.

His eternity was open wide. What was he going to do with it?

"Did what happened in Troy give you, I don't know . . ." Roland trailed off.

"Hope?" Arriane grabbed Cam's uneaten taco and downed it. "If, after all these thousands of years, Luce and Daniel can stand up to the Throne and seize a happy ending, why can't anyone? Why can't *we*?"

Cam gazed through the shattered window. "Maybe I'm not that kind of guy."

"We all carry pieces of our journeys within us," Roland said. "We all learn from our mistakes. Who's to say we don't deserve happiness?"

"Listen to us." Arriane touched the scars on her neck. "What do we three jaded birds of prey know about love?" She looked from Cam to Roland. "Right?"

"Love's not the exclusive property of Luce and Daniel," Roland said. "We've all tasted it. Maybe we will again."

Roland's optimism struck a dissonant chord with Cam. "Not me," he said.

Arriane sighed, arching her back to spread her wings and rise a few feet off the ground. A fluttering sound filled the empty church. With deft slashes of her can of white spray paint, she added the subtlest hint of wings above Lucinda's shoulders.

Before the Fall, angels' wings were made of empyreal light, all of them perfect, one pair indistinguishable from the next. In the era since, their wings had become expressive of their personalities, their mistakes and impulses. The fallen angels who had given their allegiance to Lucifer bore golden wings. Those who had returned to the fold of Heaven bore the Throne's hint of silver throughout their fibers.

Lucinda's wings had been special. They had been purely, stunningly white. Unspoiled. Innocent of the choices the rest of them had made. The only other fallen angel who had preserved his white wings was Daniel.

Arriane crumpled the second taco wrapper. "Sometimes I wonder . . ."

"What?" Roland asked.

"If you guys could go back and not screw up so epically in the love department, would you?"

"What's the point of wondering?" Cam asked. "Rosaline is dead." He saw Roland wince at the mention of his lost beloved. "Tess will never forgive you," he added, looking at Arriane. "And Lilith—"

There. He'd said her name.

Lilith was the only girl Cam had ever loved. He'd asked her to marry him.

It hadn't worked out.

He heard her song again, throbbing in his soul, blinding him with regret.

"Are you humming?" Arriane narrowed her eyes at Cam. "Since when do you hum?"

"What *about* Lilith?" Roland said.

Lilith was dead, too. Though Cam had never known how she had lived out her days on earth after they parted, he knew she would have left this world and ascended to Heaven long ago. If Cam were a different kind of guy, it might have brought him peace to imagine her enfolded in joy and light. But Heaven was so painfully distant, he found it best not to think of her at all.

Roland seemed to be reading his mind. "You could do it your own way."

"I do everything my own way," Cam said. His wings pulsed silently behind him.

"It's one of your best traits," Roland said, looking up at the stars through the ruined ceiling, then back at Cam again.

"What?" Cam asked.

Roland laughed softly. "I didn't say anything."

"Allow me," Arriane said. "Cam, this is totally when everyone expects you to make one of your dramatic exits into that pocket in the clouds." She pointed to a rope of fog dangling from Orion's Belt.

"Cam." Roland stared at Cam, alarmed. "Your wings."

Near the tip of Cam's left wing was a single, tiny white filament.

Arriane gaped. "What does it mean?"

It was one white fleck amid a field of gold, but it forced Cam to remember the moment his wings had changed from white to gold. He had long ago accepted his destiny, but now, for the first time in millennia, he imagined something else.

Thanks to Luce and Daniel, Cam had a fresh start. And only one regret.

"I have to go." He fully extended his wings, and brilliant golden light flooded the chapel as Roland and Arriane leaped out of the way. The candle tipped and shattered, its flame dwindling on the cold stone floor.

Cam shot into the sky, piercing the night, and headed toward the darkness that had been awaiting him since the moment he'd flown away from Lilith's love.

ONE

WASTELAND

LILITH

Lilith woke up coughing.

It was wildfire season—it was always wildfire season—and her lungs were thick with smoke and ash from the red blaze in the hills.

Her bedside clock flashed midnight, but her thin white curtains glowed gray with dawn. The power must be out again. She thought of the biology test awaiting her in fourth period, followed immediately by the sucky fact that last night she'd brought home her American history book by mistake. Whose idea of a cruel joke was it to assign her two textbooks with precisely the same color spine? She was going to have to wing the test and pray for a C.

She slid out of bed and stepped in something warm and soft. She drew her foot up, and the smell assaulted her.

"Alastor!"

The little blond mutt trotted into her bedroom, thinking Lilith wanted to play. Her mom called the dog a genius because of the tricks Lilith's brother, Bruce, had taught him, but Alastor was four years old and refused to learn the only trick that mattered: being housebroken.

"This is seriously uncivilized," she scolded the dog, and hopped on one foot into the bathroom. She turned on the shower.

Nothing.

Water off till 3 p.m. her mom's note proclaimed on a sheet of loose-leaf taped to the bathroom mirror. The tree roots outside were curling through their pipes, and her mom was supposed to have money to pay the plumber this afternoon, after she got a paycheck from one of her many part-time jobs.

Lilith groped for toilet paper, hoping at least to wipe her foot clean. She found only a brown cardboard tube. Just another Tuesday. The details varied, but every day of Lilith's life was more or less the same degree of awful.

She tore her mom's note from the mirror and used it to wipe her foot, then dressed in black jeans and a thin black T-shirt, not looking at her reflection. She tried to remember a single shred of what her biology teacher had said might be on the test.

By the time she got downstairs, Bruce was tilting the remains of the cereal box into his mouth. Lilith knew those stale flakes were the last morsels of food in the house.

"We're out of milk," Bruce said.

"And cereal?" Lilith said.

"And cereal. And everything." Bruce was eleven and nearly as tall as Lilith, but much slighter. He was sick. He had always been sick. He was born too soon, with a heart that couldn't keep up with his soul, Lilith's mother liked to say. Bruce's eyes were sunken and his skin had a bluish tint because his lungs could never get enough air. When the hills were on fire, like they were every day, he wheezed at the smallest exertion. He stayed home in bed more often than he went to school.

Lilith knew Bruce needed breakfast more than she did, but her stomach still growled in protest. Food, water, basic hygiene products—everything was scarce in the dilapidated dump they called home.

She glanced through the grimy kitchen window and saw her bus pulling away from the stop. She groaned, grabbing her guitar case and her backpack, making sure her black journal was inside.

"Later, Bruce," she called, and took off.

Horns blared and tires squealed as Lilith sprinted across the street without looking, like she always told Bruce not to do. Despite her terrible luck, she never worried about dying. Death would mean freedom from the panicked hamster wheel of her life, and Lilith knew she wasn't that lucky. The universe or God or *something* wanted to keep her miserable.

She watched the bus rumble off, and then started walking the three miles to school with her guitar case bouncing against her back. She hurried across her street, past the strip mall with the dollar store and the drive-through Chinese place that was always going in and out of business. Once she got a few blocks beyond her own gritty neighborhood, known around town as the Slump, the sidewalks smoothed out and the roads had fewer potholes. The people who stepped outside to get their papers were wearing business suits, not the ratty bathrobes Lilith's neighbors often wore. A well-coiffed woman walking her Great Dane waved good morning, but Lilith didn't have time for pleasantries. She ducked through the concrete pedestrian tunnel that ran beneath the highway.

Trumbull Preparatory School sat at the corner of High Meadow Road and Highway 2—which Lilith mostly associated with stressful trips to the emergency room when Bruce got really sick. Speeding down the pavement in her mother's purple minivan, her brother wheezing faintly against her shoulder, Lilith always gazed out the window at the green signs on the side of the highway, marking the miles to other cities. Even though she hadn't seen much—anything—outside of Crossroads, Lilith liked to imagine the great, wide world beyond it. She liked to think that someday, if she ever graduated, she'd escape to a better place.

The late bell was ringing when she emerged from the tunnel near the edge of campus. She was coughing, her eyes burning. The smoldering wildfires in the hills that encircled her town wreathed the school in smoke. The brown stucco building was ugly, and made even uglier by its papering of student-made banners. One advertised tomorrow's basketball game, another spelled out the details for the after-school science fair meeting, but most of them featured blown-up yearbook photos of some jock named Dean who was trying to win votes for prom king.

At Trumbull's main entrance stood Principal Tarkenton. He was barely over five feet tall and wore a burgundy polyester suit.

"Late again, Ms. Foscor," he said, studying her with distaste. "Didn't I see your name on yesterday's detention list for tardiness?"

"Funny thing about detention," Lilith said. "I seem to learn more there staring at the wall than I ever have in class."

"Get to first period," Tarkenton said, taking a step toward Lilith, "and if you give your mother one second of trouble in class today—"

Lilith swallowed. "My mom's here?"

Her mom substituted a few days a month at Trumbull, earning a tuition waiver that was the only reason she could afford to send Lilith to the school. Lilith never knew when she might find her mom waiting ahead of her in the cafeteria line or blotting her lipstick in the ladies' room. She never told Lilith when she would be gracing Trumbull's campus, and she never offered her daughter a ride to school.

It was always a horrible surprise, but at least Lilith had never walked in on her mother substituting in one of her own classes.

Until today, it seemed. She groaned and headed inside, wondering which of her classes her mom would turn up in.

She was spared in homeroom, where Mrs. Richards had already finished the roll and was furiously writing on the board about ways students could help with her hopeless campaign to bring recycling to campus. When Lilith walked in, the teacher shook her head wordlessly, as if she were simply bored by Lilith's habitual lateness.

She slid into her seat, dropped her guitar case at her feet, and took out the biology book she'd just grabbed from her locker. There were ten precious minutes left in homeroom, and Lilith needed them all to cram for her test.

"Mrs. Richards," the girl next to Lilith said, glaring in her direction. "Something suddenly smells awful in here."

Lilith rolled her eyes. She and Chloe King had been enemies since day one of elementary school, though she couldn't remember why. It wasn't like Lilith was any kind of threat to the rich, gorgeous senior. Chloe modeled for

Crossroads Apparel and was the lead singer of a pop band called the Perceived Slights, not to mention the president of at least half of Trumbull's extracurricular clubs.

After more than a decade of Chloe's nastiness, Lilith was used to the constant rain of attacks. On a good day, she ignored them. Today she focused on the genomes and phonemes in her bio book and tried to tune Chloe out.

But now the other kids around Lilith were pinching their noses. The kid in front of her mimed a retching motion.

Chloe swiveled in her seat. "Is that your cheap idea of perfume, Lilith, or did you just crap your pants?"

Lilith remembered the mess Alastor had left by her bedside and the shower she hadn't been able to take, and felt her cheeks burn. She grabbed her things and bolted from the classroom, ignoring Mrs. Richards's ravings about a hall pass, and ducked into the closest bathroom.

Inside, alone, she leaned against the red door and closed her eyes. She wished she could hide in here all day, but she knew once the bell rang, this place would be flooded with students. She forced herself to the sink. She turned on the hot water, kicked off her shoe, raised her offending foot into the basin, and pumped the cheap pink soap dispenser. She glanced up, expecting to see her sad reflection, and instead she found a glittery poster taped over the mirror. *Vote King for Queen,* it read below a professional head shot of a beaming Chloe King.

Prom was later this month, and the anticipation seemed to consume every other kid at school. Lilith had seen a hundred of these kinds of posters in the halls. She'd walked behind girls showing each other pictures of their dream corsages on their phones on their way to class. She'd heard the boys joke about what happened after prom. All of it made Lilith gag. Even if she had money for a dress, and even if there were a guy she actually wanted to go with, there was no way she would ever set foot in her high school when she wasn't legally required to be there.

She tore Chloe's poster from the mirror and used it to clean the inside of her shoe, then tossed it into the sink, letting the water run over it until Chloe's face was nothing but wet pulp.

⸙

In poetry, Mr. Davidson was so engrossed in writing Shakespeare's Sonnet 20 on the board that he didn't even notice Lilith come in late.

She sat down cautiously, watching the other kids, waiting for someone to hold their nose or gag, but luckily they only seemed to notice Lilith as a means for passing notes. Paige, the sporty blond girl to Lilith's left, would nudge her, then slide a folded note onto her desk. It wasn't labeled, but Lilith knew, of course, that it wasn't meant for her. It was for Kimi Grace, the cool half Korean, half

Mexican girl sitting to her right. Lilith had passed enough notes between these two to glimpse snatches of their plans for prom—the epic after-party and the sick stretch limo they were pooling their allowances to hire. Lilith had never been given an allowance. If her mom had any cash to spare, it went straight to Bruce's medical bills.

"Right, Lilith?" Mr. Davidson asked, making Lilith flinch. She shoved the note under her desk so she wouldn't get caught.

"Could you say that again?" Lilith asked. She really did not want to piss off Mr. Davidson. Poetry was the only class she liked, mostly because she wasn't failing it, and Mr. Davidson was the only teacher she'd ever met who seemed to enjoy his job. He'd even liked some of the song lyrics Lilith had turned in as poetry assignments. She still had the loose-leaf paper on which Mr. Davidson had written simply *Wow!* beneath the lyrics for a song she called "Exile."

"I said you've signed up for the open mic, I hope?" Davidson asked.

"Yeah, sure," she mumbled, but she hadn't and hoped not to. She didn't even know when it was.

Davidson smiled, pleased and surprised. He turned to the rest of the class. "Then we all have something to look forward to!"

As soon as Davidson turned back to his board, Kimi Grace nudged Lilith. When Lilith met Kimi's dark, pretty eyes, she wondered for a moment if Kimi wanted to talk about the open mic, if the idea of reading in front of an audience made her nervous, too. But all Kimi wanted from Lilith was the folded note in her hand.

Lilith sighed and passed it to her.

She tried to skip gym to study for her bio test, but of course she got caught and ended up having to do laps in her gym uniform and her combat boots. The school didn't issue tennis shoes, and her mom never had the cash to get her any, so the sound of her feet, running circles around the other kids who were playing volleyball in the gym, was deafening.

Everyone was looking at her. No one had to say the word *freak* out loud. She knew they were thinking it.

By the time Lilith made it to biology, she was beat down and worn out. And that was where she found her mom, wearing a lime-green skirt, her hair in a tight bun, handing out the tests.

"Just perfect," Lilith said with a groan.

"Shhhhhh!" a dozen students replied.

Her mom was tall and dark, with an angular beauty. Lilith was fair, her hair as red as the fire in the hills. Her nose was shorter than her mother's, her eyes and mouth less fine. Their cheekbones sat at different angles.

Her mom smiled. "Won't you please take a seat?"

As if she didn't even know her daughter's name.

But her daughter knew hers. "Sure thing, Janet," Lilith

said, dropping into an empty desk in the row nearest the door.

Her mom's angry gaze flicked to Lilith's face; then she smiled and looked away.

Kill them with kindness was one of her mom's favorite sayings, at least in public. At home, she wore a harsher manner. All that her mom loathed about her life she blamed on Lilith, because Lilith had been born when her mom was nineteen and beautiful, on her way to a remarkable future. By the time Bruce came along, her mom had recovered enough from the trauma of Lilith to become an actual mother. The fact that their dad was out of the picture—no one knew where he was—gave her mother all the more reason to live for her son.

The first page of the biology test was a grid in which they were expected to map dominant and recessive genes. The girl to her left was rapidly filling in boxes. Suddenly Lilith could not remember a single thing she had learned all year. Her throat itched, and she could feel the back of her neck begin to sweat.

The door to the hallway was open. It had to be cooler out there. Almost before she knew what she was doing, Lilith was standing in the doorway, her backpack in one hand, her guitar case in the other.

"Leaving class without a hall pass is an automatic detention!" Janet called. "Lilith, put down that guitar and come back here!"

Lilith's experience with authority had taught her to listen carefully to what she was told—and then do the opposite.

She bumped down the hall and hit the door running.

⚜

Outside, the air was white and hot. Ash twisted down from the sky, drifting onto Lilith's hair and the brittle gray-green grass. The most inconspicuous way to leave school grounds was through one of the exits beyond the cafeteria, which led out to a small area of gravel where kids ate lunch when the weather was okay. The area was "secured" with a flimsy chain-link fence that was easy enough to climb over.

She made it over the fence, then stopped herself. What was she doing? Bailing on an exam proctored by her own mother was a horrible idea. There would be no escaping punishment. But it was too late now.

If she kept going this way, she'd end up back at her rusting, peeling eyesore of a house. No thanks. She gazed up at the few cars zipping across the highway, then turned and crossed the parking lot on the west side of campus, where the carob trees grew thick and tall. She entered the little forest and moved toward the shady, hidden edge of Rattlesnake Creek.

She ducked between two heavy branches on the bank

and let out her breath. Sanctuary. Sort of. This was what passed for nature, anyway, in the tiny town of Crossroads.

Lilith rested her guitar case in its customary place in the crook of a tree trunk, kicked up her feet atop a heap of crisp orange leaves, and let the sound of the creek trickling in its cement bed relax her.

At school she'd seen pictures of "beautiful" places in her textbooks—Niagara Falls, Mount Everest, waterfalls in Hawaii—but she liked Rattlesnake Creek better than any of those because she didn't know a soul beside herself who thought this little grove of withered trees was beautiful.

She opened her case and took out the guitar. It was a dark orange Martin 000-45 with a crack slanted down its body. Someone on her street had thrown it away, and Lilith couldn't afford to be picky. Besides, she thought the flaw made the instrument sound richer.

Her fingers strummed the strings, and as chords filled the air, she felt an invisible hand smoothing her rough edges. When she played, she felt surrounded by friends she didn't have.

What would it be like to meet someone who actually shared her taste in music? she wondered. Someone who didn't think the Four Horsemen sang "like whipped dogs," as a cheerleader had once described Lilith's favorite band. It was Lilith's dream to see them play live, but it was impossible to imagine actually attending a Four Horsemen show. They were too big to play Crossroads. Even if they did come here, how could Lilith afford a ticket when her family barely had enough money for food?

She didn't notice when she tumbled into a song. It wasn't fully formed yet—just her sorrow melding with her guitar—but a few minutes later, when she stopped singing, someone behind her started clapping.

"Whoa." Lilith spun around to face a black-haired boy leaning against a nearby tree. He wore a leather jacket, and his black jeans disappeared into scuffed combat boots.

"Hey," he said as if he knew her.

Lilith didn't answer. They *didn't* know each other. Why was he talking to her?

He studied her intensely, his gaze penetrating. "You're still beautiful," he said softly.

"You're . . . really creepy," Lilith replied.

"You don't recognize me?" He sounded disappointed.

Lilith shrugged. "I don't watch *America's Most Wanted.*"

The boy looked down, laughed, then nodded at her guitar. "Aren't you afraid of making that worse?"

She flinched, confused. "My song?"

"Your song was a revelation," he said, pushing off the tree and walking toward her. "I mean that crack in your guitar."

Lilith watched the easy way he moved—coolly, slowly, as if no one had ever made him feel insecure about anything in his life. He stopped right in front of her and slid a canvas bag from his shoulder. The strap landed on Lilith's boot and she stared at it, as if the boy had put it there, touching her, intentionally. She kicked it off.

"I'm careful." She cradled her guitar. "Right now, the ratio of guitar to crack is just right. If it ever became more crack than guitar, then it would be worse."

"Sounds like you have it all figured out." The boy stared at her long enough for Lilith to grow uncomfortable. His eyes were a spellbinding green. He clearly wasn't from around here. Lilith didn't know if she'd ever met anyone who wasn't from Crossroads.

He was gorgeous and intriguing, and therefore too good to be true. She hated him immediately. "This is my spot. Find your own," she said.

But instead of going away, he sat down. Next to her. Close. Like they were friends. Or more than friends. "Do you ever play with anyone else?" the boy asked.

He tilted his head, and Lilith caught a glimpse of a starburst tattoo on his neck. She realized she was holding her breath.

"What, music? Like a band?" She shook her head. "No. Not that it's any of your business." This guy was invading her turf, interrupting the only real time she had to herself. She wanted him gone.

"What do you think of The Devil's Business?" he asked.

"What?"

"As a band name."

Lilith's instinct was to get up and walk away, but nobody ever talked to her about music. "What kind of band is it?" she asked.

He picked up a carob leaf from the ground and studied it, twirling its stem between his fingers. "You tell me. It's your band."

"I don't have a band," she said.

He raised a dark eyebrow. "Maybe it's time you got one."

Lilith had never dared allow herself to dream of what it might be like to play in an actual band. She shifted her weight to put more space between them.

"My name's Cam."

"I'm Lilith." She wasn't sure why telling this boy her name felt so monumental, but it did. She wished he weren't here, that he hadn't heard her play. She didn't share her music with anyone.

"I love that name," Cam said. "It suits you."

Now it really was time to leave. She didn't know what this guy wanted, but it definitely wasn't anything good. She picked up her guitar and got to her feet.

Cam went to stop her. "Where are you going?"

"Why are you talking to me?" she asked. Something about him made her blood boil. Why was he horning in on her private space? Who did he think he was? "You don't know me. Leave me alone."

Lilith's bluntness usually made people uncomfortable. But not this guy. He laughed a little under his breath.

"I'm talking to you because you and your song are the most interesting things I've stumbled upon in ages."

"Your life must be really boring," Lilith said.

She started to walk away. She had to stop herself from looking back. Cam didn't ask where she was going or seem surprised that she was leaving in the middle of their conversation.

"Hey," he called.

"Hey what?" Lilith didn't even turn around. Cam was the kind of boy who hurt girls foolish enough to let him. And she didn't need any more hurt in her life.

"I play guitar, too," he said as she started back through the forest. "All we'd need is a drummer."

TWO

DEAD SOULS

CAM

Cam watched Lilith disappear into the woods of Rattle-snake Creek, suppressing an overwhelming urge to race after her. She was as magnificent as she had been in Canaan, with the same bright, expressive soul shining through her outer beauty. He was amazed, and massively relieved, because when he'd discovered the shocking news that Lilith's soul was not in Heaven, as he'd expected, but in Hell with Lucifer, Cam had imagined the worst.

It was Annabelle who'd finally told him. He'd gone to her thinking she could slip him some details about Lilith's state in Heaven. The pink-haired angel had shaken her head and looked so sad when she pointed down, *way* down, and said to him, "You didn't know?"

Cam burned with questions about how Lilith—pure, kind Lilith—had ended up in Hell, but the most important one was this: Was she still the girl he loved, or had Lucifer broken her?

Five minutes with her had brought him right back to Canaan, to the breathtaking love they'd once known. Being next to her had filled him with hope. Except—

There was something different about Lilith. She wore a razor-sharp bitterness like a coat of armor.

"Enjoying yourself?" The voice came from somewhere above him.

Lucifer.

"Thanks for the glimpse," Cam said. "Now get her out of here."

Warm laughter shook the trees. "You came to me begging to know the state of her soul," Lucifer said. "I offered to let you visit her—but only because you're one of my favorites. Now why don't we talk business?"

Before Cam could respond, the ground dropped out from underneath him. His stomach hurtled upward, a sensation only the devil could trigger, and as Cam plunged down, he pondered the limits of angelic strength. He rarely questioned his instincts, but this instinct, to love Lilith and be loved by her again—powerful as it was— would either require the devil's clemency or would pit Cam directly against Lucifer. He unpinned his wings and looked down as a blue spot grew and sharpened beneath his feet. He landed on a linoleum floor.

The forest and Rattlesnake Creek were gone, and Cam found himself standing in the center of a food court in a deserted mall. He folded his wings against his sides and took a seat on a stool at an orange laminate table.

The food court atrium was huge, filled with a hundred ugly tables identical to his. It was impossible to tell where it began and where it ended. A long skylight spanned the ceiling, but it was so dirty, Cam could see nothing beyond the gray grime coating its glass. The floor was strewn with trash—empty plates, greasy napkins, crushed to-go cups and their chewed-on plastic straws. A stale odor hung in the air.

Around him were typical vendors—Chinese food, pizza, wings—but the stores were all run-down: the burger place was shuttered, the lights of the sandwich shop were burned out, and the glass case at the yogurt stop was smashed. Only one vendor's lights were on. Its awning was black with the word *Aevum* spelled out in bold gold letters.

A youthful figure with wavy auburn hair stood behind its counter, wearing a white T-shirt, jeans, and a flat white chef's hat. He was cooking something Cam couldn't see.

The devil's post-Fall guise could be anything, but Cam always recognized Lucifer by the searing heat that emanated from him. Though twenty feet separated them, it felt like Cam was standing right over a hot grill.

"Where are we?" Cam called.

Lucifer glanced over and gave Cam a strange, alluring smile. He had the face of a handsome, charismatic twenty-two-year-old, a dusting of freckles on his nose.

"This is Aevum—sometimes referred to as Limbo," the devil said, picking up a large spatula. "It is a state of being between time and eternity, and I'm running a special for first-time customers."

"I'm not hungry," Cam said.

Lucifer's wild eyes sparkled as he used the spatula to flip something sizzling onto a brown cafeteria tray. Then he moved behind a beige cash register and raised the plastic divider separating the little kitchen from the food court.

He rolled his shoulders and released his wings, which were huge and stiff and greenish-gold, like ancient, tarnished jewelry. Cam held his breath against their repulsive, musty smell and the tiny black damned critters that scuttled and nested in the folds.

With the cafeteria tray held high, Lucifer approached Cam. He narrowed his eyes at Cam's wings, where the fissure of white still glowed against the gold. "White's not a good color on you. Something you want to tell me?"

"What's she doing in Hell, Lucifer?"

Lilith had been one of the most virtuous people Cam had ever known. He couldn't fathom how she could ever have become one of Lucifer's subjects.

"You know I can't betray a confidence." Lucifer smiled

and set the plastic tray down in front of Cam. On it was a tiny snow globe with a golden base.

"What is this?" he asked. Dark gray ash filled the snow globe. It fell ceaselessly, magically, nearly obscuring the tiny lyre floating inside.

"See for yourself," Lucifer said. "Turn it over."

He turned the globe upside down and found a little golden knob at its base. He wound it and let the lyre's music wash over him. It was the same melody he'd been humming since he flew away from Troy: Lilith's song. That was how he thought of it.

He closed his eyes and was back on the riverbank in Canaan, three millennia ago, listening to her play.

This cheap music-box version was more piercing than Cam could have anticipated. His fingers tensed around the globe. Then—

Pop.

The snow globe shattered. The music dwindled as blood trickled down Cam's palm.

Lucifer tossed him a reeking gray dishrag and gestured for him to clean up the mess. "Lucky for you I have so many." He nodded at the table behind Cam. "Go ahead, try another. Each one's a little different!"

Cam set down the shards of the first snow globe, wiped his hands, and watched the cuts in his palms heal. Then he turned and looked again at the food court: in the center of each of the once-empty orange tables was a snow globe atop a brown plastic tray. The number of tables in the food court had grown—there was now a sea of them, stretching into the dim distance.

Cam reached for the globe on the table behind him.

"Gently," Lucifer said.

Inside this globe was a tiny violin. Cam turned the knob and heard a different version of the same bittersweet song.

The third globe contained a miniature cello.

Lucifer sat down and kicked his feet up as Cam moved around the food court, winding each snow globe into music. There were sitars, harps, violas. Lap steel guitars, balalaikas, mandolins—each one playing an ode to Lilith's broken heart. "These globes . . . ," Cam said slowly. "They represent all the different Hells you've trapped her in."

"And every time she dies in one of them," Lucifer said, "she ends up back here, where she is reminded anew of your betrayal." He stood and paced the aisles between tables, taking in his creations with pride. "And then, to keep things interesting, I banish her to a new Hell crafted especially for her." Lucifer grinned, exposing rows of razor-sharp teeth. "I really can't say what's worse—the endless Hells I subject her to again and again, or having to come back here and remember how much she hates you. But that's what keeps her going—her anger and her hatred."

"Of me." Cam swallowed.

"I work with the material I'm given. It's not my fault

you betrayed her." Lucifer let out a laugh that made Cam's eardrums pulse. "Want to know my favorite twist in Lilith's current Hell? No weekends! School every day of the year. Can you imagine?" Lucifer lifted a snow globe into the air, then let it fall to the ground and shatter. "As far as she's concerned, she's a typically gloomy teenager, suffering through a typically gloomy high school experience."

"Why Lilith?" Cam asked. "Do you craft everyone's Hell this way?"

Lucifer smiled. "The dull ones make their own dull hells, fire and brimstone and all that crap. They need no help from me. But Lilith—she's special. Not that I have to tell you that."

"What about the people suffering with her? Those kids at her school, her family—"

"Pawns," Lucifer said. "Brought here from Purgatory to play a bit part in someone else's story—which is a hell of another sort."

"I don't get it," Cam said. "You've made her existence utterly miserable—"

"Oh, I can't take all the credit," Lucifer said. "You helped!"

Cam ignored the guilt he felt lest it choke him. "But you've allowed her one thing she dearly loves. Why do you let her play music?"

"Existence is never so miserable as when you have a

taste of something beautiful," Lucifer said. "It serves to remind you of everything you can never have."

Everything you can never have.

Luce and Daniel had shaken something loose in Cam, something he thought was lost for good: his ability to love. The realization that such a thing was possible for him, that he might have a second chance, had made him yearn to see Lilith.

Now that he had, now that he knew she was here . . .

He had to *do* something.

"I need to see her again," Cam said. "That was too short—"

"I've done you enough favors," Lucifer said with a snarl. "I showed you what eternity is like for her. I didn't have to do even that."

Cam scanned the endless snow globes. "I can't believe you hid all this from me."

"I didn't hide her; you didn't care," Lucifer said. "You were always too busy. Luce and Daniel, the popular crowd at Sword and Cross, all that jazz. But now . . . well, would you like to see some of Lilith's previous Hells? It'll be fun."

Without waiting for an answer, Lucifer put his palm on the back of Cam's head and pushed it at one of the snow globes. Cam squeezed his eyes shut, bracing for his face to smash into the glass—

Instead:

He stood with Lucifer beside a vast river delta. Torrential rain poured from the sky. People ran from a row of huts, clutching belongings, panic on their faces as the river swelled against its banks. Across the river, a girl with a sad, calm expression walked slowly, carrying a sitar, in stark contrast to the chaos around her. Though she looked nothing like the Lilith he had loved in Canaan or the girl he had just met in Crossroads, Cam recognized her instantly.

She was walking *toward* the surging river.

"Ah, Lilith," Lucifer said with a sigh. "She really knows when to pack it in."

She sat in the mud on the riverbank and began to play. Her hands flew over the long-necked instrument, producing sad, sonorous music.

"A blues for drowning," Lucifer said with a hint of admiration.

"No—it's a blues for the moments before drowning," Cam said. "Big difference."

Then the river was over its banks, over Lilith and her sitar, over the houses, over the heads of all the fleeing people, over Cam and Lucifer.

Seconds later, Cam and Lucifer stood on a mountain bluff. Wisps of fog curled like fingers around the pine trees.

"This is one of my favorites," Lucifer said.

Mournful banjo music sounded behind them. They

turned and saw seven rail-thin children sitting on the porch of a sagging log cabin. They were barefoot, and their stomachs were bloated. A girl with strawberry-blond hair held the banjo in her lap, her fingers moving over the strings.

"I'm not going to stand here and watch Lilith play along to her starvation," Cam said.

"It's not so bad—it's just like going to sleep," Lucifer said.

The smallest boy now appeared to be doing just that. One of his sisters laid her head on his shoulder and followed suit. Then Lilith stopped playing and closed her eyes.

"That's enough," Cam said.

He thought about the Lilith he'd just encountered at Rattlesnake Creek. All this past suffering, the imprint of all these deaths, was in her somewhere, but she had no conscious memory of it. Just like Luce.

No, he realized, Lilith was nothing like Luce. They were as far from each other as east from west. Luce had been an archangel, living a cursed mortal life. Lilith was a mortal cursed by immortal influences, blown across the universe by eternal winds she could not perceive. But she felt those winds nonetheless. They were there in the way she sang with her eyes closed and strummed her cracked guitar.

She was doomed. Unless . . .

"Send me back in," Cam said to the devil. They were back in Hell's food court, snow globes atop the tables everywhere Cam looked, each one full of Lilith's pain.

"You liked Crossroads that much?" Lucifer asked. "I'm touched."

He looked deep into the devil's eyes and shuddered at the wildness he found there. All this time, Lilith had been under Lucifer's spell. *Why?* "What would it take to make you release her?" Cam asked Lucifer. "I'll do anything."

"*Anything?* I like the sound of that." Lucifer slid his hands into his back pockets, tilted his head, and stared at Cam, considering. "Lilith's current Hell is set to expire in fifteen days. I'd enjoy watching you make her even more miserable for those two weeks." He paused. "We could make it interesting."

"You have a bad habit of making things interesting," Cam said.

"A wager," Lucifer proposed. "If, in the fifteen days remaining, you can cleanse Lilith's dark heart of her hatred for you and convince her to fall in love with you again—truly fall in love—I'll close up shop, at least where she's concerned. No more bespoke Hells for her."

Cam narrowed his eyes. "It's too easy. What's the catch?"

"Easy?" Lucifer repeated, cackling. "Didn't you notice the gigantic chip on her shoulder? That's all you. She hates you, pal." He blinked. "And she doesn't even know why."

"She hates that miserable world," Cam said. "Anyone would. That doesn't mean she hates me. She doesn't even remember who I am."

Lucifer shook his head. "The hatred for her miserable world is a front for the older, blacker hatred for you." He poked Cam in the chest. "When a soul is hurt as deeply as Lilith, the pain is permanent. Even if she no longer recognizes your face, she recognizes your soul. The core of who you are." Lucifer spat on the floor. "And she loathes you."

Cam winced. It couldn't be true. But then he remembered how cold she'd been to him. "I'll fix her."

"Sure you will," Lucifer said, nodding. "Give it a try."

"And after I win her back," Cam asked, "then what?"

Lucifer smiled patronizingly. "You'll be free to live out the rest of her mortal days with her. Happily ever after. Is that what you want to hear?" He snapped his fingers as if he'd just remembered something. "You asked about the catch."

Cam waited. His wings burned with the need to fly to Lilith.

"I have indulged you too much for too long," Lucifer said, suddenly cold and serious. "*When* you *fail*, you must return to where you belong. Here, with me. No more gallivanting through the galaxies. No more white in your wings." Lucifer narrowed his blood-red eyes. "You will join me behind the Wall of Darkness, on my right-hand side. Eternally."

Cam eyed the devil evenly. Thanks to Luce and Daniel, Cam had an opportunity—he could rewrite his fate. How could he give that up again so easily?

Then he thought of Lilith. Of the despair she'd wallowed in for millennia.

No. He couldn't entertain what it would mean to lose. He would focus on winning her love and easing her pain. If there was any hope of saving her, it was worth everything to try.

"Agreed," Cam said, and held out his hand.

Lucifer swiped it away. "Save that crap for Daniel. I don't need a handshake to hold you to your word. You'll see."

"Fine," Cam said. "How do I get back to her?"

"Take the door to the left of the hot-dog-on-a-stick stand." Lucifer pointed at the row of vendors, which were now far in the distance. "Once you set foot in Crossroads, the countdown begins."

Cam was already moving toward the door, toward Lilith. But as he passed out of Hell's food court, Lucifer's voice seemed to follow him.

"Just fifteen days, old boy. Tick-tock!"

THREE

ATMOSPHERE

LILITH

Fifteen Days

Lilith could not be late to school again today.

Bailing on the bio test yesterday had already earned her detention after last period—her mother had silently handed her the detention slip when Lilith got home. So this morning, she made it a point to get to homeroom before Mrs. Richards had even finished adding creamer to the coffee in her biodegradable cup.

She was two pages into her poetry homework before the bell rang, and so pleased with her small accomplishment that she didn't even flinch when a familiar shadow darkened her desk.

"Brought you a present," Chloe said.

Lilith looked up. The senior reached into her zebra-striped purse and plucked out something white, then slapped it on Lilith's desk. It was one of those adult diapers, the kind meant for really ancient, incontinent people.

"In case you crap your pants again," Chloe said. "Try it on."

Lilith's cheeks warmed, and she pushed the diaper off her desk, pretending she didn't care that it was on the floor now, that other kids had to step over it to get to their desks. She glanced up to see whether Mrs. Richards had noticed, but to her dismay, Chloe was now having a tête-à-tête with their smiling homeroom teacher.

"I can recycle my shampoo bottles *and* my conditioner bottles, too?" Chloe was saying. "I never knew! Now, may I please have a hall pass? I'm supposed to meet with Principal Tarkenton."

Lilith watched with envy as Mrs. Richards dashed out a pass to Chloe, who took it and skipped out of the room. Lilith sighed. Teachers doled out hall passes to Chloe like they doled out detentions to Lilith.

Then the bell rang, and the intercom crackled to life.

"Good morning, Bulls," Tarkenton said. "As you know, today is the day we reveal the much-anticipated theme of this year's prom."

The kids around Lilith all hooted and clapped. She felt alone among them once again. It wasn't that she thought she was smarter or had better taste than these kids who cared so much about a high school dance. Something deeper and more important divided her from everyone she'd ever met. She didn't know what it was, but it made her feel like an alien most of the time.

"You voted, we tallied," the principal's voice continued, "and this year's prom theme is . . . Battle of the Bands!"

Lilith scowled at the intercom. *Battle of the Bands?*

She hadn't filled out the ballot for this year's prom, but she found it hard to believe that her classmates would have selected a theme that was actually almost interesting. Then she remembered that Chloe King was in a band, and that the girl had somehow brainwashed the student body into thinking that whatever she did was cool. Last spring, she'd made playing bingo an actual thing the in-crowd did every Thursday night. Lilith, of course, had never gone to Bingo Babes, as it was called, but come on—who between the ages of eight and eighty actually enjoyed the game of bingo?

The prom theme could have been worse. But still, Lilith was sure Tarkenton and his high school henchmen would figure out a way to make sure it sucked.

"And now a message from your prom chair, Chloe King," Tarkenton said.

A scuffling noise came from the intercom as the principal passed the microphone.

"Hey, Bulls," Chloe said in a voice that managed to be both peppy and sultry at the same time. "Buy your prom tickets and get ready to dance the night away to am*az*ing music played by your am*az*ing friends. That's right—prom is going to be part Coachella, part reality TV show, with a panel of snarky judges and everything. It's all sponsored by King Media—thanks, Daddy! So save the date: Wednesday, April thirtieth—just fifteen days away! I've already signed up *my* band to do battle, so what are you waiting for?"

The intercom clicked off. Lilith had never been to one of Chloe's shows, but she liked to think the girl had about as much musical talent as a lobster.

Lilith thought back to the boy she'd met the day before at Rattlesnake Creek. Out of nowhere he'd suggested she form a band. She'd tried to put the encounter out of her mind, but with Chloe going on about how to sign up to play at prom, Lilith was surprised to feel regret about the total nonexistence of her band.

Then the homeroom door swung open—and in walked the boy from Rattlesnake Creek. He sauntered down the row next to hers and took Chloe King's seat.

Heat coursed through Lilith's body as she studied his motorcycle jacket and the vintage Kinks T-shirt that fit tightly across his chest. She wondered where they sold clothes like that in Crossroads. No store she knew. She'd never met anyone who dressed like him.

He brushed his dark hair from his eyes and gazed at her.

Lilith liked the way Cam looked, but she did not like the way he looked at her. There was a sparkle in his eyes that made her uneasy. Like he knew all of her secrets. He probably looked at all the girls that way, and some of them probably loved it. Lilith didn't—at all—but she forced herself to hold his gaze. She didn't want him to think he made her nervous.

"May I help you?" Mrs. Richards asked.

"I'm new here," Cam said, still staring at Lilith. "What's the drill?"

When he flashed his Trumbull student ID, Lilith was so stunned she fell into a coughing fit. She struggled for control, mortified.

"Cameron Briel." Mrs. Richards read from the ID card, then scrutinized Cam from head to toe. "The drill is you sit over there and be quiet." She pointed at the desk farthest from Lilith, who was still coughing.

"Lilith," Mrs. Richards said, "do you know the statistics on the rise of asthma due to increased carbon emissions in the past decade? When you finish coughing, I want you to get out a sheet of paper and write a letter to your congresswoman demanding reform."

Seriously? She was getting in trouble for coughing?

Cam gave Lilith two light thumps on the back, the way her mother did to Bruce when he was having one of his fits. Then he bent down, picked up the diaper, raised an eyebrow at Lilith, and stuffed it inside Chloe's purse.

"She might need that later," he said, and smiled at Lilith as he walked to the other side of the room.

Trumbull wasn't a big school, but it was big enough for Lilith to be surprised that Cam was also in her poetry class. She was even more surprised when Mr. Davidson sat him in the empty seat next to her, since Kimi Grace was out sick.

"Hey," Cam had said when he slid into the seat.

Lilith pretended she hadn't heard him.

Ten minutes into class, as Mr. Davidson was reading a love sonnet by the Italian poet Petrarch, Cam leaned over and dropped a note onto her desk.

Lilith looked at the note, then at Cam, then glanced to her right, certain it was meant for someone else. But Paige wasn't reaching out to take the note from her, and Cam was smirking, nodding at the face of the note on which he'd written in neat black script, *Lilith*.

She opened it and felt a strange rush, the kind she felt when she dipped into a really good book or heard a great song for the first time.

In ten minutes of class, Teach has faced his blackboard an impressive total of eight minutes and forty-eight seconds. By my calculations, you and I could absolutely sneak out the next time he turns

around and not be missed until we're already at
Rattlesnake Creek. Wink twice if you're game.

Lilith did not even know where to start with this. Wink twice? More like drop dead three times, she wanted to tell him. When she looked up he was wearing a strange, tranquil expression, as if they were the kind of friends who did stuff like this all the time, as if they were any kind of friends. The weird thing was, Lilith skipped class all the time—she'd done it twice yesterday, in homeroom and biology. But she never did it for a fun reason. Escape was always her only option, a survival mechanism. Cam seemed to think he knew who she was and how she lived her life, and that annoyed her. She didn't want him to think about her at all.

No, she scrawled back, right over the words of Cam's note. She crumpled it up and pitched it at him the next time Mr. Davidson turned around.

The rest of her day was long and dreary, but at least she got a break from Cam. She didn't see him at lunch or in the hallways or in any of her other classes. Lilith reasoned that if she had to have two classes with him, it was best to have them back-to-back first thing in the morning and get the squirrelly sensation he made her feel out of the way. Why was he so casual with her? He seemed to think she enjoyed his presence. Something about him filled her with rage.

When the final bell rang, when she most wanted to be slinking behind the carob branches to play her guitar alone at Rattlesnake Creek, Lilith trudged to detention.

The detention room was spare—only a few desks and one poster on the wall that featured a kitten clinging to a tree branch. For what felt like the three thousandth time, Lilith read the words printed beneath its calico tail:

YOU ONLY LIVE ONCE,

BUT IF YOU DO IT RIGHT, ONCE IS ENOUGH.

The way to survive detention was to go into a trance. Lilith stared at the kitten poster until it took on an otherworldly quality. The kitten looked terrified, hanging there with its claws puncturing the branch. Was it supposed to embody "living right"? Not even the decor in this school made sense.

"Room sweep!" Coach Burroughs announced as he burst through the door. He checked in every fifteen minutes, like clockwork. The assistant basketball coach wore his silver hair in a greased-back pompadour, like an aging Elvis impersonator. The kids called him Crotch Burroughs, in honor of his borderline indecent shorts.

Even though Lilith was the only one in detention today, Burroughs paced as though disciplining a room full of invisible delinquents. When he got to Lilith, he slapped a stapled packet on her desk. "Your makeup biology test, Highness. It's different from the one you skipped out on yesterday."

The same or different, it didn't matter—Lilith was going to fail this one, too. She wondered why she was never called into a counselor's office, why no one seemed interested in how her appalling grades were threatening her college prospects.

When the door opened and Cam walked in, Lilith actually smacked her forehead.

"Are you kidding me?" she muttered under her breath when he handed Burroughs a yellow detention slip.

Burroughs nodded at Cam, sent him to a desk across the room, and said, "You got an assignment to keep you occupied?"

"I can't begin to tell you how much I have to do," Cam said.

Burroughs rolled his eyes. "Kids these days think they have it so hard. You wouldn't know real work if it bit you. I'll be back in fifteen minutes. In the meantime, the intercom is on, so the office will hear everything that happens in this room. Understand?"

From his desk, Cam winked at Lilith. She turned to face the wall. They were not on winking terms.

As soon as the door closed behind Burroughs, Cam walked to the teacher's desk, switched off the intercom, then sidled over to the chair in front of Lilith. He sat down and put his feet up on her desk, nudging her fingers with his boots.

She shoved his feet away. "I have a test to take," she said. "Excuse me."

"And I have a better idea. Where's your guitar?"

"How did you manage to get a detention on your first day of school? Going for a new record?" she asked, so that she wouldn't say what she was really thinking, which was, *You're the first new kid I can remember. Where are you from? Where do you shop? What's the rest of the world like?*

"Don't worry about that," Cam said. "Now, about your guitar. We don't have a lot of time."

"Weird thing to say to a girl sitting in detention for eternity."

"This is your notion of eternity?" Cam looked around, his green eyes pausing on the kitten poster. "Wouldn't be my first choice," he finally said. "Besides, you don't notice forever when you're having fun. Time only exists in sports and sorrow."

Cam stared at her until a shiver ran across her skin. Lilith felt her face flush; she couldn't tell whether she was embarrassed or angry. She realized what he was doing, trying to soften her by talking about music. Did he think she was so easy to play? She felt another inexplicable surge of fury. She *hated* this boy.

He pulled a black object the size of a single-serving cereal box from his bag and placed it on Lilith's desk.

"What's that?" she asked.

Cam shook his head. "I'm going to pretend you didn't just ask that. It's a miniature guitar amp."

She nodded, like *of course*. "I've just never seen one so, um . . ."

"Square?" Cam prompted. "All we need is a guitar to plug it into."

"Burroughs will be back in fifteen minutes," Lilith said, glancing at the clock. "Twelve. I don't know how detention works where you come from, but around here, you don't get to play guitar."

Cam was the new kid, yet he strode in here like he owned the place. Lilith was the one who'd been stuck here all her life, who knew how things worked and how crappy this school was, so Cam could just back off.

"Twelve minutes, huh?" He threw the mini amp back into his bag, stood up, and held out his hand. "We'd better hurry."

"I'm not going with you—" Lilith protested as she let him drag her out the door. Then they were in the hallway, where it was quiet, so she shut up. She looked down at his hand in hers for a second before jerking away.

"See how easy that was?" Cam asked.

"Don't touch me ever again."

The words seemed to punch Cam in the gut. He frowned, then said, "Follow me."

Lilith knew she should go back to detention, but she

liked the idea of a little mischief—even if she didn't like her partner in crime.

Grumbling, she followed Cam, keeping close to the wall, as if she could blend in with the student-made posters supporting Trumbull's terrible basketball team. Cam pulled a Sharpie from his bag and added the letters *HIT* to the end of a message that stated GO BULLS!

Lilith was surprised.

"What?" He raised an eyebrow. "Once you go bullshit, you never go back."

On the second floor, they came to a door marked BAND ROOM. For someone who had only been here a day, Cam sure seemed to know his way around. He reached for the knob.

"What if someone's in there?" Lilith asked.

"Band meets first period. I checked."

Someone *was* in there. Jean Rah was a half-French, half-Korean boy who, like Lilith, was a social pariah. They should have been friends: like her, he was obsessed with music, he was mean, he was weird. But they weren't friends. Lilith wished Jean Rah would permanently evaporate, and she could see in his eyes that he wished the same about her.

Jean looked up from a drum kit, where he was tuning the snare. He could play every instrument there was. "Get out," he said. "Or I'll page Mr. Mobley."

Cam grinned. Lilith could tell Cam instantly liked this

scowling kid with his Buddy Holly glasses, which made her hate them both even more.

"Do you guys know each other?" Cam asked.

"I make it a point not to know him," Lilith said.

"I'm unknowable," Jean said, "to idiots like you."

"Talk crap and get the crap beaten out of you," Lilith said, glad to have a target for her anger. Her body tensed, and the next thing she knew she was lunging at Jean—

"Whoa, whoa, whoa," Cam said, catching her by the waist.

She writhed against the strong arms restraining her, not knowing which boy she wanted to hit first. Cam had gotten her all riled up, interrupting a peaceful detention hour, bringing her here. . . . And that wink. She got pissed off all over again thinking about the way he'd winked at her.

"Let. Me. Go," she seethed.

"Lilith," Cam said quietly. "Everything's cool."

"Shut up," she said, yanking herself away. "I don't want your help, or your pity, or whatever it is you're trying to do."

Cam shook his head. "I'm not—"

"Yes, you are," Lilith said. "And you'd better stop."

Her palm itched to slap Cam. Not even his expression, which was an unsettling mixture of confusion and hurt, eased her feelings. The only reason she didn't hit him was that Jean was watching.

"Uhh . . ." Jean raised his eyebrows and glanced at Lilith, then Cam. "You two are kind of wigging me out. I'm calling Mobley."

"Go ahead," Lilith snapped. "Do it."

But the boy was so shocked that he stayed put.

Lilith's first instinct was to leave the band room immediately, yet—oddly—she found herself wanting to stay. She didn't know why she'd never come in here before. It felt comforting to be surrounded by instruments. Even though they weren't fancy instruments—the trumpets were dented, the drum skins were worn so thin they were translucent, the metal triangles were coated with rust—nothing else at this school was even half as intriguing.

A gentle smirk crossed Cam's face. "I'm getting an idea."

"Probably a first for you," said Jean.

"Forgive us if we're not impressed," Lilith said, surprised to find herself siding with Jean.

"You guys share a common enemy," Cam stated.

Lilith snorted. "You pick up on people's hatred of you quickly. That was what, ten minutes?"

"Not me," Cam said. "I mean the school. The town." He paused. "The world."

Lilith couldn't decide if Cam was wise or a cliché. "What's your point?"

"Why don't you combine forces and channel your rage?" Cam said. He handed Lilith a guitar from a stand

and put his hand on Jean's shoulder. "Lilith and I are starting a band."

"We are not," Lilith said. What was *with* this guy?

"We are too," Cam said to Jean as if it was already a done deal. "Prom's in fifteen days, and we need a drummer if we're going to win the Battle of the Bands."

"What's your band name?" Jean asked skeptically.

Cam winked at Lilith. *Again.* "The Devil's Business."

Lilith groaned. "There is no way I'd ever be in a band called The Devil's Business. Any band I start is going to be called Revenge."

She hadn't meant to say any of that. It was true, she'd kept that band name like a secret for ages, ever since she'd decided that the best way to get revenge on all the jerks at school would be to get famous and have an actual band with legit musicians and never be seen by anyone from Crossroads again, except for the sold-out shows they'd have to stream online because her band would never, ever play her hometown.

But she'd never planned on saying the name out loud.

Cam's eyes widened. "A band with that name's gonna need a big-ass synthesizer. And a disco ball."

Jean narrowed his eyes. "I'd love to synthesize the shit out of this school," he said after a moment. "I'm in."

"I'm not," Lilith said.

Cam smiled at Lilith. "She's in."

Smile back, Lilith. Other girls would have mirrored

his expression, but Lilith wasn't like any other girl she knew. A thick ball of rage settled in her stomach, pulsing at Cam's smugness, his certainty. She scowled and left the band room without another word.

※

"I'm starving," Cam said as he followed her out of school.

They had made it back to detention in time to switch the intercom back on just before Burroughs did his final room sweep. She'd turned in her exam, mostly blank, and they'd both been excused.

Why wouldn't Cam leave her alone?

In his right hand swung a guitar case he had borrowed from the band room. His canvas bag was over his shoulder.

"Where do you like to eat around here?"

Lilith shrugged. "A nice little spot called *none of your business.*"

"Sounds exotic," Cam said. "Where is it?" As they walked, his smooth fingertips grazed Lilith's calloused ones. She pulled away swiftly, instinctively, with a look that said if that hadn't been an accident, he'd better not try it again.

"I'm going that way." She pointed in the direction of Rattlesnake Creek, wishing she hadn't just divulged her plan. She wasn't suggesting he join her.

But that was exactly what Cam did.

At the edge of the woods, he held aside a carob branch so she could duck underneath. Lilith watched him study the branch, as if he'd never seen this kind of tree before.

"Don't they have carobs where you're from?" she asked. They were everywhere in Crossroads.

"Yes and no," Cam said.

He muttered something under his breath as she made her way to her tree. She sat down and watched the water trickle over the rocks jutting up from the creek bed. A moment later, Cam joined her.

"Where *are* you from?" she asked.

"Around?" Cam reached between the crooked branches where Lilith stashed her guitar. Sometimes she came here and played when she cut lunch; it helped her to not think about how hungry she was.

"Mysterious?" she said, mimicking his tone and taking the guitar from him.

"Not as cool as it sounds," Cam said. "Last night I slept in the doorway of a TV repair shop."

"O'Malley's on Hill Street?" Lilith said, tuning her high E string. "That's weird. I slept there once when I was grounded and had to get away from Janet." She felt his eyes on her, yearning for her to elaborate. "Janet is my mom." But that was a dead-end topic, so she changed the subject. "How'd you end up here?"

Cam's jaw tensed, and a vein appeared on his forehead,

between his eyes. It was clearly the last thing he wanted to discuss, which made Lilith suspicious. He was hiding something, just like she was.

"Enough *Behind the Music*." Cam opened the guitar case he'd lifted from the band room and took out a green Fender Jaguar, property of Trumbull Prep. "Let's play something."

Lilith sneezed and hugged her stomach. Hunger was running with rusty scissors through her insides.

"A hunger sneeze," Cam said. "I should never have let you talk us out of getting something to eat. Good thing you're with me."

"Why?"

"Because we're good together." He brushed his dark hair from his eyes. "And because I travel with exquisite snacks."

From his canvas bag he produced a sleeve of water crackers and a short, fat jar with foreign writing on it. He put his hand on the lid and tried to turn it. It didn't budge. He tried once more. The vein appeared on his forehead again.

"Here." Lilith took the jar from him and slid it up her guitar strings, letting one of them pop the vacuum seal. She'd done it once at home when Bruce was hungry and a jar of pickles was the very last thing they had to eat.

The lid twisted open in her hands.

Cam ran the tip of his tongue across his teeth and nodded slightly. "I loosened it for you."

Lilith peered into the jar. It was crammed with tiny, wet, black eggs.

"Ossetra," Cam said. "The finest caviar."

Lilith had no idea what to do with caviar. Where did he get it—especially if he'd slept on the street the night before? Cam opened the package of crackers and used one to scoop out a mound of the glistening black stuff.

"Close your eyes and open your mouth," he said.

She didn't want to, but hunger got the better of her.

The cracker was brittle, the caviar soft and lush. Then the brininess of the eggs struck her, and at first she thought she didn't like it. But she let it sit on her tongue for a moment as a rich sensation spread through her mouth, buttery with an edge of sharpness. She swallowed, already addicted.

When she opened her eyes, Cam was smiling at her.

"Is this expensive?" she asked, feeling guilty.

"Tastes best if you eat it slow."

A calm silence fell between them as they ate. She was grateful for the food, but it bothered her that this guy acted like they were closer than they were. "I should get home," she said. "I'm grounded."

"In that case, you should stay out as long as you can." Cam tilted his head, looking at her the way guys in movies looked at girls they were about to kiss. He stayed like that for a moment; then he picked up her guitar.

"Hey!" Lilith said as a chord filled the air. Her guitar was her most prized possession. No one touched it but

Lilith. But as Cam's fingers strummed her strings and he began to hum, she watched him, mesmerized. His song was beautiful—and familiar. She didn't know where she'd heard it before.

"Did you write that?" she couldn't help asking.

"Maybe." He stopped playing. "It needs a female vocalist."

"I'm sure Chloe King's available," Lilith said.

"Speaking of which," Cam said, "how about that prom theme? Battle of the Bands?" He tossed his head. "Could be cool."

"Cool is the very last thing it could ever be," Lilith said.

"I'll sign up if you sign up."

Lilith burst out laughing. "That's supposed to entice me? Has anyone ever told you you're a little bit conceited?"

"Not in the past five minutes," Cam said. "Just think about it. We've got two weeks to throw a decent band together. We could do it." He paused. "You could do it. And you know what they say about Revenge."

"What?" she said, waiting to hear what he'd say next to piss her off.

He gazed into the distance, at something that seemed to make him sad. When he spoke, his voice was soft. "It's sweet."

FOUR

HOLDING OUT

CAM

Fourteen Days

The next morning, as the sun broke over the hills, Cam peeled himself off the roof of the Trumbull gym, where he'd slept the night before. His neck was stiff, and he needed a hot shower to loosen it. He glanced around, making sure the coast was clear, then swooped down until he was level with the high windows of the gym. He found an unlocked pane and slipped inside.

It was quiet in the boys' locker room, and Cam paused for a moment to stare at his reflection in the mirror. His face looked . . . older—his features more angular, his eyes more recessed. Over the millennia he had changed his appearance many times to blend in to his surroundings, letting the sun bronze his pale skin or adding muscle to his naturally slim frame, but he was always the one to make those changes. They didn't just *happen*. Never before had he been startled by his own reflection.

What was going on?

The question nagged at him as he showered, stole a clean white T-shirt from some kid's locker, slipped into his jeans and motorcycle jacket, and headed outside to wait for Lilith's bus.

Near the cul-de-sac where the buses pulled in, Cam leaned against a glass-encased bulletin board promoting the school's various extracurricular activities. There was a German club meeting at three o'clock. LEARN HOW TO ASK YOUR DATE TO PROM IN GERMAN!, the flyer boasted. Another held details for cross-country tryouts. GET IN SHAPE AND LOOK GREAT IN YOUR PROM DRESS!, it promised. In the center was a glittery flyer promoting a gig for Chloe King's band, the Perceived Slights, the following week. They were opening for a local band called Ho Hum. BE ABLE TO SAY YOU SAW THEM BEFORE THEY WON THE BATTLE OF THE BANDS AT PROM!

Cam had only been in Crossroads one full day and already he was feeling the school's prom-mania. He had been to a prom before, once, decades ago, with a cool girl from Miami who'd had a crush on him. Even though they'd disabled the fire alarm and spent most of the night up on the roof watching shooting stars, they'd also danced to a few fast songs, and Cam had enjoyed himself. Of course, he'd had to fly before anything got too serious.

He wondered what Lilith thought of prom, whether she had any desire to go. It dawned on him that he would need to ask her to be his date. The idea was thrillingly old-fashioned. He would have to make it special. He'd have to do everything just right.

At the moment, winning Lilith's love was looking like a losing bet. Lucifer was right, she hated him. But the girl he'd fallen in love with was there, somewhere, buried underneath all that pain. He just had to reach her somehow.

The squeal of brakes startled him, and Cam turned to watch the caravan of yellow buses lining up. Students filed down their steps. Most of them walked toward the building in clusters of twos and threes.

Only Lilith walked alone. She had her head down, her red hair covering her face, the white wires of her earbuds dangling. Her shoulders were hunched forward, which made her look smaller than she was. When he couldn't see the fire in her eyes, Lilith looked so defeated Cam could hardly stand it. He caught up to her as she walked through the doors to the school's main hallway.

He tapped her shoulder. She spun around.

"Hey," he said, suddenly breathless.

He wasn't used to having her so close, after all this

time spent so far away. She was different from the girl he'd loved in Canaan, but just as wondrous. When he'd made this wager with Lucifer, he hadn't anticipated how difficult it would be not to touch her as he used to. He had to restrain every impulse to reach for her, to caress her cheek, to take her into his arms and kiss her and never let her go.

Lilith looked at him and flinched. Her face twisted with disgust or something worse as she removed her earbuds. He'd done nothing to her in this life, but she was hardwired to despise him.

"What?" Lilith asked.

"What are you listening to?" he asked.

"Nothing you'd like."

"Try me."

"No thanks," she said. "Can I go now, or did you want to make more painfully awkward small talk?"

Cam's eyes caught another flyer for the Perceived Slights gig taped to a nearby locker. He ripped it off and thrust it at her. "This band's playing next week," he said. "Wanna go together?"

She glanced briefly at the flyer and shook her head. "Not really my kind of music. But if you like bubblegum pop, have a blast."

"The Slights are just the opening act. I've heard Ho Hum is pretty good," he lied. "I think it'd be fun." He paused. "I think it'd be fun to go with you."

Lilith squinted, adjusting the strap of her backpack on her shoulder. "Like a date?"

"Now you're feeling me," Cam said.

"I am absolutely *not* feeling you," she said, walking away. "The answer is no."

"Come on," Cam said, following. The halls were a chaos of students at their lockers getting ready for the day, tossing in books, putting on lip gloss, and gossiping about prom. "What if I can get us backstage?"

Cam doubted there was a backstage at this gig, but he'd pull whatever strings needed pulling if Lilith would say yes.

"Did somebody say 'backstage'?" came a sibilant voice. "I've got passes to whatever backstage you want."

Lilith and Cam stopped and turned. Behind them, in the middle of the hallway, stood a boy with auburn hair and a smirk on his square, almost handsome face. He wore distressed jeans, an argyle-printed T-shirt with subtle gray skulls inside its diamonds, and a thin gold chain around his neck. In one hand he held a tablet.

Lucifer wasn't supposed to be here. This wasn't part of their bet.

"Who are you?" Lilith asked.

"I'm Luc," Lucifer said. "I'm with King Media. We've partnered with Trumbull Prep to put on the best prom this school has ever seen. I'm the intern, but I think they might take me on full-time—"

"I'm not going to prom," Lilith said drily. "You're wasting your time."

"But you *are* interested in music, right?" Lucifer asked.

"How'd you know that?" Lilith asked.

Luc smiled. "You just have that look." He tapped a password into his tablet and pulled up an electronic sign-up sheet. "I'm facilitating the student sign-up for the Battle of the Bands." He glanced at Cam. "You gonna sign up, bro?"

"Isn't this beneath even you?" Cam asked.

"Oh, Cam," Luc said, "if you refuse to do things that are beneath you, you'll never get much accomplished in this world."

Lilith studied Cam. "You know this guy?"

"We're old friends," Luc said. "But where are my manners?" He extended his hand. "Nice to meet you, Lilith."

"You know my name?" Lilith stared at Luc with a look of equal parts wonder and disgust. Cam knew the perverse appeal of the devil. It was what kept Lucifer's ranks overflowing.

"What else could your name be?" Luc asked. "Or . . . King Media does its research," he added with a smile as Lilith awkwardly shook his hand.

Cam tensed. This wasn't fair. He had two weeks to get Lilith to fall in love with him. He didn't have time for Lucifer's interference.

"What are you doing here?" Cam asked Lucifer, unable to hide the venom in his voice.

"Let's just say I wasn't being challenged enough," Luc said. "Then I landed this internship with King Media—"

"I have no idea what that means," Cam said.

Luc's smirk deepened. "Any questions or concerns about prom and the Battle of the Bands go through me. I want the students here to get to know me, to see me as a friend, not an authority figure. By the time prom rolls around, we'll all feel like besties."

The intercom clicked on, filling the hall with even more noise. "Good morning, Bulls!"

Luc pointed a finger at the ceiling. "You two should really listen to this announcement."

"At six o'clock this evening," Tarkenton said, "there will be an open mic in the cafeteria. It's open to all, but mandatory for students in Mr. Davidson's poetry class."

Lilith groaned. "I'd rather die than read some dreary poem in public," she said, miserable. "But Mr. Davidson's class is the only one I'm passing—and I'm only barely doing that."

"You heard Tarkenton," Cam said to Lilith. "*Open* mic. You don't have to read a poem—you could sing one. We could make tonight Revenge's first gig."

"*We're* not doing anything, because *we* don't have a band," Lilith said.

By now the hallways had mostly emptied out. In another minute, they'd be late for class. But Cam felt glued to the ground: He was close enough to smell her skin, and it made him dizzy with desire. "Screw homeroom," he said. "Let's sneak out right now and go practice."

Long ago, in Canaan, music had connected Lilith and Cam; Cam needed it to perform its magic a second time, here, in Crossroads. If they could just perform together, the chemistry between them would break down Lilith's defenses for long enough for him to win her heart again. He knew it would. And if he had to attend a high school prom to play with her again, so be it.

"I, for one, would love to hear you sing, Lilith," Luc chimed in.

"Stay out of this," Cam said. "Don't you have somewhere to go? Freshmen to corrupt or something?"

"Sure," Luc said. "But not before I add Lilith to my list." He held the tablet out to her again, waiting until she keyed in her email address. Then he flipped its cover closed and headed for the door. "Later, loser," he called to Cam. "And, Lilith, you'll be hearing from me."

❧❦

The day passed quickly. Too quickly.

Lilith had ignored Cam in homeroom and in poetry, and he didn't see her for the rest of the school day. He'd snuck out to Rattlesnake Creek at lunch, hoping he would find her there, strumming her guitar, but all he'd found was the tuneless trickle of April water in the creek bed.

No Lilith.

He'd hung around the band room after the bell, hoping she might return there after class.

She hadn't.

As the sun sank in the sky, he made his way alone to the Trumbull open mic. He walked across the bleak campus toward the cafeteria, coughing from the smoky air. The burning hillsides—the barely disguised flames of Lilith's Hell—encircled all of Crossroads, and no one here seemed to care. Cam had seen a fire truck drive toward the blaze that morning and noted the blank expressions on the firefighters' faces. They probably spent every day hosing water on those smoldering trees, unconcerned that the fire never dwindled.

Everyone in this town was one of Lucifer's pawns. Nothing and no one would change in Crossroads until the devil wanted it to change.

Except, Cam hoped, for Lilith.

When he reached the cafeteria, Cam held the door open for a couple holding hands. The boy whispered something in the girl's ear, and she laughed and pulled him in for a kiss. Cam looked away, feeling a stab in his chest. He stuffed his hands inside his jacket pockets and ducked inside.

The cafeteria's daytime drabness was barely disguised. A makeshift stage had been set up at one end, with ragged black curtains hanging between two poles for a backdrop. Mr. Davidson stood center stage behind a microphone.

"Welcome," he said, adjusting his glasses. He appeared

to be in his thirties, with a mop of dark brown hair and a rail-thin frame that radiated nervousness. "There's nothing more exciting than discovering vital new pieces of art. I can't wait for you all to share your work with each other tonight."

Above the audience's groans and grumbles, he added, "Also, you have to perform or else you'll get a zero. So without further ado, put your hands together for our first performer, Sabrina Burke!"

As the audience applauded weakly, Cam slid into an empty seat next to Jean Rah, who offered Cam his fist to bump. Jean was Cam's kind of guy—dark, funny, with a kindness you had to dig for. Cam wondered what Jean had done to end up in Lucifer's domain. Some of the most interesting mortals—and angels—had a way of pissing off the Throne.

On the stage, Sabrina's hands shook as she reached for the microphone. She whispered, "Thank you," as she unfolded a handwritten poem. "This poem is called . . . 'Matrimony.' Thank you, Mr. Davidson, for your help. You're the best teacher ever." She cleared her throat and began:

> *"A wedding is a prehistoric ritual for two people*
> *a man and a woman—*
> OR SO THEY SAY!"

She looked up from her paper.

"YOU CANNOT TAKE AWAY MY FREEDOM!
  FREE? DUMB!
I am woman, watch me soar!"

She looked down. "Thank you."

The rest of the students applauded. "So brave," a girl sitting next to Cam said. "So true."

Cam's eyes wandered over the audience until he found Lilith in the third row, chewing her nails. He knew she was imagining herself up there, alone. The Lilith he remembered was a natural performer, once she got past the initial panic of stepping onto a stage.

But this Lilith was different.

Now the audience was clapping for a towering black boy who walked confidently onstage. He didn't bother to adjust the microphone, which was way too short for him. He just opened his notebook and projected.

"This one's sort of like a haiku," he said.

"Some birds never land.
They've got to do all of their
Business in the clouds."

A contingent of girls in the back row hooted and cheered, calling out to the boy, "You're so fine, James!" He waved at them, as if he got that kind of reaction buying a soda or getting out of his car, and exited the stage.

A spoken-word performance and three poets later,

Mr. Davidson took the stage again. "Good job, everyone. Next up? *Lilith.*"

A few boos echoed across the cafeteria, and Mr. Davidson attempted to shush them. Lilith took her place on the stage. The spotlight made her hair look brighter, her face paler as she held her black journal under her arm, ready to read her poem. She cleared her throat. The microphone howled with feedback.

Several of the students covered their ears. One yelled, "Get off the stage! Loser!"

"Hey, now!" Mr. Davidson called out. "That's not nice."

"Um—" Lilith tried to adjust the microphone but only got a squeal of feedback.

Cam was off his seat by then and rushing up to the stage.

Lilith glared as he approached. "What are you doing?" she whispered.

"This," he said. With a deft twist of his wrist, he adjusted the microphone so it was the perfect distance from Lilith's lips. Now she wouldn't have to hunch. She could speak in her low, natural voice and be heard clearly throughout the cafeteria.

"Get off the stage." She cupped her palm over the mic. "You're embarrassing me." She turned out to the audience. "Um, I'm Lilith, and I—"

"And you suck!" shouted a girl at the back of the cafeteria.

Lilith sighed and flipped through the pages of her notebook. It was clear to Cam how much the other students hated Lilith, and how terrible she felt because of it. He didn't want to be one more thing making her miserable right now.

He started backing off the stage when the look in her eyes made him stop.

"What is it?" he asked.

"I can't do this," she mouthed.

Cam came close again, stopping before instinct took over and he embraced her. "Yes, you can."

"I'll take the zero." She backed away from the microphone, clutching her journal. "I can't read in front of all these people who hate me."

"Then don't," Cam said. At the foot of the chair where Lilith had been sitting in the audience, Cam had spied her guitar case. Luckily she hadn't stowed it at the creek today.

"Huh?" she asked.

"Lilith," Mr. Davidson called from the back of the cafeteria. "Is there a problem?"

"Yes," Lilith said.

"No," Cam said at the same time.

He jumped off the stage, opened the silver clasps of her guitar case, and raised the lovely, cracked instrument in his arms. He heard snickering from the crowd and saw the flash of someone photographing Lilith as she stood caught in the grip of her stage fright.

Cam ignored them all. He pressed the guitar into

Lilith's hands and eased the strap over her shoulder, taking care not to catch her long red hair beneath it. He took her journal from her, and it felt warm where her hands had been.

"This is a disaster," she said.

"Most great things start out that way," he said, so that only she could hear. "Now, close your eyes. Imagine you're alone. Imagine it's sunset, and you've got all night."

"Get a room!" someone yelled out. "You both suck!"

"This isn't going to work," Lilith said, but Cam noticed the way her fingers naturally moved into strumming position. The guitar was like a shield between her and the audience. Already she was more comfortable than she'd been a moment before.

So Cam kept going.

"Imagine you've just thought up this new song, and you're proud of it—"

Lilith started to interrupt. "But—"

"Let yourself be proud," Cam told her. "Not because you think it's better than any other song, but because it comes as close as anything ever could to expressing how you feel right now, what you're about."

Lilith closed her eyes. She leaned in to the mic. Cam held his breath.

"Boo," someone hooted.

Lilith's eyes shot open. Her face went white.

Cam homed in on Luc in the center of the audience,

hands cupped around his mouth, jeering at Lilith. Cam had never punched the devil, but he wasn't afraid to change that tonight. He stared out coolly at the audience, raised both his fists, and flipped them off.

"That's enough, Cam," Mr. Davidson said. "Please exit the stage."

The sound of very quiet laughter made Cam turn to Lilith. She was watching him, chuckling, the ghost of a smile on her face.

"Showing them who's boss?" she asked.

He shook his head. "Play that guitar and show them yourself."

Lilith didn't answer, but Cam could tell from the change in her expression that he'd said something right. She leaned in to the mic again. Her voice came soft and clear. "This one's called 'Exile,'" she said, and began to sing.

"Where love spurs me I must turn
My rhymes, my rhymes,
Which follow my afflicted mind
My mind, my mind.
What shall be last, what shall be first?
Shall I drown from this thirst?"

The song poured out of her like she'd been born to sing it. At the microphone, with her eyes closed, Lilith didn't seem so twisted by anger. There was the hint of the girl she'd once been, the girl Cam had fallen in love with.

The girl he was still in love with.

When she finished, Cam was trembling with emotion. Her song was a version of the one he'd been humming as he left Troy. She still knew it. Some remnant of their love story was still alive in her. Just as he'd hoped it would be.

Lilith's fingers lifted off the strings of her guitar. The audience was silent. She waited for applause, hope in her eyes.

But all she got was laughter.

"Your song sucks worse than you!" someone hollered, throwing an empty soda bottle on stage. It hit Lilith in the knees, and the hope in her eyes died.

"Cut it out!" Mr. Davison said, returning to the stage. He turned to Lilith. "Nice job."

But Lilith was rushing off the stage and out of the cafeteria. Cam ran after her, but she was too fast, and it was too dark outside to see where she had gone. She knew this place better than he did.

The door closed behind him, silencing the distant sound of another student reading poetry. He sighed and leaned against the stucco wall. He thought of Daniel, who had suffered through so many bleak periods when his longing for Luce consumed him, made him wish he could die and escape their curse, only to be rewarded with a single brush of her fingertips in the next life before she was gone again.

Is it worth it? Cam had often asked his friend.

Now Cam understood Daniel's unchanging answer. *Of course it is,* he'd say. *It's the* only *thing that makes my existence worthwhile.*

"Rookie mistake."

Cam turned his head and saw Luc emerge from the shadows.

"What?" Cam muttered.

"Getting cocky on the first day." Lucifer snarled. "We've got two more weeks together, and there are so many ways for you to lose."

Cam was feeling far from cocky. If the devil got his way, Cam wasn't the only one who would lose.

"Up your game at any time," he told Lucifer through his teeth. "I'm ready."

"We'll see how ready you are," Lucifer snickered just before he disappeared, leaving Cam alone.

INTERLUDE

SPARKS

TRIBE OF DAN, NORTHERN CANAAN

Approximately 1000 BCE

In the moonlight, the blond boy dove into the Jordan River. His name was Dani, and though he had been in the village for only a month, his loveliness was already legendary from here to southern Beer-sheba.

From the banks of the river, a dark-haired girl watched him, fingering her necklace. Tomorrow she would turn seventeen.

And—out of sight—Cam was watching her. She seemed more beautiful now that she'd fallen for the night swimmer. Of course, Cam knew what the girl's fate would be, but nothing could stop her from loving Dani. Her love, Cam thought to himself, was pure.

"He's like a religion," a soft voice said from behind him. He turned to find a stunning redhead. "She is devoted to him."

Cam stepped toward the girl on the riverbank. He had never seen a mortal like her. Her waist-length red hair shimmered like a garnet. She was as tall as he was and graceful even standing still. Freckles kissed her slender shoulders and her smooth cheeks. He marveled at the intimacy in her blue eyes, as if the two of them were already complicit in some delightful brand of mischief. When she smiled, the tiny gap between her front teeth thrilled him in a way he'd never known.

"Do you know them?" Cam asked. This marvelous girl was only talking to him because she'd caught him watching Daniel and Lucinda.

Her laughter was clear as rainwater. "I grew up with Liat. And everyone knows Dani, though he only found our tribe near the end of the last moon. There is something unforgettable about him, don't you think?"

"Perhaps," Cam said. "If you like that type."

The girl studied Cam. "Did you travel here on the giant star that fell through the sky last night?" she asked. "My sisters and I were sitting by the fire, and we thought the star bore the wondrous shape of a man."

Cam knew she was teasing, flirting, but he was

impressed that she had guessed correctly. His wings had carried him here the night before; he'd been chasing the tail of a shooting star.

"What's your name?" he asked.

"My friends call me Lilith."

"What do your enemies call you?"

"Lilith," she growled, baring her teeth. Then she laughed.

When Cam laughed, too, Liat whirled around a few feet below. "Who's there?" she called from the bank into the darkness.

"Let's get out of here," Lilith said quietly to Cam, and held out her hand.

This girl was amazing. Fierce, full of life. He took her hand and let her lead him, a little worried he might do so forever, following wherever she went.

Lilith guided him to a bank of irises farther down the curving river, then reached inside the hollow trunk of an enormous carob tree and pulled out a lyre. Sitting among the flowers, she tuned the instrument by ear, so deftly Cam could see that she did it every day.

"Will you play for me?" Cam asked.

She nodded. "If you'll listen." Then she began to play a series of notes that entwined like lovers, curled like the bends in the river. Miraculously, her glorious, humming melody assumed the shape of words.

She sang a sad love song that made everything else vanish from his mind.

Wrapped in her song, he couldn't care less about

Lucifer or the Throne, Daniel or Lucinda. There was only Lilith's breathtaking, lingering song.

Had she composed it here, among the irises by the river? Which came to her first, melody or lyric? Who had been the inspiration?

"You had your heart broken?" he asked her, hoping to mask his jealousy. He lifted the lyre from her hands, but his fingers were clumsy. He was unable to play anything remotely as beautiful as the music that had flowed from Lilith.

She leaned close to Cam, her eyelids lowering as she gazed at his lips. "Not yet." She reached for her instrument and strummed a twinkling chord. "No one's broken my lyre yet either, but a girl can't be too careful."

"Will you teach me to play?" he asked.

He wanted more time with Lilith—a strange feeling for him. He wanted to sit close and watch the sunlight sparkle in her hair, to memorize the graceful rhythms of her fingers as she pulled beauty from string and wood. He wanted her to look at him the way Liat looked at Dani. And he wanted to kiss those lips every day, all the time.

"Something tells me you already know how to play," she said. "Meet me here tomorrow night." She glanced at the sky. "When the moon sits in the same place, *you* sit in the same place."

Then she laughed, tucked her lyre into the tree, and skipped away, leaving a dark-haired, green-eyed angel falling madly in love for the very first time.

FIVE

MARKED

LILITH

Thirteen Days

Lilith wasn't expecting her world to change after her performance at the open mic. And it didn't. Not really.

Life still sucked.

"Lilith?" Her mother screamed before Lilith's alarm clock had even gone off. "Where is my marigold cardigan with the cheetah-print elbow patches?"

Lilith groaned and buried her head beneath her pillow. "The fashion police swung by to pick it up yesterday," she muttered to herself. "It was a menace to society."

Three soft raps on her open door made Lilith's head pop up. That was her brother's knock.

"Hey, Bruce," she said to the bed-headed boy chewing on a frozen waffle.

"Mom thinks you stole her fancy knockoff yellow sweater. She's getting kinda Incredible Hulk–y about it."

"Does she honestly think I would be caught dead in 'marigold'?" Lilith asked, and Bruce chuckled. "How you feeling, kid?"

Bruce shrugged. "Okay."

People often called Lilith's younger brother fragile because he was so thin and pale. But Bruce was the strongest force in Lilith's life. He was hopeful against all odds. He was fun just sitting around on the couch. He knew how to make her laugh. She wished he had a better life.

"Just okay?" Lilith asked, sitting up in bed.

Bruce shrugged. "Not great. My oxygen read was low today, so I have to stay home again." He sighed. "You're lucky."

A brutal laugh escaped Lilith's lips. "I'm lucky?"

"You get to go to school every day and hang out with your friends."

Bruce was so sincere Lilith couldn't even think of describing at length all the ways her entire school hated her.

"My only friend is Alastor," Bruce added, and at the sound of his name, the little dog trotted into Lilith's room. "And all he does is poop on the rug."

"Oh no you don't." Lilith scooped the mutt up before he ruined the pile of laundry she hadn't folded yet. Her one clean pair of jeans was in there. On her way into the bathroom, she touched her brother's shoulder. "Maybe your oxygen read will be better tomorrow. There's always hope."

As she got into the shower—the water was back on, but ever since the pipes had been shut off, the water smelled like rust—she thought about what she'd said to Bruce. Since when did Lilith believe there was *always hope* that tomorrow might be better?

She must have said it because she was trying to cheer him up. Her brother brought out the soft side no one else knew Lilith had. Bruce had such a good heart, and he so rarely got out of this house that only Lilith and her mom ever felt its warmth. He made it virtually impossible for Lilith to feel sorry for herself.

As Lilith got dressed, she closed her door and hummed the song she'd sung last night. It made her think, accidentally, about the longing in Cam's eyes when he'd handed her that guitar. As if she mattered to him. As if he needed her—or needed something from her.

Lilith scowled. Whatever Cam wanted from her, she wasn't going to give it up.

"Out of my way, poser." Some football jock with a square head knocked Lilith sideways into a row of beaten-up metal lockers. No one even blinked.

"Ow." Lilith rubbed her arm.

The fluorescent light above her flickered and buzzed. She kneeled on the snot-green tile to enter her combination and get her books for the day. A few lockers over, Chloe King was showing off the new angel-wing tattoo on her right shoulder to her latest boyfriend and as many of her friends as could crowd around.

When Chloe spotted Lilith, she smiled a big, suspicious smile. "Great performance last night, Lil!" she sang.

No way was Chloe actually being nice. Lilith knew she should exit the scene before this got nasty. "Um, thanks," she said, hurrying to unlock her locker.

"Oh my God, you thought I was being serious? That was a joke. Like your performance." Chloe burst out laughing and was joined by her entire clique.

"And . . . another awful day," Lilith muttered, turning back to her locker.

"Doesn't have to be."

Lilith looked up.

Luc, the intern she'd met the day before, was standing right over her. He leaned against the lockers, flipping a strange golden coin into the air.

"I heard you were always late to school," he said.

Lilith's chronic tardiness didn't strike her as fascinating gossip. Aside from Tarkenton, a few teachers, Jean, and now Cam, no one at Trumbull had ever cared to notice Lilith. "If you were expecting me to be late, why are you waiting for me before the bell?"

"Isn't that what one does in high school?" Luc glanced

around the hallway. "Wait at a classmate's locker in hopes of being asked to prom?"

"You're not a classmate. And I hope you're not trying to get me to ask you to prom. Because you would be waiting a long time." Lilith opened her locker and tossed in some books. Luc rested his elbows on the locker door and stared down at her. She glared up at him, waiting for him to move so she could close it.

"Have you ever heard of the Four Horsemen?" he asked.

"Everyone's heard of them." Chloe King turned away from her admirers to face Luc. Silver eyeliner glittered against her flawless dark skin, and she wore her hair in a hundred tiny braids. She glanced down at Lilith. "Even trash like her."

"Since when do you listen to the Four Horsemen?" Lilith asked.

The Four Horsemen were haunting and profound. Their rock ballads were smart and sad, and every album was different from the last, so true fans could see a real evolution in their style. Their lead singer, Ike Ligon, wrote songs that were the reason Lilith wanted to be a musician. There was no way a girl like Chloe could relate to the pain they expressed in their music.

"It's cruel to get her hopes up," Chloe said to Luc, and started humming the chorus of the Four Horsemen's latest single, "Sequins of Events."

Lilith shut her locker and stood. "Get my hopes up about what?"

"If you didn't skip school so often," Luc said to Lilith, "you might have heard the news."

"What news?" Lilith asked.

"The Four Horsemen are the closing band at prom," Chloe said. Behind her, her three girlfriends squealed. One of them had a soft guitar case slung over her shoulder, and Lilith realized these girls were probably in Chloe's band.

Lilith's blood drummed in her ears. "No way."

"I'm getting Ike's name tattooed right here." Chloe turned back to her boyfriend and his friends, undoing a button over her cleavage to show off her future ink site. "Right above my heart. See?"

The boys definitely saw.

"The Four Horsemen are coming to Crossroads?" Lilith said. *"Why?"*

Chloe shrugged, as if she couldn't imagine an amazing band not wanting to visit their dismal town. "They're helping Tarkenton judge the Battle of the Bands."

"Wait. You mean the Four Horsemen are going to watch bands from this school perform?" Lilith asked quietly. "At prom?"

Luc nodded as if he understood how world-altering this news was. "I pitched the idea to Ike myself."

"You know Ike Ligon?" Lilith blinked at Luc.

"We were texting last night," Luc said. "I hope this

doesn't embarrass you, but your performance at the open mic got me thinking about how amazing it would be for the Four Horsemen to perform a song written by a Trumbull student."

Luc had been there last night? Lilith was about to ask why, but all that came out of her mouth was, "Whoa." It had finally hit her: The Four Horsemen were going to be *here,* in Crossroads. At Trumbull. This was the closest she'd ever come to fangirling in public.

"Ike loved the idea," Luc said. "Starting today, we're accepting lyrics, even MP3s of student-written material, and Ike will sing the winning song to close out the prom."

"Daddy thinks it's a way to make prom more inclusive," Chloe added. "Except for freaks like you."

But Lilith was barely listening to Chloe. In her mind, she imagined Ike Ligon's scruffy face lighting up at her lyrics. For a split second she even imagined meeting him, and soon her fantasy had flown her to a real recording studio, with Ike producing her first album.

Chloe squinted at Lilith. "I'm sorry. Are you, like, imagining one of *your* songs getting picked?" Chloe turned back to her friends and laughed.

Lilith felt herself flush. "I don't—"

"You don't even have a *band,*" Chloe said. "Whereas mine already has three singles Ike is going to love." She slammed her locker. "It will be so amazing to be prom queen *and* win the battle *and* have the Four Horsemen cover one of my songs."

"Don't you mean one of *our* songs?" the girl with the guitar asked Chloe.

"Sure," Chloe said with a snort. "Whatever. Let's go." She snapped her fingers and started down the hallway, her friends nipping at her heels.

"She's not going to win," Luc whispered in Lilith's ear as Chloe walked away.

"She wins everything," Lilith murmured as she slung her backpack over her shoulder.

"Not this." Something in Luc's tone made Lilith stop and turn around. "You have a real shot at winning, Lilith, only . . . Never mind."

"What?"

Luc frowned. "Cam." He glanced at the other students flowing past them toward their classes. "I know he pressured you to start a band with him yesterday. Don't do it."

"I wasn't planning to," Lilith said. "But why do you care?"

"You don't know Cam like I do."

"No," Lilith agreed. "But I don't need to know him to know I hate him." Saying it out loud made her realize how strange it sounded. She *did* hate Cam, and she didn't even know why. He hadn't done anything to her, and yet the thought of him made her tense up and want to break something.

"Don't tell anyone I told you this"—Luc leaned in—"but a while back, Cam was in a band with this chick singer—"

"*Chick singer?*" Lilith narrowed her eyes. Guys sucked.

"Female vocalist, I mean," Luc said with a slight eye roll. "She wrote all the songs. And she was totally in love with him."

Lilith wasn't interested in Cam, but it wasn't a huge surprise that other girls were. She got it: Cam was sexy and magnetic, but he wasn't her type. When he turned his charm on her, it only made Lilith despise him more.

"Who cares?" she asked.

"You should," Luc replied. "Especially if you're going to get into bed with him—musically speaking."

"I'm not getting into bed with Cam in any sense," Lilith said. "I just want to be left alone."

"Good," Luc said with a cryptic smile. "Because Cam is . . . how should I put this? He's more the love-'em-and-leave-'em type."

Lilith thought she might throw up. "So what?"

"So one day, after things had been going so well—or at least so this young girl thought," Luc said, "Cam just disappeared. No one heard from him for months. Though we did hear *of* him, eventually. You remember that song 'Death of Stars'?"

"By Dysmorphia?" Lilith nodded. She'd only ever heard that one single, but she'd loved it. "It was never not on the radio last summer."

"That's because of Cam." Luc frowned. "He stole the girl's lyrics, claimed them as his own, and sold the song to Lowercase Records."

"Why would he do that?" Lilith said. She thought back to that moment the day before when he'd gently coaxed her from paralyzing stage fright into song. She loathed him, and yet . . . that had been one of the nicest things anyone had ever done for her.

The bell rang, and the crowd in the hall thinned as students filtered into classrooms. Over Luc's shoulder, Lilith saw Tarkenton sweeping the halls for tardy students. "I have to go," she said.

"I'm just saying," Luc said, beginning to walk away, "your songs are good. Too good to let Cam strike again."

⚹

Lilith walked toward her homeroom, her mind spinning. How could she waste her time in class when there was a songwriting competition judged by Ike Ligon coming up? She didn't even care that it was happening at prom. She could show up just for the Battle of the Bands. She didn't need a date or a dress. She only needed to be in the same room as Ike Ligon.

She should be practicing right now. She should be writing more songs.

Before she knew it, her feet had led her to the band room.

Cam sat on the floor, tuning the slim green electric

guitar she'd seen him play the other day. Jean Rah was tapping out a rhythm on his jeans with his drumsticks. What were they doing in here?

"We were just talking about you," Jean Rah said.

"You guys aren't supposed to be here," Lilith said.

"Neither are you," Cam said, and gave her another infuriating wink.

"Do you have some sort of tic?" Lilith asked. "Like a muscle spasm in your eye?"

Cam looked taken aback. "It's called a wink, Lilith. Some people actually find it charming."

"Other people think it makes you look like a huge perv," Lilith said.

Cam stared at her, and she waited for him to say something snarky, but instead he said, "Sorry. Won't happen again."

Lilith sighed. She needed to focus on her music, and Cam was a distraction. Everything about him was distracting, from the way his fingers moved over his guitar, to the inscrutable smile crinkling his green eyes when he glanced up at her. She didn't like it.

And she'd never liked Jean. She wanted them both out. Her mouth pinched into a scowl. "Please leave," she said. "Both of you."

"We were here first," Jean said. "If anyone needs to leave, it's you."

"Both of you, chill," Cam said. "Let's just jam. Wait until you hear this groove Jean and I just made up."

"No," Lilith said. "I came to work on something. Privately. I don't even have my guitar."

Cam was already inside the band closet, pulling one from a case. He walked toward Lilith and rested the guitar in her hands, reaching behind her head to drape the strap over her shoulders. It was a Les Paul, with a thin neck and a cool silver spray-paint job on its fingerboard. She'd never held such a nice guitar before.

"Now what's your excuse?" Cam asked softly. His hands stayed at the nape of her neck longer than they needed to, like he didn't want to pull away.

So she did.

The smile on Cam's lips vanished, as if she'd hurt him somehow.

If she had, she told herself she didn't care. She didn't know why he was being so forward, what he meant by encouraging her music.

She thought about Chloe King, how rude she'd been to her about the open mic performance. It was the only time Lilith had ever played in public. Holding this guitar, she realized that she didn't want it to be the last.

It didn't mean they were starting a band. They could just, as Cam said, *jam*.

"What do I do?" she said, feeling vulnerable. She didn't like being at anyone's mercy—especially Cam's.

Silently, Cam guided her hand up the guitar's warm neck. His right hand traced hers over the strings. She swayed a little.

"You know what to do," Cam said.

"I don't. I've never—with other people—I . . ."

"Just start playing," Cam said. "Wherever you go, we'll follow you."

He nodded at Jean, who tapped his drumsticks together four times as Cam grabbed the slim green Jaguar bass with the vintage-style tremolo arm.

And then, like it was no big deal, Lilith set her fingers free.

Her guitar locked in with Jean Ra's kick drum like a heartbeat. Cam's scratchy chords crisscrossed the heavy rhythm like a Kurt-Cobain-and-Joe-Strummer hybrid. Every now and then, Jean fingered the short, black Moog synthesizer that sat next to his drum kit. The synth chords buzzed like fat and friendly bees, their vibrations finding safe homes in the spaces left by the other instruments.

After a while, Cam lifted his hand into the air. Lilith and Jean stopped playing. They could all sense they were onto something.

"Let's move on to some vocals," Cam said.

"You mean, like, now?" Lilith asked. "Just like that?"

"Just like that." Cam flipped a switch and tested the mic with a fingertip, then aimed the mic at Lilith and stepped back. "How about the song you sang yesterday?"

" 'Exile,' " Lilith said, her heart racing. She took out her journal, the one with all her lyrics, but then she thought back to the day before, how much everyone had hated her performance. What was she doing? Performing in front of anyone else was only going to cause her more humiliation.

Then she thought of Ike Ligon singing her song in front of the entire school.

"I'm ready," she said.

Softly, Cam said, "One, two, three, four," and he and Jean began. Cam motioned for Lilith to start singing.

She couldn't.

"What's wrong?" Cam asked.

Everything, she wanted to say. The only thing Lilith had ever known was disappointment. Nothing in her life ever worked out. Which, for the most part, was okay, because she never let herself expect anything, so she never really cared.

But this? Music?

It mattered to her. If she sang and she sucked, or if her song wasn't chosen for the battle, or if she, Cam, and Jean started a band and it all fell apart, Lilith would lose the only thing she cared about. The stakes were too high.

Best to back away now.

"I can't," she said.

"Why not?" Cam asked. "We're good together. You know that—"

"I *don't* know that." Her eyes met Cam's, and she felt tense, like a wire about to snap. She remembered her conversation with Luc that morning, and the chorus of Dismorphia's "Death of Stars" started playing in her mind:

The stars are on your face tonight
There is no outer space tonight

"What is it?" Cam said.

Should she ask him about the song? And the girl? Was that crazy?

What if Cam *was* a lyric thief? What if that was the real, secret reason he wanted to start a band with her? Aside from her guitar, Lilith's songs were the only things she valued. Without them, she had nothing.

"I have to go," Lilith said. She set down the guitar and grabbed her bag. "And I'm not entering my lyrics in the competition. It's over."

"Wait—" Cam called, but she was already out the band room door.

Outside, Lilith crossed the school parking lot toward the smoke-filled woods. She coughed, trying not to think about how good it had felt to make music with Cam and Jean. It was stupid to have jammed with them, stupid to hope for anything, because she was Lilith and everything always sucked and she never, ever got what she wanted in life.

Other kids didn't hesitate when they were asked about their dreams. "College," they'd say, "then a career in finance." Or, "Backpack in Europe for two years," or, "Join the marines." It was as if everyone but Lilith had gotten an email that explained which schools to apply to, and how to join Tri Delt once you were there, and what to do if you wanted to be a doctor.

Lilith wanted to be a musician, a singer of her own songs—but she knew better than to believe it was possible.

She sat down at her spot by the creek and unzipped her backpack, reaching inside for her journal. Her fingers groped for the book. She reached deeper, pushing aside her history textbook, her pencil bag, her key ring. Where was her journal? She opened the bag wide and dumped out its contents, but the bound black book wasn't there.

Then she remembered she'd taken it out in the band room when she thought she was going to sing. It was still in there. With Cam.

In a heartbeat, Lilith was on her feet and sprinting back to the band room, running faster than she knew she could. She shoved open the door, gasping for breath.

The band room was empty. Cam and Jean—and her black notebook—were gone.

SIX

GOING UNDER

CAM

Twelve Days

Lilith's black notebook lay open on a bench in the boys' locker room the next morning as Cam got dressed for school. When she'd run out of the band room yesterday, his intention had been to return the journal to her immediately. He'd looked for her at Rattlesnake Creek, but she wasn't there, and he couldn't drop it at her house because he didn't know where she lived.

The longer he held the journal in his hands, though, the deeper the temptation became to open it. By sundown, he broke, and he'd stayed on the roof of the Trumbull gym all night, reading and rereading every one of Lilith's brilliant, devastating songs by the light of his cell phone.

He knew it was wrong. A violation of her privacy. But he couldn't stop himself. It was like someone had lifted the velvet rope outside Lilith's heart and given him VIP access. Once, long ago, Cam had touched this tender, vulnerable side of Lilith, but now he could only glimpse it through her songs.

And these songs? They wrecked him. Each one— from "Misery Loves" to "Standing at the Cliff's Edge" to Cam's personal favorite, "Somebody's Other Blues"— was dominated by suffering, humiliation, and betrayal. The worst part was knowing precisely where all this pain came from. Bearing the memories for both of them was torture.

The way Lilith looked at him now, like he was a stranger, was torture, too. Cam could finally empathize with Daniel, who'd had to start over with Lucinda every time they met.

Dressing in another stolen T-shirt and his usual jeans and leather jacket, Cam was so ashamed of the pain he'd caused Lilith that he found it hard to meet his own eyes in the mirror. He finger-combed his wet hair and was surprised to find that it felt a little thinner. And, now that he thought about it, his jeans felt a little tighter around the waist.

He leaned in to look at his reflection and was taken

aback by a few age spots near his hairline—which, he could see, had receded a half inch. What was happening?

Then it hit him: *Lucifer* was happening to him, manipulating Cam's mortal appearance to make winning Lilith's love even harder. As if it wasn't hard enough already.

If the devil was slowly stripping away the good looks Cam took for granted, what advantage would he have left? He would have to up his game. His gaze fell on Lilith's journal, and suddenly he knew what he had to do.

The dismal, dusty library was the one place on Trumbull's campus that actually had reliable Wi-Fi. Cam grabbed a chair by the window so he could see when Lilith's bus arrived. It was a Saturday morning, which meant that under other circumstances Lilith might still be sleeping, but Saturday meant nothing in Crossroads. Lucifer had bragged that there were no weekends in this Hell. None of the other students noticed or cared, for instance, that their prom was taking place on a Wednesday.

Cam pitied them. They had no idea of the particular joy of a Friday afternoon at four o'clock, or the hedonistic thrill of a Saturday-midnight joyride that took all of Sunday to recover from—and they never would.

Through the library window Cam could see hints of orange light given off by the wildfires encircling Crossroads. He knew Lilith's temper would rival their blaze if she discovered what he was about to do, but he had to risk it.

He Googled the Four Horsemen and soon found an

email address for Ike Ligon. It was a long shot that his email would reach the lead singer and not some assistant, but the only other way to reach Ike—through Lucifer—was not an option.

All the other songs submitted to the prom lyrics contest would be vetted by Luc. Cam knew the Four Horsemen wouldn't judge a thing, and that, as of yesterday, Lilith wasn't planning on submitting a song. She was more talented than everyone in Crossroads put together, and Cam wanted her favorite singer to hear her music—without being swayed by the devil.

He settled into his chair, and into Lilith's voice, as he crafted an email on his phone.

Dear Mr. Ligon,

    I hope you don't mind me reaching out directly, but your songs have always inspired me, so I wanted to share one of mine with you. I can't wait to see you perform when you visit Crossroads. My bio and lyrics for the Battle of the Bands competition are attached. Thanks for everything.

The black journal sat on Cam's lap, but he found he didn't need to open it. He typed out the lyrics of his favorite, "Somebody's Other Blues," from memory:

I dreamed life was a dream
Someone was having in my eyes

I was outside looking in
And all I saw was lies
It's not my life, it's not my life
I'm not the one not having fun

Cam typing out the rest of the lyrics, impressed by the power of Lilith's songwriting. The bio was trickier. No musician was candid in a bio. They listed their albums, maybe an influence, whether they had been lucky enough to hit the charts, then they said where they lived, and that was it.

But Cam found it impossible to write about Lilith's life and Lilith's unique situation from an objective point of view. Instead, he wrote:

I wrote this song at the creek behind my school, where I go to escape when the world gets suffocating. I go there every day. I'd live there if I could. I wrote this song after I got my heart broken, but not right after. I got hurt so bad that it took a long time before I could put what it felt like into words. There are still some things about my broken heart that I don't understand, and I don't know if I ever will. But music helps. That's why I write, and that's why I listen to music all the time. For what it's worth, your songs are my favorites.

I don't expect to win this contest. I've learned never to expect anything at all. It's an honor just to think of you reading something I wrote.

As he typed the final words, Cam's vision blurred. His eyes filled with tears.

He hadn't cried when he was exiled from the presence of the Throne, or when he'd fallen through the Void. He hadn't even cried when he'd first lost Lilith all those millennia ago.

But now he couldn't stop himself. Lilith had suffered so much. And Cam had been the cause of it. He'd known she was hurt when they split up—how could he not have known?—but he'd never expected the pain and anger to stay with her for so long, to dominate her as it did in Crossroads. The spirit of the girl he loved was still there, but it had been tortured, ruthlessly.

His tears came, hard and steady. He was glad to be alone in the library.

Hzzzzzz.

One of Cam's tears had fallen onto the table, making a sizzling sound. He watched it burn a hole through the Formica, and then through the carpet underneath. Black smoke swirled up from the floor.

Cam leapt to his feet, wiping his eyes on the sleeve of his leather jacket—and watched his tears eat through the leather, too. What was happening?

"Demons should never cry."

Cam turned to find Luc wearing a wireless headset, playing *Doom* on his tablet at the table behind Cam. How long had he been there?

The devil threw off his headset. "Don't you know what demon tears are made of?"

"I've never had a reason to know," Cam said.

"Nasty stuff," Luc said. "Toxic in the extreme. So be careful. Or don't be—your call."

Cam glanced back at his phone, glad his tears hadn't fallen on it. He quickly hit Send. Lucifer whistled under his breath.

"You're losing it," Luc said. "Lilith's going to hate that you just did that."

"If you interfere with this," Cam said, "it invalidates our wager."

Lucifer chuckled. "You're doing enough damage on your own, bud. You don't need my help." He paused. "In fact, your performance thus far is so pathetic, I feel sorry for you. So I'm going to throw you a bone."

The devil held out a Post-it note, which Cam snatched. "What is this?"

"Lilith's address," Luc said. "She's going to straight-up whale on you when you return the journal. Might be best to do it in private, not in front of the whole school."

Cam grabbed his messenger bag and pushed past the devil and through the library doors. There was an hour until the bell. Maybe Lilith would still be at home.

He jogged to the back lot of the school, waited for a garbage truck to drive by, and then unpinned his wings. He felt good with his wings out. His hair could thin and his waist could thicken at Lucifer's whim, but his wings would always be his most beautiful feature. Broad and strong and glittering in the smoky light and—

Cam winced when he saw the tips of his wings looking thin and webbed, more like batwings than those of a glorious fallen angel. Another of Lucifer's attacks on his vanity. Cam couldn't let it paralyze him. He had twelve days left with Lilith, and far too much to do.

Clouds of ash drifted over his wings as he soared into the sky. He felt the heat of the burning hills lick his body, so he flew higher, until suddenly, above him, the sky seemed to curve, and a translucent barrier appeared before him, just like the glass encasing the snow globes Lucifer had shown him in Aevum.

He had reached the upper limits of Lilith's Hell.

From here, he could see everything. There wasn't much. The main roads in the town—even the highway next to school—were all loops, which sent the cars that drove on them in endless, pointless circles. Beyond the widest ring of road was the ring of burning hills.

Claustrophobia made his wings twitch. He had to break Lilith free of this place.

Cam banked left and soared downward, toward a run-down neighborhood near the end of High Meadow Road. He pulled up short and hovered in the air, twenty feet above Lilith's house. The roof was caving in in a few places, and the landscaping looked like it had been abandoned a decade ago. The air was particularly smoky in this part of town. It must have been an awful place to grow up.

He heard her voice from below. She sounded angry. She always sounded angry. He quickly furled his wings and landed on the dead brown grass of her backyard.

Lilith was sitting on the porch with a young boy who must have been her brother. At the sight of Cam rounding the corner, Lilith rose and balled her fists. "Where's my journal?"

Without speaking, Cam reached into his bag and handed the black book over. Their fingers touched as she took it from him, and Cam felt an electric surge through his body.

He wished suddenly that he could keep that journal. Having it with him last night had been almost like having Lilith with him. Tonight, he'd sleep alone again.

"Who's he?" her brother asked, nodding at Cam.

Cam held out his hand to the boy. "I'm Cam. What's your name?"

"Bruce," the boy said brightly, before falling into a coughing fit. His hands and feet were big compared with the rest of him, like he should have been much larger but hadn't managed to grow.

"Don't talk to him," Lilith said to her brother, clutching Bruce with one arm and her journal with the other. She glanced up at Cam. "See what you did?"

"Is he okay?" Cam asked.

"Like you care." She glanced at her journal. "You didn't read it, did you?"

He had memorized every word. "Of course not," Cam said. He didn't want to make a habit of lying to her, but this was different. She deserved to win that lyrics contest. If she did, Cam wanted her to be surprised. If she didn't—because of Lucifer's meddling—he didn't want her to be disappointed.

"Then why did you take it?" she asked.

"So that I could give it back," he said, which was true. "I know it's important to you." He dared a step closer and studied the way her hair caught the sunlight. "While I'm here, I also wanted to apologize."

Lilith tilted her head, suspicious. "I don't have time for all the things you need to apologize for."

"That's probably true," Cam said. "I know I can come on strong sometimes. But when I bug you about starting a band, it's only because I believe in you and your music. I like playing with you. But I'll back off. At least I'll try to. If you want me to." He met her eyes. "Do you want me to?"

For a moment Cam thought he saw a ray of light come into Lilith's eyes. But maybe it was only wishful thinking.

"I thought you'd never ask," she said coldly. "Come on, Bruce. It's time to check your oxygen."

The boy had stopped coughing by then. He was petting a little white dog who'd trotted out from the house. "Are you Lilith's boyfriend?"

Cam grinned. "I like this kid."

"Shut up," Lilith said.

"Well, is he?" Bruce asked Lilith. "Because if he's your boyfriend, he's going to have to win me over, too. Like with arcade games and ice cream and, like, teaching me to throw a baseball."

"Why stop there?" Cam asked. "I'll teach you to throw a football, a punch, a poker match, and even"—he glanced at Lilith—"the coolest girl off her game."

"Poker," Bruce whispered.

"How about teaching yourself the fine art of leaving?" Lilith said to Cam.

Cam heard a woman hollering Lilith's name from inside the house. She got to her feet and guided Bruce toward the door.

"Nice to meet you, Bruce."

"You too, Cam," the little boy said. "I've never heard that name before. I'll remember it."

"Don't bother," Lilith said, glaring at Cam before ushering the boy back inside. "You'll never see him again."

SEVEN

LOVE WILL TEAR US APART

LILITH

Eleven Days

Lilith had decided long ago that Trumbull's lunchroom was nothing short of a torture chamber, but the next morning Cam slipped a note in her locker asking her to meet him in the band room during lunch—so there was no way she was going there. And while Rattlesnake Creek was always calling her name, today she was actually hungry.

So the cafeteria it was. Just before noon, she entered the noisy labyrinth of sticky lunch tables. Conversations quieted and benches creaked the moment she stepped inside.

For a second, she saw herself through their eyes: A hostile scowl pinching her lips. The feral look in her blue eyes. Cheap black jeans so busted they were more hole than denim. The tangled bright red hair no brush could tame. Even Lilith wouldn't want to eat lunch with Lilith.

"Did you find a dollar on the street? Or did you come to beg for scraps?" Chloe King said, appearing in Lilith's path. Chloe held her tray casually with one hand. Her fingernails were lilac. Her mane of braids swished as she walked.

"Leave me alone." Lilith pushed past, knocking the tray out of Chloe's hands, spilling her burger and fries to the floor and a carton of milk onto Chloe's tight white suede minidress.

"You'd better be glad this is white, or your broke-ass mom would be at the bank taking out a loan to buy me a new one."

The girls from her band, the Slights, came to Chloe's side, each one in a different-colored pastel minidress. Suddenly, as if a spotlight had found them, Lilith could visualize their band onstage. They probably couldn't play their instruments, but Chloe's band would win the battle because everyone would think they looked hot. It wasn't like Lilith even had a band anyway, but the thought of Chloe winning made her furious.

"Are you listening?" Chloe said. "Hello?" She nudged her burger with the toe of her boot. "Maybe we should thank Lilith for reminding us not to eat the crap they serve here."

Her friends laughed predictably.

Out of the corner of her eye, Lilith saw Cam enter the cafeteria, guitar case in hand. "I wouldn't be caught dead at prom. I'm not entering the Battle of the Bands, so even someone who sings like you has a chance."

"Your mom came by my house the other night looking for work," Chloe said. "Daddy felt sorry for her. I offered to let her clean my toilet—"

"That's a lie," Lilith snarled.

"Someone's gotta pay the medical bills for your sick runt brother."

"Shut up," Lilith said.

"Of course, Daddy didn't give your mom a dime." Chloe buffed her nails against her dress. "He knows a bad investment when he sees one, and anyone can tell that kid's a goner."

Lilith lunged forward, grabbed Chloe's braids, and yanked them hard.

Chloe's head snapped back and her eyes watered as she fell to her knees. "Stop," she said. "Please stop."

Lilith tightened her grip. People could say whatever they wanted about *her*, but no one put down her brother.

"Let go, you animal!" The blond one—Kara—wailed, bouncing on her toes like she'd been sprung.

"Should I be filming this for, like, evidence?" Chloe's friend June asked, pulling out her phone.

"Lilith—" Cam rested his hand on the nape of her neck. At his touch, something rushed through her, immobilizing her.

Then her brain engaged. This was none of Cam's business. She'd known from the moment she saw him that he was the kind of guy who hurt people. She took her fury out on Chloe's head, tugging her braids harder. "Go away, Cam."

He didn't. *You're better than this,* his hand seemed to be telling her.

Cam didn't know the pain and stress and humiliation Lilith had to deal with on a daily basis. He didn't know her at all.

"What?" she demanded, turning to look at him. "What do you want?"

He nodded toward Chloe. "Kick her ass."

June dropped her cell phone and leaped at Lilith, but Cam slipped between them and held her back. June bit his arm like a piranha.

"Let her go!" Kara screamed at Cam. "Principal Tarkenton? Somebody? Help!"

Lilith didn't know if Tarkenton was in the cafeteria. It was hard to see much beyond the tight circle of twenty or so students that had gathered around them.

"Fight! Fight! Fight!" the crowd chanted.

And then—suddenly—it all just felt so stupid.

Fighting Chloe wasn't going to change anything. It wouldn't make Lilith's life better. If anything, it would make it worse. She could be expelled, and they could find an even worse place to send her to school. Lilith loosened her fingers and let go of Chloe, who slumped to the ground, rubbing her scalp.

Kara, June, and Teresa rushed to help Chloe up.

"Honey, are you hurt?" Kara asked.

"How's your strumming hand?" Teresa asked, lifting and flexing Chloe's guitar-playing hand.

Chloe reared up, baring her teeth at Lilith and Cam. "Why don't you two run away and start your worthless lives together? I hear a meth lab calling your name." She touched her temple and winced. "You've got top billing on my shit list, Lilith. You'd better watch yourself."

Chloe and her band stalked away. The crowd dispersed slowly, disappointed that there hadn't been more of a fight.

Lilith stood next to Cam, not feeling the need to say anything. She should have just let Chloe's insults slide off her like she did every other day. Her mother would be furious when she heard about this.

Cam pulled Lilith against the nearest cafeteria table to let a few students walk past. But when the students were gone, he didn't let her go. She felt his hand on the small of her back and, for some reason, she didn't flick it off.

"Don't let the bitches get you down," he said.

Lilith rolled her eyes. "Transcend girls who think they're better than me by pretending I'm better than them? Thanks for the advice."

"That's not what I meant," Cam said.

"But you just called them bitches."

"Chloe is playing a role," Cam said, "like an actress."

"What are you doing, Cam?" she said, feeling tired. "Why egg me on to fight Chloe? Why try to cheer me up now? Why pretend to be interested in my music? You don't know me, so why do you care?"

"Did it ever occur to you that I might *want* to know you?" Cam said.

Lilith crossed her arms and looked down, uncomfortable. "There's nothing to know."

"I doubt that," he said. "For example . . . what do you think about before you fall asleep at night? How dark do you like your toast? Where would you go if you could travel anywhere in the world?" He stepped closer, his voice dropping almost to a whisper as he reached out to touch her face below her left cheekbone. "How'd you get that scar?" He smiled a little. "See? Plenty of fascinating secrets in there."

Lilith opened her mouth. Closed it. Was he serious?

She studied his face. His features were relaxed, like he wasn't trying to persuade her to do something for once, like he was content just to stand next to her. He was serious, she decided. And she had no idea how to respond.

She felt something within her stir. A memory, a flash of recognition, she wasn't sure. But something about Cam seemed suddenly, strangely familiar. She looked down and noticed her hands were trembling.

"You can trust me," Cam told her.

"No," she said softly. "I don't do trust."

Cam leaned closer, tilting his head until the tips of their noses almost touched. "I'll never hurt you, Lilith."

What was happening? Lilith closed her eyes. She felt like she might faint.

When she opened them, Cam was even closer. His lips came close to hers—

And then Jean Rah's voice broke the spell between them. "Hey, dudes."

Lilith stepped back, stumbling over her own feet. Her knees were weak, and her heart was racing. She looked at Cam, who wiped his forehead with the back of his hand and exhaled. Jean Rah was oblivious to anything that might have been about to happen.

He held up his phone. "Band room's open till one. Just saying."

A text chimed on Jean's phone, and his eyebrows shot up. "You pulled out Chloe King's weave and I missed it?"

Lilith laughed, and then something crazy happened: Jean joined in, and Cam did, too, and suddenly the three of them were laughing so hard they were crying, like it was the most natural thing in the world.

Like they were friends.

Were they friends? It felt good to laugh, that was all Lilith knew. It felt light, like springtime, the first day you go outside without a coat. She looked at Jean and couldn't remember why she'd ever hated him.

And then it was over. They stopped laughing. Everything went back to dreary normality.

"Lilith," Cam said, "can I talk to you alone?"

There was something about the way he asked that made her want to say yes. But *yes* was a dangerous word all of a sudden. Lilith didn't want to be alone with Cam. Not now. Whatever he'd been trying to do a moment ago had been too much.

"Hey, Jean?" she said.

"Yeah?"

"Let's go jam."

Jean shrugged and followed Lilith out of the cafeteria. "Later, Cam."

⚜

In the band room, a scrawny, dark-haired freshman in a tie-dyed T-shirt was struggling to set a huge copper timpani drum onto its base. The kid had long hair that nearly covered his eyes, and almond-colored skin. Jean watched the spectacle with interest, scratching his chin. "Yo, Luis. Need a hand?"

"I'm cool," the boy wheezed.

Jean turned to Lilith like she was a calculus problem he didn't know where to begin solving. "Did you really want to jam, or were you just trying to make Cam jealous?"

"Why would us playing together make Cam jealous?" Lilith started to say, but she stopped. "I really want to jam."

"Cool," Jean said. "You know, I was at that stupid open mic. Your song was good."

Lilith felt herself blush. "It was a real crowd-pleaser," she said darkly.

"Screw this school," Jean said, shrugging. "I was clapping for you." Then he motioned toward Luis. "The three of us should start a band. There's still time to sign up for prom—"

"I'm not going to prom," Lilith said. She felt confused about a lot of things lately, but that was one truth she knew for certain.

Jean frowned. "But you have to. You're awesome."

The compliment was so direct Lilith didn't know how to respond.

"I mean, whatever," Jean said. "Skip the *prom* part of prom, bring a date or rock it solo, but at least show up for the battle. I have to go to the whole thing, because my insane girlfriend has been obsessing about this 'cranberry satin maxidress' since our first date. See? She's texting me right now."

He held up his phone. The lock screen displayed a photo of Kimi Grace, the sassy half-Korean, half-Mexican girl who sat next to Lilith in poetry. Lilith hadn't known she was with Jean—but now, she could totally see it.

In the photo, Kimi was beaming, holding up a piece of paper that read, in bubble letters, ELEVEN DAYS TILL THE BEST NIGHT OF OUR LIVES.

"She's cute," Lilith offered. "She's excited."

"She's all kinds of crazy," Jean said. "My point is, everyone makes such a big deal about how prom is this *epic* night. Well, it actually might exceed the hype if you showed up and played some epic music."

Lilith rolled her eyes. "Nothing about Trumbull is 'epic' . . . I promise."

Jean wiggled one of his eyebrows. "Maybe not yet." He patted Luis on the shoulder. The freshman threw his head back and shook some hair out of his face. "Luis here plays drums, not terribly."

"Yeah," Luis said. "What he said."

"Luis," Jean said. "You got a date to prom yet?"

"I'm weighing my options," he said, turning red. "I know a couple senior girls who might invite me. But even if they don't, I'll be there to play. No doubt. I can totally drum."

"See? He's dedicated," Jean Rah said. "So, Luis on drums"—Jean rustled through the instruments in the closet and pulled out a black Moog synthesizer—"you singing and playing guitar. And I'll drop in on the synth. Sounds like a band to me."

It did sound like a band. And Lilith had always dreamed of playing in one. But . . .

"Why are you hesitating?" Jean asked. "This is a slam dunk."

Maybe Jean was right. Maybe it really was just a simple decision. Some kids. Some instruments. A band. She bit her lip so Jean wouldn't see her smiling.

"Okay," she said. "Let's do it."

"Sweet!" Luis shouted. "I mean . . . cool."

"Yeah," Jean said. "Cool. Now grab a guitar from the closet."

Lilith followed his instructions, watching as Jean Rah placed the guitar on its stand, then pulled the stand next to the mic. He disappeared into the closet and came out with a brown card table. He set it up next to Lilith and sat the Moog keyboard on it.

"Try it," he said.

She played a C on the keyboard with her left hand. Her guitar growled out a punchy C. Her fingers danced a quick ascending riff on the MIDI keys, and her guitar responded perfectly. "Cool, huh?" Jean said. "Keep the audience on their toes."

"Yeah," Lilith said, impressed with Jean Rah's musical ingenuity. "Definitely."

"Hey, what's our band name?" Luis asked. "We're not really a band if we don't have a name."

Lilith inhaled and said, "Revenge."

She smiled, because all of a sudden, for the very first time, she was part of something bigger than herself.

"Radical." Luis lifted his drumsticks, then slapped a snare drum as hard as he could.

The sound was still reverberating through the band room when the door swung open and Principal Tarkenton stepped inside. He was glowering. "My office, Lilith. Now."

⁂

Hurrying into Tarkenton's office, Lilith's mom ignored her and gave the principal a hug. "I'm so sorry, Jim."

Her mom had already been on campus, subbing for the French teacher, so she was in Tarkenton's office within minutes for the emergency parent-teacher conference.

"It's not your fault, Janet," Tarkenton said, straightening his tie. "I've worked with enough bad seeds to know one when I see one."

Lilith looked around the office. Tarkenton's walls were covered with photographs of him fishing in Crossroads's one dismal lake.

"Your daughter started a fight with one of our most

promising students," Tarkenton said. "Fueled by jealousy, I imagine."

"I heard." Her mom adjusted the pink floral scarf tied tightly around her neck. "And Chloe's such a nice girl."

Lilith stared at the ceiling and tried not to show how much it hurt that her mother never even considered standing up for her.

"And with Chloe's father being so influential in the town," her mom continued, "I hope he won't pass judgment on the rest of my family. My Bruce doesn't need any more trouble, poor boy."

If Bruce were there, he would have rolled his eyes. He'd been treated like a ghost his whole life by everyone except Lilith, and he hated it.

"Detention doesn't seem to be a deterrent to her," Tarkenton went on. "But there is another option: a school for wayward students." He slid a brochure across his desk. Lilith read the gothic-printed words *Sword & Cross Reform School*.

"But what about prom?" Lilith asked. She had only just formed a band and hadn't even signed it up for prom yet—but she wanted to. More than she'd wanted anything in a long time. Maybe ever. She wished she had a mother who would understand that, a mother she could confide in about her fears and dreams. Instead she had Janet, who was still convinced Lilith had taken her stupid yellow cardigan.

"Since when are you going to prom?" her mom asked.

"Did a boy ask you? Is it that boy I saw you talking to outside yesterday? The one who didn't even ring the bell to introduce himself?"

"Mom, please." Lilith groaned. "It's not about a boy. It's about the Battle of the Bands. I want to play."

Tarkenton glanced at the enrollment sheet for the battle on the corner of his desk. "Don't see you on here, Lilith."

She grabbed the sheet and quickly wrote her new band's name. Now it was real. She stared at it and swallowed.

"Revenge?" Tarkenton snorted. "That sounds anti-authority."

"I'm not—that's not what our band is about," Lilith said. "Please, give me one more chance."

All she wanted was the opportunity to play her music, to see the Four Horsemen, to stand on a stage and sing and, for a few minutes, forget her horrible life. Performing wasn't something she had even known she wanted before she'd bonded with Jean Rah and Luis, but now it was all she could think about.

After that, Tarkenton and her mom could do whatever they wanted with her.

As they discussed Lilith's future and potential disciplinary action, Lilith looked through Tarkenton's window at the parking lot, where Luc was walking toward a red Corvette parked close to the building. What was he doing here? He slid behind the wheel and revved the engine loudly.

"What is that?" Tarkenton said, and spun toward the sound.

"It's very loud," her mom said, squinting. "Is that . . . a Corvette?"

Lilith eyed Luc with curiosity. Could he see her through the window?

"Who is that boy?" her mom asked. "He looks too old to be in high school. Do you know him, Lilith?"

Lilith glanced at her mother, wondering how to answer that question. When she looked back at the parking lot, Luc was gone, as though he'd never been there to begin with.

"No," Lilith said, turning her attention back to the sign-up sheet on Tarkenton's desk. "Now can I please be in the battle?"

She watched as her mother and the principal exchanged glances. Then Tarkenton leaned back in his chair and said, "One more chance. But even the smallest screwup and you're done," he continued. "You hear me?"

Lilith nodded. "Thank you."

Her heart was pounding. She was officially a musician.

INTERLUDE

ISOLATION

TRIBE OF DAN, NORTHERN CANAAN

Approximately 1000 BCE

Cam had been watching the moon for hours, willing it to speed its path across the desert sky. Almost a day had passed since he'd said goodbye to Lilith at the carob tree. It had all seemed so charming when she was making the plans, inviting Cam to meet her again at the river in the moonlight, but to wait all these hours to see her was a new kind of torture.

It wasn't like Cam to let a mortal girl slow him down.

"Pathetic," he muttered, unfurling his white wings and feeling a sense of freedom as they stretched toward the sky.

Who was he, Daniel Grigori?

He despised feeling bound to anyone or anything. But he couldn't seem to help himself when it came to Lilith. She made him want to stay.

Cam took to the sky, flying toward Lilith's village. He landed swiftly and folded his wings out of sight, ducking into a wine tent near the oasis, the last place he might find her. He was considering not keeping their date. He took a seat in a darkened corner, struck up a conversation with two local men, and shared the contents of their earthenware flagon.

By the time Cam and his new friends had drained the flagon, the moon hung low in the sky. He had expected to feel relieved—now there was nothing he could do. Lilith might forgive him, but she would never trust or fall in love with him now.

That was what he'd wanted, wasn't it?

⚜

In the morning, Lilith opened her eyes and sat up before memory stabbed her. Why had Cam agreed to meet her if he'd never planned to show up? Or had something happened that prevented him from coming? All she knew was that when the moon was in the center of the sky, she'd been there—and he hadn't.

The only thing to do was ask him, and the only place

Lilith could think to look for Cam was at the well. Eventually, everyone in her tribe went there. She hummed as she followed the narrow, dusty path to the center of the village. The sky was clear, the grass was high against her fingertips, and the hot air pressed down on her shoulders.

Where the northbound path met the westbound path sat the village well. It was made of packed, baked mud, with a wooden basket that dipped down to its belly on a thick, coarse rope. The water came up cool and clean even on the hottest summer day.

Lilith was surprised to find two people she'd never seen before drawing the bucket up from the well: a wiry, ebony-haired girl with a wild gleam in her eye, and a dark-skinned boy playing a strange melody on a small bone flute.

"You must come from far away," Lilith said, swaying to the flute's music. "I've never heard a song like that."

"What's the farthest place you can think of?" the wiry girl asked, helping herself to a ladle of water.

Lilith eyed the girl. "I can think of worlds made only of music, where our heavy bodies would not survive."

"A musician, eh?" The boy held the flute out to her. "See what you can make of this."

Lilith took the flute and studied it, fingering the holes. She held it to her lips, closed her eyes, and blew.

An odd song seemed to play itself, as if a spirit were

breathing through Lilith's lungs, moving her fingers. She was startled at first, but soon she relaxed into the melody, following its meandering path. When she had finished, she opened her eyes. The strangers gaped.

"I've never—" the girl said.

"I know," the boy agreed.

"What?" Lilith said. "This is obviously a magic flute. Everyone who plays it must sound like that."

"That's just it," the girl said. "We've never met anyone but Roland here who can play that thing at all."

Roland nodded. "You must have a great deal of soul."

The girl put her arm around Lilith's shoulders and leaned against the well. "Allow me to introduce myself. I'm Arriane. We've been traveling for a long time."

"My name is Lilith."

"Lilith, have you happened to see a blond kid around here, a boy?" Roland asked. "Pretty new to these parts?"

"Kind of self-righteous and vain?" Arriane added.

"Dani?" Lilith said. She glanced toward the river in the east where she'd last seen him swimming. The carob trees swayed in the breeze, sending their sweet seeds scattering through the grass.

"That's him!" Arriane squealed. "Where can we find him?"

"Oh, he's around here someplace," Lilith said. "Probably followed closely by Liat."

Roland winced. "I really hope he's got a plan."

Arriane punched Roland in the arm. "What he means is that we hope Dani is getting along—you know, prospering. In your midst, as it were. I need some water." The girl dipped the ladle into the well and took another drink.

Lilith looked at the strangers and frowned. "Are you two . . . lovers?"

Arriane spat out her water in a great burst.

"Lovers?" Roland said, laughing as he hoisted himself up to sit on the lip of the well. "Why do you ask?"

Lilith sighed. "Because I need advice."

Roland and Arriane exchanged glances.

"Tell you what," Roland said. "You teach me how to play that song, and we'll see what we can do."

※ ※

Lilith's lyre lay on the bank next to the flute, which lay next to most of the clothes the three had been wearing when they met at the well.

They splashed in the Jordan River, floated on their backs, and watched the sunlight dance on the surface of the water. Music and conversation had done their magic, and the strangers were now friends. Lilith found it easy to divulge the painful incident of the night before.

"A guy like that," Arriane said, before spitting a stream of water in a high arc. "Treat him like he doesn't exist. A wise woman knows better than to stop a bad man from disappearing."

Roland let the current carry him closer to Lilith. "There are lots of other fish in the river. And you're a great catch. Might as well try to forget about him."

"Wise," Arriane said. "Very wise."

Lilith watched the sunlight glint on Roland's shoulders and Arriane's face. She'd never met anyone like these two, except, maybe, for Cam.

Just then, something rustled on the bank. "Isn't it romantic?" asked a voice from the bushes.

Cam strode to the water's edge and frowned at Lilith. "Do you bring all your conquests here?"

"Wait," Arriane said. "*This* is the boy you've been talking about?"

Lilith was simultaneously thrilled and crestfallen. "You know him?"

"This has nothing to do with you, Arriane," Cam said.

"I thought we were discussing a young man of depth and complexity," Arriane said. "Imagine my surprise to learn it's *you*."

Cam scowled and dove into the river, his body arcing high in the air before it met the water. When he emerged, he was so close to Lilith that their faces were almost touching. She stared at the beads of water on his upper lip. She wanted to touch them. With her lips. She was angry with him, but that anger paled before the intensity of her attraction.

He took her hand. He kissed her palm. "I'm sorry about last night."

"What kept you?" she asked quietly, though at the touch of his lips on her skin, she had already forgiven him.

"Nothing that will keep me again. I'll make it up to you, I promise."

"How?" Lilith asked, breathless.

Cam smiled and looked around the river, then up at the brilliant blue sky. He smiled at his two friends, who were both shaking their heads. Then he smiled at Lilith, an alluring, complicated smile that drew her body against his underwater and told her in an unspoken language that her life would never be the same.

"A party." Cam wrapped his arms around her and started twirling her in the water. The dizziness was so delightful Lilith couldn't help but laugh. "Say you'll come?"

"Yes," Lilith said breathlessly. "I will."

Arriane leaned into Roland. "This is not going to end well."

EIGHT

THE WEEPING SONG

CAM

Ten Days

"Good morning, students."

Cam leaned back in his chair as the principal's voice crackled through the intercom in homeroom the next morning. "Topping today's announcements, the soccer team is having a car wash after school. Please come out and support them. As you know, prom tickets are available in the cafeteria until Friday, and in a moment I will announce the prom court."

The classroom, which had been buzzing a second earlier, silenced. It had been a while since Cam had seen this sort of undivided attention from a group of teens. They cared about prom. He glanced across the room at Lilith and wondered if there was a deep, hidden part of her that cared about it, too.

When Jean Rah had told Cam yesterday that Lilith had signed up to play at prom, Cam had been so excited he'd pumped his fists and leaped into the air, losing his cool for a whole three seconds.

"Damn, dude," Jean had said with a laugh. "You do realize you're not in the band, right?"

"Not yet," Cam had said, swiping his hair to the side.

Jean had shrugged amicably. "Take that up with the boss. Revenge is really Lilith's band."

"Don't mind if I do," Cam had said.

Today he was going to ask her—not just if he could be in the band, but if she'd go with him to prom. Like a date. Yesterday, in the cafeteria, right after she'd fought with Chloe, Lilith had seemed to soften. She'd let Cam in a little, hadn't shut him down, even when he'd dared to talk a little sweet to her.

He wished she'd meet his eyes now, across homeroom, but she was deep in her black journal.

"The nominees for prom queen are," Tarkenton said over the intercom, "Chloe King, June Nolton, Teresa Garcia, and Kara Clark."

Chloe—who was now wearing her hair shaved on

the sides—immediately jumped up from her desk. "The Slights strike again."

Chloe and her bandmates hugged each other, giggling, crying, their pastel minidresses riding up their thighs.

Mrs. Richards crossed the room and pried them apart, urging them to sit back down.

"As for prom king," Tarkenton said, "the nominees are Dean Miller, Terrence Gable, Sean Hsu, and Cameron Briel."

Cam winced as a few kids around him whistled and clapped. Lilith, of course, didn't look up. Cam had made no effort to get to know any of the students at Trumbull other than Lilith and Jean. This prom court appointment was clearly Lucifer's doing; he must have bet that Lilith would be disgusted by anyone who bought in to the pomp of prom court.

Tarkenton went on to list some of the prom court responsibilities, and Cam wondered how many dumb meetings he would have to bail on over the next ten days. But then the classroom door swung open and drew his full attention.

Luc, his tablet tucked under his arm, sidled in and over to Mrs. Richards. He whispered something in her ear.

To Cam's dismay but not surprise, the teacher pointed at Lilith. "That's her, in the second row."

Luc smiled gratefully, then walked toward Lilith as if they were strangers. "Ms. Foscor?"

"Yeah?" Lilith said, startled by the sight of the tall boy standing over her. She covered what she'd been writing in her book.

"This is confirmation that your entry has been received." Luc dropped the envelope on her desk.

"My entry to what?" As Lilith tore open the envelope, Luc shot Cam a cheesy thumbs-up and disappeared out the classroom door.

Cam leaned forward as she unfolded the contents: a single sheet of paper. He was desperate to read it, to be ready to perform triage for whatever trauma the devil meant to unleash on Lilith. He had leaned so far forward that the girl in front of him glanced over her shoulder, wrinkled her nose, and shoved his desk back a few inches. "As if, pervert." Cam felt her study his skin, the age spots near his forehead. "Ew. How many times did you fail freshman year—fifteen?"

He ignored her. He watched as Lilith's fingers began to shake, and the blood drained from her cheeks. She rose from her seat, grabbed her things, and bolted out the door.

Cam bolted after her, ignoring Mrs. Richards's threats about suspension, expulsion, a letter to his parents. He caught up with Lilith in the hall and took her by the elbow. "Hey—"

She whipped his hand away. "Back off."

"What happened?"

"He warned me about you."

"Who?"

"Luc." Lilith closed her eyes. "I'm so stupid."

When she thrust the paper at Cam, he saw it was a printout of his email to Ike Ligon, along with the lyrics to "Somebody's Other Blues." The only thing that wasn't included was the bio Cam had written, the words that had made him cry.

"You stole my lyrics and entered them in the contest," Lilith said.

Cam took a deep breath. "It's not that simple."

"Isn't it?" Lilith asked. "Did you or did you not go through my journal, take my lyrics, and enter them in this contest?"

How could he explain that he had done this to help her? That Lucifer was trying to drive a wedge between them? He watched her face twist with disgust. "I know it was wrong—"

"You're unbelievable!" Lilith shouted. She looked like she might strangle him.

He tried to take her hands. "I did it for you."

She pushed him off again. "You did not just say that. And *stop* touching me."

He put his hands up in surrender. "I sent the lyrics in *as* you, not me."

"What?"

"That song is brilliant," he said. "And you said yourself you weren't going to enter the contest. It's such a big opportunity to get your music out there, Lilith. I couldn't let you pass it up."

She stared at the printout. "Luc said—"

"You cannot listen to Luc, okay?" Cam said. "His goal in life is to try to turn you against me."

Lilith squinted. "And why is that?"

Cam sighed. "It's hard to explain. Look, you have every right to be mad at me, but please, don't let it get in the way of your music. You could win this, Lilith. You *should* win this."

Cam realized then just how close they were standing. Inches separated their shoulders. He could hear her breathing. Lilith had so much pain in her eyes. He would do anything for her to be the happy, carefree girl he'd once known.

"You promised to back off," she said.

Cam swallowed. "I will. But please, just think about what I said. You're too talented not to try."

Lilith blushed and averted her eyes like someone unaccustomed to compliments. He could see all the little things that made up who she was—the ink stains on her hands, the callouses on her fingertips. She was a huge talent, a bright star. Her music was the one thread that connected her to the Lilith he'd fallen in love with so long ago, which was why he had to make her understand that his intentions in entering her lyrics in the contest were good.

"Lilith," he whispered.

The bell rang.

She took a step backward, and Cam could tell the moment between them had passed. Her body was tense again, and her eyes full of hate. "Why should I take advice from someone who would do something so low?" She snatched the printout from his hand and rushed away as doors opened and students spilled into the hall.

Cam banged his head against a locker. So much for asking her to prom today.

"Ouch," Luc called as he casually walked past. "And just when I thought she was starting to warm to you. It's almost like there's an invisible force working against you at every turn." The devil's throaty laughter echoed in Cam's ears long after Luc had disappeared around the corner.

At lunchtime, Cam found out from Jean, who had found out from Kimi, that Lilith had received another note in third period, this time from the office, which mysteriously excused her from class for the rest of the day. Cam was supposed to take some joke of a calculus test in fourth period, but he had no hesitations about skipping.

He cut out the back exit, slid onto the motorcycle he'd picked up the day before, and made for the rough side of town. Soon he was knocking on Lilith's door. In front of the garage was a battered, grape-colored minivan, its back door open.

"What the—" Lilith said when she answered.

"Everything okay?" he asked.

"What a dumb question," she said.

Lilith's body language was shouting at him to stay back. He tried to respect that, but it was hard. He hated to see the rage that flooded her whenever she laid eyes on him.

It especially sucked because in his pocket were the prom tickets he'd bought for the two of them.

"There's something I've been wanting to ask you," he said.

"You heard about Revenge," she said. "You came to ask if you could be in the band."

Cam couldn't let her bluntness throw him off. He would take this nice and easy, even shoot for romantic, like he'd planned. "First of all, I want to say that I'm really glad you signed up to play at prom—"

"Can we please not call it prom?" Lilith said.

"You want to rename prom?" he asked. "It's cool with me, but it might provoke a riot at Trumbull. Those kids are pretty excited. 'Only ten days to go until the best night of our lives,' and all that crap."

"They'll kick you off prom court if they catch you mocking it," Lilith said. "It's high school heresy."

Cam smiled a little. So she *had* been listening when his name had been announced. "Is that all I have to do to get kicked off prom court?" he said. "Wait, I thought we weren't calling it prom."

Lilith thought for a moment. "Just so we're clear, I'm going because I want to play music and hear the Four Horsemen, not because I want to wear my dream corsage or a cranberry satin maxidress."

"I should hope not," Cam said. "Cranberry is so last season."

It looked, for an instant, like Lilith was going to smile, but then her eyes went cool again. "If you didn't come about the band, why are you here?"

Ask her. What are you waiting for? He felt the tickets in his pocket, but for some reason Cam was frozen. The vibe wasn't right. She'd say no. He'd better wait.

After a moment's awkward silence, Lilith pushed past him and walked across her lawn to the battered minivan. She leaned in through the open door, pulled a lever, and stepped back as a metal platform unfolded and lowered to the driveway.

Lilith's mother appeared on the front porch. She wore pink lipstick and a megawatt smile that concealed none of the exhaustion in her eyes. Her beauty had faded, but Cam could tell she'd once been a knockout, just like Lilith.

"Can I help you?" she asked Cam.

Cam opened his mouth to reply, but Lilith cut him off. "He's just someone from school. He came to drop off some work."

Her mother said, "School will have to wait. I need your help with Bruce right now." She turned away from the door and reappeared a moment later pushing a wheelchair, and in the wheelchair was Bruce. He was trembling and looked frail. He coughed into a dishrag, his eyes watering.

"Hi, Cam," Bruce called.

"I didn't know your brother was sick."

Lilith shrugged him off, going over to Bruce and running her fingers through his hair. "Now you do. What do you want, Cam?"

"I—" Cam started to say.

"Never mind. Of all the possible reasons you might have come here," Lilith said, "I can't think of a single one that matters."

Cam had to agree. But what could he do—open his wings and tell her the truth, that he was a fallen angel who'd once broken her heart so deeply she'd never recovered? That the devil had assigned her to millennia of serial Hells? That her rage toward Cam ran so much deeper than anger about stolen song lyrics? That he would lose everything if he failed to win her heart again?

"Lilith, time to go," her mother said, pulling the lever and then walking around to the driver's seat. As the wheelchair rose into the back of the van, Bruce met Cam's gaze and surprised him with a wink, as if to say, *Don't take things so seriously.*

"Bye, Cam," Lilith said as she closed the back doors behind her brother and got in on the passenger side.

"Where are you going?" Cam asked.

"The emergency room," Lilith called out the window.

"Let me go with you. I can help—"

But Lilith and her family were already backing down the driveway. He waited until the van had turned the corner before letting his wings out again.

❊

The sun was setting by the time Cam found them in the ER.

Lilith and her mom were asleep in a hallway, leaning against each other on stained orange chairs. He watched Lilith for a moment, marveling at her beauty and her stolen peacefulness.

He waited until the security guard left his post, then snuck back toward the rooms for patients. Cam peeked behind several curtains before he found the boy, sitting on a cot with his shirt off, oxygen tubes running through his nose, an IV hooked up to his arm. *Bruce* had been written in blue marker on a dry-erase board over his head.

"I knew you'd come," he said, without turning away from the window.

"How'd you know that?"

"Because you love my sister," he said.

Cam reached for Bruce's hand, realizing that he was

holding it as much for his own sake as for the boy's. It struck him that he had not seen a friendly face since he'd entered Lilith's Hell. He'd been toiling nonstop, with no sign that he was making any progress and no one to tell him to keep going. He squeezed the boy's hand gratefully.

"I do love her," he said over the soft beeps of the machines Bruce was hooked up to. "I love her more than anything, anywhere, in this world and beyond."

"Easy, that's my sister you're talking about." Bruce smiled weakly. For a moment, his breath halted. Cam was about to call for a nurse when the boy's chest eased into a steady rhythm. "Just kidding. Hey, Cam?"

"Yeah?"

"Do you think I'll be around long enough to feel that way about someone someday?"

Cam had to look away, because he couldn't lie to Bruce and say that yes, he would someday love a girl as deeply as Cam loved Lilith. In another week and a half, there would be nothing left of this world. Regardless of what Lilith chose and how Cam and Lucifer's deal played out, Bruce and all the other sad souls in Crossroads would likely be recycled for future punishments.

Still, Cam wished there were a way to give the boy some comfort in the little time he had left. He felt a lump forming in his throat and his wings burning at the base of his shoulders. An idea formed in his mind. It was risky, but then so was Cam.

He glanced at the kid, who was looking out the window and seemed to be in a faraway place. He likely had only minutes before a nurse came in or Lilith and her mother woke up.

He took a deep breath, closed his eyes, tilted his head toward the ceiling, and unfurled his wings. Usually there was a delicious abandon to throwing out his wings, but this time Cam was careful not to let them strike any of the medical equipment keeping Bruce stable.

When Cam opened his eyes, he saw that his wings filled the small curtained space and made the walls shimmer with golden light. Bruce was gazing at him with great reverence and only a little fear. An angel's glory was the most incredible sight a mortal could see—and this time Cam knew it was especially remarkable because, aside from Lilith, Bruce hadn't seen much beauty in his brief life.

"Any questions?" Cam asked. It was only fair to give the kid a moment to try to catch up.

Ever so slightly, the boy shook his head, but he didn't scream, and he didn't burst into flames. It helped that Bruce was young, his heart and mind still open to the possibility of angels. This was all Cam had hoped for. Now he could proceed.

He ran his hands along the inside of his wings, surprised to feel that the new white fibers felt different to the touch than the golden ones. They were thicker, sturdier, and, Cam realized, perfect for what he had in mind.

He grimaced as he plucked a single filament from his

wings. In his hand it became a huge white feather, a foot long and as soft as a kiss. It was called a *pennon*. At the base of the feather, at the end of its pointed quill, was a single drop of iridescent blood. It was impossible to say what color the blood was, for it was every color all at once.

"Hold this," he said to Bruce, handing him the feather with the quill pointing up.

"Wow," Bruce whispered, running his fingers along the soft white edges as Cam moved to the IV dripping medicine into Bruce. He unscrewed the tube at the bottom of the bag, then reached to take the pennon back from Bruce. He dipped its quill into the IV and watched the clear bag of liquid swirl with a trillion colors for a moment before the angelic blood dispersed into it. Cam reattached the IV and handed the feather back to Bruce. He didn't need it anymore.

"Did you just save my life?" Bruce asked, tucking the feather under his pillow.

"For today," Cam said, trying to sound brighter than he felt. He folded his wings into themselves and out of sight.

"Thanks."

"Our secret?"

"Sure," Bruce said, and Cam started for the door. "Hey, Cam," the boy called softly when Cam was just about to turn into the hallway.

"Yeah?"

"Don't tell her I said this," the boy whispered, "but you should tell Lilith that you love her."

"Oh, yeah?" Cam said. "Why is that?"

"Because," Bruce said, "I think she loves you, too."

NINE

LOVE MORE

LILITH

Nine Days

Revenge met in the band room the next morning before school.

When Lilith walked in, bearing photocopies of her latest song, "Flying Upside Down," Jean was trying out some crazy new riffs on the synthesizer while Luis tore through a supersized sack of Doritos. He held out the bag for Lilith and rattled the chips inside.

"I usually try to hold off on my artificial-cheese fix until at least nine a.m.," she said, waving him off.

"This is brain food, Lilith," Luis insisted. "Get some."

Jean walked by and grabbed a fistful on his way to set up Lilith's microphone. "He's right," he said with his mouth full.

Lilith succumbed and took a chip. She was surprised by how delicious it tasted. She took a second chip, and a third.

"Now you're ready to rock," Luis said after she'd polished off a couple of handfuls, and it was true. She wasn't so hungry, so edgy anymore.

She smiled at Luis. "Thanks."

"No sweat," he said, then nodded at Lilith's outfit. "Nice duds today, by the way."

Lilith glanced down at her dress. That morning, for the first time she could remember, she hadn't felt like wearing black. She'd raided her mother's closet before school and found a tight white dress with big green polka dots, cinched with a wide purple patent-leather belt. She'd paused in front of her mother's full-length mirror, surprised at how cool the ensemble looked with her broken-in combat boots, how the green in the dress brightened her red hair.

When she'd come into the kitchen wearing it, Bruce had looked up from his Pop-Tart and whistled.

Lilith still didn't know exactly what had happened, but Bruce had been discharged early, and when her family returned from the hospital yesterday, he said he felt better than he had in years. The doctor couldn't explain why her brother's breathing had suddenly returned to normal; he could say only that Bruce was better than he'd been in a long, long time.

"How many times do I have to tell you that my closet is not your personal playground?" her mom had asked, even though Lilith had never before raided her closet. She put down her coffee and pushed up the sleeves of her yellow cardigan—the one she'd accused Lilith of stealing but had since found at the bottom of her dresser.

"I've always loved this dress on you," Lilith said, and meant it. "Is it okay if I borrow it? Just for today. I'll be careful."

Her mother's mouth twitched, and Lilith knew an insult was brewing, but maybe Lilith's compliment had thrown her off. Because instead of lashing out, her mother scrutinized Lilith's look, then reached across the counter for her purse.

"It'll look better with a little color on your lips," she said, handing Lilith a tube of matte pink lipstick.

Now, in the band room, being careful not to get lipstick on the microphone, Lilith waited for Jean's cue, then leaned in and started singing her new song. She was nervous, so she closed her eyes and let Luis's backbeat and Jean's psychedelic chords come at her sideways in the dark.

It had been so easy to imagine how the song might sound when she was alone in her room, writing lyrics and inventing melodies. But now that she was singing it in front of other people, she felt exposed. What if they hated it? What if it sucked?

Her voice trembled. She considered stopping, running out of the room.

She opened her eyes and looked over at Luis, who was nodding at her with a smile plastered across his face, his drumsticks alternating between the snare and the cymbals. Jean picked up the slack on the guitar, plucking notes on the strings as though each one told a story.

Lilith felt a burst of energy rush through her. A band that hadn't existed two days ago had found a sound that was rich and nimble. Suddenly, she was singing her song like it was worthy of an audience. She had never sung so loudly or so freely.

Luis was feeling it, too. He ended the song with a slamming, cataclysmic racket on the drums.

When it was over, all three of them wore the same expression: smiling, a little dazed.

"Magic Doritos," Luis said, gazing reverently at the bag. "I'll have to stock up on these before prom."

Lilith laughed, but she knew it was more than the Doritos. It was the three of them relaxing into their sound together, not just as bandmates but as friends. And it was Lilith, and the change that had come over her the day before, knowing Bruce was feeling better.

After the hospital, Lilith's mom had suggested they all

go out for pizza, a treat that happened only once or twice a year. They'd shared a large pepperoni-and-olive and made each other laugh playing pinball on the old Scared Stiff machine.

When Lilith had tucked Bruce into bed, he'd lain back on his pillow and said, "Cam's pretty cool."

"What are you talking about?" Lilith asked.

Bruce shrugged. "He visited me at the hospital. He cheered me up."

Her instinct had been to get mad at Cam for visiting Bruce without telling her. But she sat on her brother's bed a moment longer, watching him fade into sleep, and he seemed so peaceful, so unlike the sick boy she was used to, that Lilith found she could muster nothing but gratitude for whatever Cam had done.

"What song do you want to do next, Lilith?" Jean asked now. "We need to ride this wave."

Lilith thought a moment. She wanted to work on "Somebody's Other Blues," but thinking about it, and about what Cam had done with her lyrics, still smarted.

"We could try—" she said, but three loud knocks on the door made her stop. "What was that?"

"Nothing!" Luis said. "Let's keep playing."

"Might be Tarkenton," Jean said. "We're not supposed to be in here."

The knock sounded again. Only it wasn't coming from the door. It was coming from outside. The window.

"Dude!" Jean Rah said. "It's Cam."

The boys rushed to open the window, but Lilith turned away. Cam's face was the last thing she wanted to see right now. The feeling she'd had playing her music moments before had been simple, good. The feeling she got when she looked at Cam was so complicated she didn't know where to begin unpacking it. She was drawn to him. She was mad at him. She was grateful to him. She didn't trust him. And it was hard to feel so many things for one person at once.

"What are you doing out there?" Luis asked. "We're on the second story."

"Trying to lose Tarkenton," Cam said. "He wants my head for skipping another prom court meeting."

Lilith couldn't help herself: She snickered at the thought of Cam in those meetings with all those stuck-up kids. When she accidentally caught Cam's eye, he smiled at her and held out his hand, and before she knew it, she found herself moving toward him to help him climb in through the window.

He stood up but didn't let go of her hand. In fact, he gave it a squeeze. Her stomach fluttered, and she didn't know why. She pulled her hand away, but not before glancing at Jean and Luis, wondering what they'd think about Cam standing there like a weirdo, holding her hand. The boys weren't paying attention. They'd moved back to Jean's synth and were working on a groove together.

"Hey," Cam whispered now that the two of them were more or less alone.

"Hey," she said. Why did she feel so awkward? She looked up at Cam and remembered there was something she wanted to say. "My brother's been in the hospital sixteen times. He's never had a visitor besides my mom and me." She paused. "I don't know why you did that—"

"Lilith, let me explain—"

"But thank you," Lilith said. "It cheered him up. What did you say to him?"

"Actually," he said, "we talked about you."

"Me?" she asked.

"It's a little embarrassing," Cam said, smiling at her like he wasn't embarrassed at all. "He kind of guessed that I liked you. He's very protective of you, but I'm trying not to let his size intimidate me."

Cam liked her? How could he just say that like it was no big deal? The words rolled off his tongue so easily, Lilith wondered how many girls Cam had said it to before. How many hearts he'd broken.

"You still with me?" Cam asked, waving his hand in front of her face.

"Yeah," Lilith said. "Um, don't underestimate Bruce. He could kick your ass."

Cam smiled. "I'm glad he's feeling better."

"It's like a miracle," she said, because it was.

"Earth to Lilith." Luis's voice sounded distorted through the microphone Jean had hooked up to his Moog.

"Bell's gonna ring in fifteen minutes. We've got time to work on one more song, and we need to schedule our next practice."

"About that," Cam said, scratching his head. "You guys got any extra room in this band for an electric-guitar player who can hang high in a three-part harmony?"

"I don't know, man," Jean said, grinning. "You're good, but last I heard the lead singer hated your guts. Stealing her journal was a dick move."

"Even if it means Lilith wins the lyrics contest," Luis added. "Personally, I think it was kind of a genius hack."

Lilith slugged him. "You stay out of it."

"What?" Luis asked. "Admit it, Lilith. You would never have entered that contest if it hadn't been for Cam. If you win, it'll be great exposure for the band."

"What can I say?" Cam shrugged. "I believe in Lilith."

He'd said it as easily as he'd said he liked her, but this sounded different, more palatable, like he wasn't just trying to get in her pants. Like he honestly believed in her. Her cheeks grew warm as Cam bent down and picked up one of the photocopied pages she'd brought in for Luis and Jean. He read the lyrics of "Flying Upside Down," a smile spreading across his face.

"This your latest?"

Lilith was about to explain a few changes she already wanted to make, but Cam surprised her by saying, "I love it. Don't change a word."

"Oh."

Cam put down the paper, unzipped his bag, and pulled out a large, spherical object, wrapped in butcher paper.

"Is that Tarkenton's head?" Luis asked.

Cam glanced at the freshman drummer. "Morbid. I like it. You can stay in the band."

"I'm a founding member, bro!" Luis said. "What are you?"

"The best electric-guitar player this school's ever seen," Jean said, shrugging at Lilith. "Sorry, but Cam could really round out our sound."

"A vote, then," Cam suggested eagerly. "All those in favor of letting me into Revenge?"

The three boys raised their hands.

Lilith rolled her eyes. "This is not a democracy. I don't . . . I don't—"

"You don't have a good reason to say no?" Cam asked.

It was true. She didn't. Lilith had a million dumb reasons to tell Cam to leave the rehearsal, to go away forever. But she didn't have a single legitimate one.

"Trial period," she said finally, through gritted teeth. "One practice. Then I make the final decision."

"Good enough for me," Cam said.

Lilith jerked the butcher paper off the mystery object—and found herself holding a glittering disco ball. Even in the dingy light of the band room, it sparkled. She glanced at Cam, remembering that the first time she'd said she wanted to name her band Revenge, Cam had laughed and said they'd need a big synthesizer and a disco ball. Jean had contributed the Moog, and now Cam had brought the disco.

"Can we stop staring at that thing and play?" Luis asked.

Cam pulled his guitar case from the closet and winked at Lilith. That same annoying wink, only . . . this time she didn't mind so much. "Let us rock."

⧻⧼

"Bitch, you're standing in my way," Chloe King said.

For the first time, Lilith had been looking forward to lunch in the cafeteria, because she would have people to sit with. Her band.

She'd forgotten about Chloe.

"I was just admiring your new ink," Lilith said, nodding at Chloe's chest, which bore a brand-new tattoo. The skin around it was still red and raw, but she recognized the scrawling letters of Ike Ligon's signature just above the neckline of Chloe's low-cut shirt. Lilith thought the tattoo was ugly, but it ignited a flash of envy in her anyway. She didn't have the money to make such an obvious suck-up gesture to the Four Horsemen. She barely had enough money for the turkey sandwich on her tray.

The three Perceived Slights fanned out behind Chloe. Kara crossed her arms over her chest, and Teresa had a hungry look in her hazel eyes, like she'd pounce on Lilith if she tried to attack Chloe again. June was the only one slacking at being a stereotypical mean girl, plucking split ends distractedly from her blond hair.

Chloe put a hand up to keep Lilith at a distance. "If you can read my tattoo, you're too close. I should get a restraining order after what you did the other day."

A part of Lilith wanted to throw down her tray and rip Chloe's tattoo right out of her skin.

But it was a smaller, quieter part of her today. The bigger part of Lilith was preoccupied with thoughts of her band: changes she wanted to make to one chorus, ideas for a drum solo she wanted to bounce off Luis, even—she had to admit—a question she wanted to ask Cam about his guitar technique. For the first time, Lilith had too much good stuff knocking around in her mind to let rage overtake her.

I believe in Lilith, Cam had said earlier, in the band room. And it had stuck with her. Maybe it was time Lilith started believing in herself.

"You're a straight-up bitch clown, Lilith," Chloe said. "Always have been, always will be."

"What does that even mean?" Lilith asked. "No, never mind." She swallowed. "I'm sorry I pulled out your weave. I thought I was defending my brother, but I was just being a jerk."

Kara nudged June, who let go of the split end she was picking and started paying attention.

"I know," Chloe said, a little stunned. "Thank you for

saying that." Then, wordlessly, she summoned her friends, nodded once at Lilith, and left the cafeteria, leaving Lilith with the new experience of eating lunch in peace.

※

When Lilith swung by her homeroom class after lunch, Mrs. Richards looked up from her computer guardedly. "Your detention is nonnegotiable, Ms. Foscor."

"I'm not here to try to get out of it." Lilith pulled up a chair next to her teacher. "I came to apologize for skipping class, for being late so much, for generally being the kind of student teachers dread."

Mrs. Richards blinked, then took off her glasses. "What brought on this change of attitude?"

Lilith wasn't sure where to start. Bruce was back in school. Her mother had been treating her like a human. Her band felt whole and right. She'd even attempted to reconcile with Chloe King. Things were going so well, Lilith didn't want it to stop.

"My brother's been sick," she said.

"I'm aware of that," Mrs. Richards said. "If you need time off or extensions on your assignments, the faculty can work with you, but you'll need documentation from your mother or a doctor. You can't just run out of class whenever you feel like it."

"I know," Lilith said. "There is something I thought you might be able to help with. See, Bruce is feeling better, and I want to keep it that way. You know so much about the environment, I thought maybe you could help me make some changes around my house."

Mrs. Richards's eyes softened as she studied Lilith. "I'm a big believer that we can all change our world for the better, but sometimes, Lilith, these things are out of our control. I know how sick Bruce gets. I just don't want you to expect a miracle." She smiled, and Lilith could tell her teacher felt genuinely bad for her. "Of course, it wouldn't hurt to throw out any harsh cleaning products, and start cooking good, wholesome meals for the whole family. Homemade chicken soup. Iron-rich leafy greens. That sort of thing."

Lilith nodded. "I'll do that." She didn't know where she would get the money. Ramen noodles were her mom's idea of a good, wholesome meal. But she would find a way. "Thanks."

"You're welcome," Mrs. Richards said as Lilith moved toward the door to head to history class. "You still have detention this afternoon. But maybe we can try to make it your last."

❄

As Lilith stepped outside after detention, the huge student parking lot was empty. It gave the school a ghostly feel. Ash gathered like gray snow along the curb, and Lilith wondered if she would ever see or smell or taste real snow.

She walked toward the edge of campus, putting on her headphones, listening to some old Four Horsemen songs about broken hearts and dreams.

She was used to being one of the last kids to leave school—detention let out after soccer practice ended and the choir went home for the day—but she never really stopped to look around as she left campus. A sharp wind had loosed several of the prom court posters from the walls of the school. They swirled around the pavement like fallen leaves wearing her classmates' faces.

The sun was going down, but it was still hot. The wildfires on the hills seemed fiercer than usual as Lilith neared the cluster of trees marking the entrance to Rattlesnake Creek. She hadn't been to her spot in a few days, and she wanted a quiet place to study for her biology quiz before she headed home.

She heard a rustling in the trees and looked around but didn't see anyone. Then she heard a voice.

"I knew you couldn't stay away." Luc appeared between the carob trees. His arms were crossed, and he was looking up through the branches at the smoky sky.

"I can't talk right now," Lilith said. There was something strange about the intern, and it wasn't just the stabbing memory of opening that envelope and seeing her emailed lyrics inside. Why was he hanging out at Trumball so much anyway? This internship couldn't require his presence here full-time.

Luc smiled. "I'll make it quick. I just got off the phone

with Ike Ligon, and I thought you might be interested in our conversation."

Without meaning to, Lilith stepped toward him.

"As you know," Luc said, "the Four Horsemen are coming to town to play at prom and judge the Battle of the Bands. Now, I know all the cool kids are going to Chloe's after-party, but—"

"I'm not going to Chloe's after-party," Lilith said.

"Good." Luc smiled. "Because I was thinking I'd have a few people back to my place afterward. Something intimate. Would you like to come?"

"No, thanks—"

"Ike Ligon will be there," Luc said.

Lilith inhaled sharply. How could she pass up an opportunity to spend time with Ike Ligon? She could ask him where he got the ideas for his songs, what his approach to writing music was . . . It would be like a crash course in rock-stardom.

"Yeah, okay."

"Great," Luc said. "Just you, though. Not Cam. I heard you let him into your band. Personally, I think that's a career mistake."

"I get it, you hate Cam." Lilith wondered how Luc had heard this news. It had only happened this morning, and he didn't even go to school with them.

"He's got a reputation," Luc said. "He's been around the block. He's been *under* the block. I mean, *look* at that guy. You know the saying *live fast, die young, and leave an attractive corpse*? I guess old Cam is proving the lie to that. His sins are wearing him down—he even *looks* like a sinner."

"I hear looks are only skin-deep," Lilith said.

"With skin like Cam's, I hope so." Luc laughed. "King Media also caught wind that Cam was the one who submitted your lyrics to the contest. If he did it without your approval, that would be grounds for disqualification."

"It's okay," Lilith said, realizing quickly that she didn't want to be disqualified. "He, um, had my approval. Can I ask you something?"

Luc raised an eyebrow. "Anything."

"It seems like you and Cam have history. What is it with you two?"

Luc's gaze burned into Lilith as his voice went icy cold. "He thinks he's the exception to every rule. But some rules, Lilith, *must* be followed."

Lilith swallowed. "It sounds like you do go back a ways."

"The past is the past," Luc said, softening again. "But if you care about your future, you'll kick Cam out of the band."

"Thanks for the tip." Lilith left Luc and ducked under the branches. She found her favorite place by the creek. As she neared her carob tree, she saw something unusual: a pocked and battered antique rolltop desk sat beside it. It had a heavy wrought-iron frame and must have weighed a ton. Who had brought it here? And how? Whoever they were, they'd covered its wooden top with iris petals.

Lilith had always adored irises, even though she'd only ever seen pictures of them online. She'd been inside Crossroads's one junky florist, Kay's Blooms, dozens of times to pick up a bouquet of yellow carnations—Bruce's favorite—when he was feeling bad. Mr. Kay and his sons owned the business, and ever since Mrs. Kay had died, they stocked the basics only. Red roses, carnations, tulips. Lilith hadn't ever seen anything as exotic as irises in there.

She admired the blue-and-yellow blossoms, and she slid into the low-backed chair and rolled back the top of the desk. Inside was a handwritten note:

Every songwriter needs a proper desk. Found this on the curb in front of the Palace of Versailles. Pour toi.

He must have found it on someone's curb in the fancy part of Crossroads, waiting to be picked up and taken to the dump. But she liked that Cam had seen the desk and thought of her. She liked that he'd probably cleaned it up so she could use it. She read the last line of the note:

Love, Cam

"Love," Lilith said, tracing the letters with a finger. "Cam."

She couldn't remember a single time anyone had used

that word with her. Her family didn't talk like that, and she'd certainly never gotten anywhere near close enough to a boy for him to say it. Had Cam dashed the word out casually, like he did so many things? She shifted uncomfortably in the desk and could barely look at the word on the page.

She wanted to ask him what the deal was with this note, this desk—but it wasn't the note or the desk, it was the word. It did something to her, stirred something deep in her soul. It made her sweat. She wanted to confront Cam, but she didn't know where he lived. Instead, she took out her black notebook and let it come out as a song.

That word. What could it mean?

TEN

SLOW DIVE

CAM

Eight Days

High above Lilith, Cam spread his wings and watched her read the note he'd left on the antique desk. He'd stolen it from Chloe King, of all people—from the attic of her family's house in the fancy part of Crossroads. He would have gone to Versailles to bring Lilith back a present, he would have gone anywhere—but right now he was stuck in her Hell, so this would have to do.

He studied the way she ran her fingers over the paper several times. He watched her smell the irises—her old favorite, he knew—then take her notebook out of her backpack. When she started writing a new song, Cam smiled. This had been his vision when he'd brought the desk there for her.

It was nice just to watch Lilith at peace for a little while. Since Cam had arrived in Crossroads, it seemed like all he ever did was try to smooth over Lucifer's interventions, each one geared to make Lilith despise Cam a little more. He shouldn't complain—after all, Lilith had suffered far more and for far longer than Cam—but it was hard to get close to Lilith when she so rarely showed him anything but rage.

He looked down from the clouds and knew that even if he showered Lilith with presents and love notes every hour, every day, it wouldn't be enough. Once in a while Cam broke through to her—that day, band practice had been pretty good—and he relished those moments. But he knew they wouldn't last, that tomorrow Lucifer would find a way to undo Cam's progress and the cycle would continue until Lilith's Hell expired.

He'd torn up his first draft of the note, which asked her to go to prom with him. Lilith backed away swiftly whenever Cam came on too strong. He would save that question, plan something special, and ask her in person. He mouthed the memorized words of the note he had left on the desk. He hoped the word *love* hadn't scared her.

He thought about Daniel and Lucinda. They had

embodied *love* for so long, as far as the fallen angels were concerned. He wished they were beside him now, playing the role of the happy couple offering sage advice to their suffering friend.

Fight for her, they would tell him. *Even when it seems like all is lost, do not give up the fight for love.*

How had Luce and Daniel done it for so long? It took a strength Cam wasn't sure he had. The pain when she refused him—and, so far, almost all she did was refuse him—was staggering. And yet he went for it again and again and again. Why?

To save her. To help her. Because he loved her. Because if he gave up . . .

He could not give up.

❧❦

When dawn beckoned, Cam shot down to Trumbull's campus. Wings unfurled, he alit on a dead carob tree and caught the sun rising over a hulking new structure in the center of the football field. He shook the falling ash from his hair and perched at the end of a long, sturdy branch to get a better view.

The half-constructed amphitheater had been modeled after the Roman Colosseum. It was only a couple of stories tall, but it had the same architectural features: three tiers of stylized arches encircling a space as big as the cafeteria. Cam understood instantly what Lucifer had in mind.

"Like it?" Lucifer asked, appearing as Luc on the branch behind Cam. He wore sunglasses to battle the glare, and not being able to see the devil's eyes made Cam nervous.

"This is for prom?" Cam asked.

"King Media thought the students deserved a grander venue for their gladiatorial battle," Lucifer said. "It's all made of ash, but it *looks* impressive, right? No mortal architect could have done this. It's a shame. That Gehry guy showed promise."

"Do you want an award?" Cam asked.

"I wouldn't turn one down," Lucifer said. "And it wouldn't kill you to acknowledge my other work from time to time." The devil pulled a small square mirror from his jeans' pocket and flashed it before Cam.

Cam pushed the mirror away. He didn't have to look at his reflection to know what he would find. By now he could feel the effects of whatever curse the devil had cast upon his body. He was haggard, puffy, pathetic to look at. Girls at Trumbull who'd stopped mid-conversation just to watch him walk down the hall on his first day here now only noticed Cam when he was standing in their way. He wasn't used to this. His good looks had always been a part of the package, just like with all the angels. Not anymore.

It nagged at him, though he tried not to let it. He would have to meet this challenge and prove, once and for all, that he was more than just a beautiful face.

"Pretty boy is becoming an ugly boy." Lucifer bellowed a laugh layered with darkness. "I've often wondered whether you had any depth. Without those muscles, what will the ladies see in you?"

Cam touched the place where he was accustomed to finding his taut, firm abdomen. It had gone soft and flabby. He knew his hair was thinning, too, his face filling out, his cheeks growing jowly. He'd never thought of himself as particularly shallow; his confidence had always come from somewhere deep within. But would he be able to attract Lilith now that he looked like this?

"Lilith didn't fall in love with me in Canaan because of the way I looked," Cam told the devil. "You can make me as hideous as you want. It won't stop her from falling for me again." He was deeply worried that this wasn't true, but he'd never give Lucifer the satisfaction of knowing he was throwing Cam off his game.

"Sure about that?" The devil's angry laugh shot a chill up Cam's spine. "You've got eight days to open her heart, and none of your old tender glances will change her mind now. But if this gentle makeover isn't enough of an obstacle, you'll be pleased to know this isn't the only trick I've got up my sleeve."

"Of course not," Cam muttered. "That would be too easy."

"Exactly." Lucifer's eyes narrowed. "Ah, there she is."

The devil pointed through the trees, to where Lilith was stepping off her school bus, with a girl Cam didn't know.

Lilith was dressed all in black except for a colorful scarf around her neck. Her long hair was pulled back in a braid today instead of hiding her face. She looked happier than she had the first time Cam saw her in Crossroads. There was even a bounce in her step as she carried her guitar.

Cam smiled at first, but then a dark thought entered his mind. What if she became so happy here she lost her sense of rebellion, her desire to flee Crossroads?

What if she started to actually *like* it here?

He leaped from the tree, drawing his wings back in and untucking his T-shirt to hide his gut. He could feel the students' eyes on him as he jogged across the parking lot.

"Lilith—"

But before Lilith heard him, a red Escalade lurched forward and Chloe King climbed out from the backseat, an expensive-looking patent-leather backpack slung over her shoulder. Her bandmates slid out behind her, each sporting a similar bag and a similar expression.

"Hey, Lilith," Chloe said.

As Cam closed in on them, he got a whiff of Chloe's perfume, which smelled like birthday cake and was accentuated by the air, which smelled like lit candles.

"Chloe," Lilith said cautiously.

"I was wondering if you'd be my guitar tech at prom," Chloe said. "As prom queen, I—"

"Um, Chloe . . ." June cleared her throat. "You haven't been named prom queen yet."

"Fine." Chloe clenched her jaw. "As a *member of the prom court,* I will have a lot of other responsibilities that night, and I need someone to tune my band's guitars."

"No, Lilith will not—" Cam started.

"What are you doing here?" Lilith spun around, noticing Cam.

Cam started to speak, but Chloe cut him off. "Lilith already confided in me that she wasn't going to prom. I assume it's because no guy wants to go with her, and she's afraid she'll look pathetic if she shows up without a date. I'm doing her a favor. She still gets to have the prom experience, but she doesn't have to look like such a loser."

Cam felt his body tense. He wanted to wreck this girl, but he held himself back for Lilith's sake and watched her face for the burst of fury Chloe's words should have incited. He waited. They all did.

"This is boring," June said, checking her phone.

Lilith looked at her feet for several seconds. When she looked back up at Chloe, her expression was clear and calm.

"I can't," Lilith said.

Chloe frowned. "You can't, or you won't?"

"I signed up for the battle," Lilith said. "My band is called Revenge."

Chloe's head shot to the left, where her friend Teresa stood. "Did you know about this?"

Teresa's shoulder twitched in a shrug. "They're not competition. Relax."

"Don't tell me to relax," Chloe barked. "It's your job to keep me updated on all prom developments." She blinked rapidly, turning back to Lilith. "Well, whatever, you can still play in your own 'band.' This would just be for extra cash." She smiled, stretching her arm around Lilith's shoulder. "What do you say?"

"What's it pay?" Lilith asked, and Cam suddenly understood why Lilith was even entertaining Chloe's request. Her family needed all the extra money they could get, for Bruce.

Chloe thought a moment. "A hundred bucks."

"And what would I have to do?" Lilith asked.

"Just come to our practices and make sure my guitar's in tune and the strings are fresh," Chloe said. "I have Bar Method today, but we have practice at my house tomorrow after school."

You're better than this, Cam wanted to say. *You're too talented to be Chloe's roadie.*

"I'll pass," Lilith said.

"You're saying *no*?" Chloe asked.

"You're my competition," Lilith said. "I need to focus on my music so we can beat you guys at the battle."

Chloe narrowed her eyes. "I'm going to squash every

single one of your precious little dreams." She glanced over her left shoulder, then her right. "Girls? Let's go."

As the Perceived Slights filed off behind their leader, Cam tried to hide his smile. Just when Cam was feeling the strain of having to fend off Lucifer's tricks, Lilith had unwittingly stood up to the devil on her own.

"What?" Lilith asked. "Why are you smirking at me?"

Cam shook his head. "I'm not."

She nodded toward the front doors of the school. "You coming to homeroom?"

"Nah," he said, letting his smile bust out. "I'm in too good a mood to go to class."

"Must be nice," Lilith said, tucking her hair behind her ears. "I'm trying this turn-over-a-new-leaf thing at school, getting to class on time and all that."

"That's great," Cam said. "I'm glad."

"What will you do all day?"

Cam gazed at the sky, where black smoke from the hills climbed toward a pale gray sun. "Stay out of trouble."

"Yeah, right." Lilith lingered before him, and Cam relished the quiet moment, trying not to hope for more. He restrained himself from touching her, and instead admired the slight slope of her nose, the cowlick that made her hair swoop up a little on the right.

"Lilith—" he started to say.

"I got your note," she said. "Those flowers. That desk. I've never been given a desk before. Very original."

Cam chuckled.

"But the note—" Lilith started to say.

"I meant it," Cam said quickly. "In case that's what you were going to ask. I don't expect anything in return, but I meant it. Every word."

She looked up at him, her blue eyes wide, her lips parted. He'd seen that look before. It was burned into his memory from the very first time they ever kissed.

Cam closed his eyes and he was back there, holding her on the banks of the Jordan River, feeling her warmth against his skin, drawing his lips toward hers. Oh, that kiss. There was no deeper ecstasy. Her lips were feather soft one minute, hungry with passion the next. He never knew what to expect from her, and he delighted in each surprise.

He needed another kiss. He wanted her now, again, always.

He opened his eyes. She was still there, gazing at him, as if three thousand years hadn't passed. Was she feeling it, too? How could she not? He leaned in. He reached to cup the back of her head. She opened her mouth—

And the bell rang.

Lilith jumped back. "I can't be late. I gotta go."

"Wait—"

And just like that, she was gone, a flash of red hair disappearing through the front doors of the school. And

Cam was alone once more, wondering if he'd ever again know the bliss of her lips—or if he would starve on memories alone for the rest of eternity.

※

After school, Cam waited at the front door of Lilith's house, holding two heavy bags of groceries. He'd spent the afternoon at the town's tiny health-food store, picking out strange, exciting things he thought she'd like. Avocados. Pomegranate. Couscous. Food that, he guessed, she had never been able to afford.

Truth was, he couldn't afford them either. He'd swiped them when the storeowner wasn't looking. But what was the worst thing that could happen—he'd end up in Hell?

"Hey," he called as Lilith trudged up the path, her head bowed under the weight of her guitar and her backpack. She didn't look up. Maybe she hadn't heard him.

"Lilith," he said loudly. "Luis told me you were surviving on Doritos for breakfast. He's under the impression that's good for a musician's stamina. You need protein, complex carbohydrates, antioxidants, and I'm here to deliver."

"Drop dead, Cam," Lilith said, not even looking at him as she marched up her porch steps. She pulled her key out of her backpack and rammed it into the lock.

"Huh?" he said. "What happened now?"

She hesitated, then turned to face him. Her eyes were an angry red. "*This* happened." Lilith thrust open her backpack and pulled out a messy stack of photocopies. Some were folded, some were stomped on, one had a piece of gum stuck to it.

Lilith tossed the pages in Cam's face. He grabbed one as they fluttered to the ground and saw the lyrics to the song they'd played together the day before, "Flying Upside Down."

"It's a great song," Cam said. "I already told you that. What's the problem?"

"The problem?" Lilith asked. "First you sent my lyrics in to the competition without my permission. Then you somehow convinced me that you'd done that for my own good. But you couldn't stop there, could you?"

Cam was confused. "Lilith, what—"

She grabbed the paper out of his hand and crumpled it into a ball. "You had to go make a thousand photocopies of my song and paper the school with them."

Suddenly, Cam realized what must have happened. Lucifer had seen him getting close to her, and the devil had stepped in. "Wait—I never . . . I don't even know where the copy machine is!"

But Lilith wasn't listening. "Now all of Trumbull not only thinks I'm a narcissistic monster, but they also hate my song." She choked back a sob. "You should have heard them laughing at me. Chloe King almost passed out, she was having such a blast shredding my lyrics. But you"—she glared at him with deep, committed rage—"you skipped school today, didn't you? You missed the whole fantastic scene."

"Yes," Cam said, "but if you'd just let me explain—"

"Don't worry," Lilith told him. "I'm sure you'll catch the recap tomorrow in the cafeteria." She slung her backpack over her shoulder and pushed open her front door. "I'm done with you, Cam. Leave me alone."

Cam felt dizzy, not only because Lilith was so angry, but also because he knew how mortifying it must have been to have her lyrics posted all over school.

"Lilith," he said. "I would never—"

"Are you going to blame Luis or Jean? You were the only other person who had a copy." When she looked up at Cam, tears shone in the corners of her eyes. "You did something today that I didn't think anyone could ever do. You made me ashamed of my music."

Cam's face fell. "Don't be. That song is *good*, Lilith."

"I used to think so." Lilith dabbed her eyes. "Until you sent it out into the world, naked and defenseless."

"Why would I do that?" Cam said. "I believe in that song. I believe in you."

"The problem is, Cam, I don't believe in you." Lilith stepped inside, staring out at Cam from her doorframe. "Take your stupid groceries and get out of here."

"The groceries are for you," he said, setting them

down on her stoop. He would make Lucifer pay for this somehow. The devil's interventions had gone too far. They were tearing Lilith apart. "I'll go."

"Wait," she said.

"Yes?" he asked, turning back around. Something in her voice gave him hope. "What is it?"

"You're out of the band," Lilith said. "For good."

INTERLUDE

DISINTEGRATION

TRIBE OF DAN, NORTHERN CANAAN

Approximately 1000 BCE

The desert sky sparkled with stars as Lilith picked up her lyre. Roland sat beside her on a mound of straw, his flute at his lips. Every bright-eyed youth in the village had gathered around them, waiting for the show to start.

The party had been Cam's idea, but the concert had been Lilith's, a demonstration of her love for Cam, whom she couldn't wait to marry when the harvest came. Their courtship had been swift and passionate, and it was clear to all those around them that these two were meant to share their lives. Iris blossoms decorated the canopy of branches that Lilith and her sisters had woven that afternoon.

Roland played first. His eyes shone as he cast a spell over the audience with his mysterious flute, playing a sweet, sad song that put everyone in the mood for romance. Cam held his bronze goblet high, leaning into Lilith and smelling the salt on her skin.

Love hung palpably in the air. Dani's arm encircled Liat, who was swaying with her dark eyes closed, savoring the music. Behind her, Arriane's head rested on the shoulder of a curly-headed girl named Tess.

Lilith played the next song. It was a lush, haunting melody she had improvised during her first encounter with Cam. When she was finished, and the applause had settled down, Cam pulled her close and kissed her deeply.

"You are a miracle," he whispered.

"As are you," Lilith replied, kissing him again. Each time their lips touched, it was like the first time. She was amazed by how much her life had changed since Cam's green eyes had first smiled upon her. Behind her, Roland had started playing again, and Lilith and Cam turned their kiss into a dance, swaying together under the stars.

A hand squeezed Lilith's, and she turned to find Liat. Growing up, the two had been friendly but not friends. Now, the girls had bonded over their parallel romances.

"There you are!" Lilith said, kissing Liat's cheek, then

turning to greet Dani, but something in his expression stopped her. He looked nervous.

"What's wrong?" Lilith asked.

"Nothing," he said quickly before turning away and raising his goblet. "I'd like to propose a toast," he said to the rowdy crowd. "To Cam and Lilith!"

"To Cam and Lilith!" the party echoed as Cam slipped his arm around her waist.

Dani gazed down at Liat. "Let us all take a minute to turn to the person we love and make sure they know how special they are to us."

"Don't do it, Dani," Cam said under his breath.

"What?" Lilith asked. Until now, the night had been as blissful as any Lilith had ever known, but Cam's tone gave her a sinking feeling. She looked up at the stars pulsing in the sky and sensed something shift, a dark energy converging over their happy gathering.

Lilith followed Cam's gaze to Dani.

"Liat Lucinda Bat Chana," Dani was saying, "I say your name to affirm that you live, you breathe, you are a wonder." His eyes filled with tears. "You are my Lucinda. You are love."

"Oh no," Arriane said, pushing through the crowd.

From the opposite side of the tent, Roland was closing in on Dani, too, shoving a dozen men out of the way. They cursed his rudeness, and two of them tossed goblets at his head.

Only, Cam did not lunge at Liat and Dani. Instead, he pulled Lilith as far away from the crowd as he could manage, as—

Liat closed the distance between her lips and Dani's. A sob broke in Dani's throat, and he jerked his face away. Something in him surrendered, like a mountain falling into the sea.

And then there was light: a pillar of flame where the lovers had stood.

Lilith saw fire, breathed smoke. The ground trembled, and she fell.

"Lilith!" Cam caught her in his arms while hurrying away, toward the river. "You're safe," he said. "I've got you."

Lilith held him tightly, her eyes filled with tears. Something terrible had happened to Liat. All she could hear were Dani's cries.

⚜

When the moon had waxed and waned and waxed again, and shock had faded to resigned grief, the tribe turned its focus to Lilith's wedding to lift their spirits. Her sisters finished weaving her special wedding robe. Her brothers rolled out barrels of wine from the family cave.

And down at a hidden bend in the Jordan River, two fallen angels sunned their glistening bodies on the lily-covered bank after a last-minute swim.

"Are you sure you don't want me to postpone this?" Cam asked, shaking out his hair.

"I'm fine," Dani said, forcing a smile. "She'll come back. And what difference does it make if you marry Lilith today or in two months?"

Cam lifted his finest robe from the branches of the carob tree and wrapped it around himself. "It makes a great deal of difference to her. She'd be devastated if I suggested postponing it."

Dani looked at the river a long time. "I finished your marriage license last night. The paint should be dry by now." He stood up and pulled on his robe. "I'll get it."

Alone for a moment, Cam sat down and stared into the river. He skipped a stone across the surface and marveled that the laws of nature still held on a day as magical as this.

He'd never dreamed he'd get married. Until he met her. Love had blossomed so quickly between them that it was startling to think how much Lilith didn't know, how much Cam still needed to tell her—

Arms around his neck surprised him. Soft hands found his chest. He closed his eyes.

Lilith started singing softly, a melody he'd been hearing her hum for weeks. At last, she'd found the words to suit the tune:

"I give my arms to you
I give my eyes to you

I give my scars to you
And all my lies to you
What will you give
to me?"

"That is the most enchanting thing I've ever heard," Cam said.

"It's my wedding vow to you." She rested her forehead on the nape of his neck. "You really like it?"

"I like wine, fine clothes, the cool kiss of this river," Cam said. "There is no word that could ever capture how I feel about that vow." He turned his head to nuzzle her and saw her for the first time in her handmade wedding gown. "Or about you. Or about that dress."

"Decorum," Dani said from behind them. "You're not married yet." He knelt before the lovers and unrolled a thick scroll of parchment.

"This is beautiful," Cam said, admiring Dani's elegant Aramaic writing and the airy paintings he'd added as a border, which depicted Cam and Lilith in a dozen embraces.

"Wait," Lilith said as her brows knit together. "This says we will be married here, by the river."

"What better place? This is where we fell in love." Cam tried to keep his voice cheerful even as dread swept over him, for he knew what she was about to say.

Lilith took a deep breath, measuring her words. "You and Dani flout convention, and I like that. But we are about to be *married,* Cam. We will be entering a long tradition, one that I respect. I want to marry in the temple."

The temple Cam couldn't set foot in. And he was too ashamed to tell her why—that he was a fallen angel, and a fallen angel could not tread on consecrated ground.

He should have told her the truth from the beginning. But if he'd told her, it would have been the end of their love, for how could someone as virtuous as Lilith accept Cam as he was?

"Please, Lilith," he said. "Try to envision a beautiful wedding by the river—"

"I told you what I want," Lilith said. "I thought we had agreed."

"I would never have agreed to a marriage in the temple," Cam said, trying to keep the tone of his voice steady, not wanting to betray himself.

"Why not?" Lilith asked, bewildered. "What secret do you bear?"

Dani stepped away, giving the couple a moment alone. Even now, Cam could not bring himself to tell her that he was not human, that he was other. He loved her so much that he could not bear to fall in her esteem. And he *would* fall if she knew the truth.

He turned to face her, memorizing every freckle, every glint of sunlight in her hair, the kaleidoscopic blue of her eyes. "You are the most remarkable creature I have ever seen—"

"We *must* marry in the temple," Lilith said emphatically. "Especially after what happened to Liat. My family and my community will not honor our union any other way."

"I'm not of your community."

"But I am," Lilith said.

Her community would never honor this union if they found out the truth about Cam. He hadn't been thinking—that was the problem. He'd been so caught up in love he hadn't stopped to realize how many barriers stood between them.

He gazed loathingly in the direction of the temple. "I won't set foot in there."

Lilith was close to tears. "Then you don't love me."

"I love you more than I ever thought possible," he said sharply. "But it doesn't change a thing."

"I don't understand," she said. "Cam—"

"It's over," he said, suddenly knowing what he had to do. They would go their separate ways today, each nursing a broken heart. There was no other way. "The wedding, everything."

He spiked his words with bitterness, and when Lilith opened her mouth, he heard words angrier than the ones she spoke. This would become his side of the story: the words he needed to hear to end everything.

"You're breaking my heart," she said.

But what Cam heard behind her words was: *You're a bad man. I know what you are.*

"Forget about me," he said. "Find someone better."

"Never," she gasped. "My heart belongs to you. Damn you for not knowing that."

But Cam knew that what she really meant was: *I hope I live a thousand years and have a thousand daughters so there will always be a woman who can curse your name.*

"Goodbye, Lilith," he said coldly.

She cried out in agony, grabbed their marriage license, and flung it in the river. She was on her knees then, weeping, her arm extended toward the water as if she wished to take it back. He watched the last evidence of their love disappear with the current. Now it was only Cam who had to disappear.

In the dark days and decades that followed, every time Cam thought of Lilith, he remembered some ugly new detail that had never happened that day by the river.

Lilith spitting on him.

Lilith pinning him furiously to the ground.

Lilith giving up on their love.

Until the truth—the one that Cam refused to tell her—sank beneath his memory of her rage. Until, in his mind, Lilith had abandoned *him*. Until it got easier for him to live without her.

He would not let himself remember the tears cutting

her cheeks or the way she touched the mighty carob tree as if saying goodbye. He waited until the sun set and the moon rose. When his white wings bloomed at his sides, they sent a burst of wind rippling across the grass.

The Cam who left the Jordan River that night would never return.

ELEVEN

BREAK ME

LILITH

Seven Days

At breakfast the next day, Lilith whipped the stale Pop-Tart out of Bruce's hand and set before him a steaming bowl of oatmeal.

"Oats à la Lilith," she said. "Bon appétit."

She was proud of her concoction, which included pomegranate seeds, coconut shavings, walnuts, and fresh cream, all courtesy of Cam's groceries.

When she'd confronted him about her photo-copied lyrics, he'd pretended not to know what she was talking about. But the groceries were a dead giveaway of a guilty conscience trying to bribe her into forgiveness.

"Smells amazing," Bruce said, raising his spoon. He was dressed for school in a slightly rumpled collared shirt and a pair of khakis, his hair clean and slicked back. Lilith still wasn't used to seeing him out of pajamas. "Where'd you get all this fancy food?"

"Cam," she said, slopping a ladleful of oatmeal into a bowl for her mother, who was blow-drying her hair.

"Why'd your face get all red and scowly when you said Cam's name?" Bruce asked. His bowl was already clean. "Is there more? And did Cam bring over any chocolate chips?"

"Because he's a jerk, and no." Lilith gave him the bowl she'd been making for her mom and started fixing a third portion. There was no use trying to ration the good food—better to eat and enjoy it, especially now that Bruce was feeling better. He needed to stay healthy.

Lilith dropped into the chair next to her brother and tried to imagine someone ever hurting Bruce the way Cam had hurt her. "You have to be careful with people. We can only really trust each other. Okay?"

"Sounds lonely," Bruce said.

"Yeah," she agreed with a sigh. "It does."

But it was better than letting people like Cam wreck your life.

※

"Go away," Lilith said, slamming her locker as Cam approached in the hall before the bell. She ignored the bouquet of irises in his hand. Their soft scent, which Lilith had loved when she'd found the flowers on the antique desk two days ago, now nauseated her. Everything Cam touched nauseated her.

"These are for you," he said, holding out the bouquet. "I'm really sorry."

"Sorry for *what*, exactly? For making the photocopies?"

"No," Cam said. "I'm sorry you had such an awful day yesterday. This is me trying to cheer you up."

"You want to do something to cheer me up?" Lilith said. "Die."

She yanked the flowers from him, threw them on the floor, and stormed away.

⚜

Cam backed off during homeroom and poetry, and after that Lilith had a lovely respite of classes without him. The black cloud over her even cleared a little in biology, because she'd actually done her homework, for a change.

"Can anyone tell me the difference between the mitochondrion and the Golgi apparatus?" Mrs. Lee asked from the whiteboard.

Lilith found herself gazing in amazement at the fingers

outstretched above her head. She couldn't believe she was raising her hand, voluntarily, in biology.

Mrs. Lee snorted coffee when she saw Lilith in the front row, waiting patiently to be called upon. "Okay, Lilith," she said, failing to mask her surprise, "give it a shot.

Lilith was only able to give it a shot because of Luis. Yesterday, during lunch, he had approached her in the lunch line.

"I was working on a new beat for 'Flying Upside Down' last night," he'd said, tapping out the syncopated rhythm on his tray.

"I was thinking we could speed up the tempo a little, too," Lilith had said.

Luis paid for his burger, and Lilith used her coupon for free lunch. At first she was nervous that he would say something judgmental or snarky about it, but he hadn't said anything at all. Then they spotted Jean sitting by himself, and Luis went to sit down across from him, like it was no big deal, even though Lilith didn't think she'd ever seen them sit together before. The two boys looked up at Lilith, who'd been standing nervously over them.

"Do you need a formal invitation?" Jean patted the seat beside him. "Pop a squat."

So she did. Lilith realized that from this vantage point, seated among friends, the cafeteria felt completely different. It was warm and bright and loud and fun and, for the first time, lunch went by too quickly.

They had lots to say about music, but what surprised Lilith most about that lunch period was that they had things to talk about *other* than music. Like how Jean was nervous Kimi's parents wouldn't extend her curfew on prom night.

"You gotta go over there, dude," Luis said. "You gotta sit down on the awkward couch with her awkward dad, tell him about your college prospects or whatever. Pump yourself up, but be respectable and respectful. Girls' dads love that crap."

"I can't believe I'm taking advice from a freshman," Jean joked, taking a fry in the eye from Luis.

But the freshman turned out to be something close to a genius at biology. When Lilith moaned about her homework, Luis started singing: *"The plasma membrane is the bouncer keeping all the riffraff out."*

"What's that?" Lilith had asked.

"It's, like, my version of *Schoolhouse Rock!*" he'd said, and sang the rest of the song, which was catchy and contained a mnemonic device for every part of a cell. When he finished, Jean started clapping, and Lilith hugged Luis before she even realized what she was doing.

"I don't know why I never thought to make up songs to help me study," she said.

"You don't have to." Luis grinned. "I'll teach you everything I know. Which is, like, everything."

Now, in biology, Lilith remembered Luis's low voice singing to her the day before—and amazingly, she got the answer right. She couldn't wait to tell him.

⚸

At lunchtime, she found him in the cafeteria, pumping the soda dispenser for more ice. She trotted up and started singing. He turned and grinned and harmonized the final line with her.

"Lifesaver," she said. "Thank you."

"More where that came from," Luis said with a lop-sided grin.

"Really?" Lilith asked. She would love this to become a regular thing. She couldn't afford to hire a tutor for all the subjects she was failing.

"What do you got after lunch?" Luis asked, sipping the foam from his Coke before it spilled.

"American history," she groaned.

"I have an amazing rock opera breaking down the battles of the Civil War," he said. "It's one of my best."

"Lilith?" A tap on her shoulder made Lilith spin around. Cam was holding out a lunch tray of her favorite: lasagna.

"I'm not hungry," she said. "What part of 'die' did you not understand? Do I need to say it louder?"

"Dude, I'll eat that lasagna," Luis said.

Jean Rah had gotten up from his table. "What's going on, guys?" he asked.

Cam passed the tray to Luis as Lilith said, "Cam's out of the band."

"What'd you do this time?" Jean said, shaking his head. Next to him, Luis was forking lasagna into his mouth, wide-eyed.

"Lilith thinks I photocopied her lyrics and spread them all around the school," Cam said, tugging at the collar of his T-shirt. "It's unclear *why* she thinks I would do that, but she does."

"Naw, Lilith," Luis said, wiping sauce from his lips with his hand. "I'm the library aide, and I had to make some copies yesterday. That copy job was right ahead of me in the queue. All I knew was it was like a thousand pages long." Luis rolled his eyes. "You have to have a code when a job's that big. This one was sent from an external computer. It came from the account 'King Media.'"

Jean frowned. "So it was either Chloe King or—"

"The intern," Cam muttered. "Luc."

"Whatever," Lilith said, weirdly angry that the story she'd believed about Cam was falling apart. "Cam's still out of the band. Jean, Luis, I'll see you guys after school for practice."

But when Lilith got to the band room after school, her friends weren't there. Instead, the Perceived Slights were getting ready to practice.

Or rather, their new guitar tech—a quiet girl named Karen Walker, who sat next to Lilith in biology—was setting up their instruments. She chewed her lip as she plucked the strings and turned the pegs of Chloe's gleaming electric guitar. Lilith could tell Karen didn't really know what she was doing, but the band members weren't paying much attention. They were lounging on the risers, drinking smoothies and playing on their phones.

"Um, June, did you just send me your geeky classical Spotify station?" Teresa asked the blonde to her left.

"It's Chopin, and I listen to it when I fall asleep," June said.

"Dork!" Chloe said without looking up from her phone. "My lucky station right now is All Prince All the Time. Dean and I listened to it last Friday night."

Lilith thought about angelic-looking June lying in bed, dreaming to Chopin's waltz concertos. Lilith had tried sleeping to music. It was torturous. She hung on every note, marveling at the chord changes, trying to discern the various instruments.

Maybe music left other people alone, allowing them to relax. Music never left Lilith alone.

"Did somebody take down the sign outside that said No Freaks Allowed?" Chloe said when she noticed Lilith standing in the doorway. "Are you here to dump more of your crappy lyrics on unsuspecting victims?"

Lilith didn't like Chloe, but she knew her well enough to realize that Chloe wasn't lying—she actually thought Lilith had passed around those photocopies herself.

Which meant Chloe wasn't the culprit.

Yet Luis said the copy job had come from a King Media computer. She remembered Cam suggesting that Luc might have made the photocopies. But that didn't make sense. Why would the Battle of the Bands intern try to sabotage her?

"Have you seen Luis and Jean?" she asked Chloe. "We've got practice in here."

"Not anymore," Chloe said, her lips twisted into a venomous grin. "We kicked those losers out. This is *our* turf now."

"But—"

"You guys can use the concrete slab out by the dumpster. Go on," Chloe said, making a shooing gesture with her hands. "Skedaddle. We're about to get started, and I don't want you stealing our sound."

"Right," Lilith deadpanned as she shoved open the band-room door. "Because I might be tempted to copy the groundbreaking way you show off your cleavage when you play guitar."

❄❄

Lilith found Jean and Luis in the parking lot, sitting on the hood of Jean's baby-blue Honda. The temperature had soared since lunchtime, and a haze of heat rose from the pavement. The sun was a muted orange dot behind a smoky cloud. Luis's brow was damp with sweat when he offered Lilith the dregs of the huge bag of Doritos he was holding.

"I could use some Cool Ranch right about now," Lilith said.

"Chloe kicked you out, too?" Jean asked, kicking his feet up onto his car's headlight.

She nodded. "Where are we going to practice now? My house is definitely not an option."

"Mine neither," Luis said between chomps. "My parents would kill me if they found out I was in a band. They think I'm staying late today for an extra SAT prep course."

"My place is no good either," Jean said. "I'm the oldest of five kids, and you guys do not want to deal with my siblings. Especially not the twins. They're psycho."

"So basically we're screwed," Lilith said. She thought about Rattlesnake Creek, but they'd need a generator to power the mics, the speakers, the synthesizer. It would never work.

"What about Cam's place?" Jean said. "Anyone know where he lives?"

"I'm sorry, are you referring to the Cam who's no longer in the band?" Lilith said, narrowing her eyes.

"He didn't sabotage you, Lilith," Jean said. "I know you're embarrassed, but it wasn't Cam. You should talk to him, clear the air. We need him."

Lilith didn't answer. She liked having Jean and Luis as friends, and she didn't want to mess that up, but she'd draw the line if they forced her to let Cam back in the band. Still, now that Jean mentioned it, Lilith *was* curious about where Cam lived.

"Library aide to the rescue," Luis said, scrolling through his phone. "I have access to the student database with everyone's address." He tilted his head back, shaking some of the hair away from his eyes. "Here it is, Two Hundred and Forty-One Dobbs Street." He shoved the last of the Doritos into his mouth, then tossed the wadded-up bag into a nearby trash can. "Let's go."

"This doesn't mean I'm letting him back in Revenge," Lilith said to the boys who were already climbing into the car. "We'll just go check it out."

❇

Luis offered Lilith shotgun, which she thought was a chivalrous gesture, and Jean's GPS directed them toward the gritty side of town. He cranked up the stereo—insisting on introducing them to one of his favorite new albums, which they all loved—and drove past the strip mall Lilith always passed on her way to school. They turned into Lilith's neighborhood and drove right past her street.

She held her breath until she could no longer see her driveway in the side-view mirror, as if Jean or Luis might be able to tell that the hideous house at the end of the lane was the one Lilith called home. She thought about Bruce inside, watching old episodes of *Jeopardy!* with Alastor on the couch beside him, and she felt like she was betraying him simply by being ashamed of where she came from.

It surprised her that Cam would live on this side of town. She remembered an early conversation when he'd told her he'd slept outside the night before. At the time, she thought he'd been joking. He seemed to have plenty of money. He drove his own motorcycle, and his leather jacket looked expensive. He'd brought her groceries, served her caviar, tried to give her flowers just this morning.

Jean turned sharply left and braked. "This can't be right."

Lilith didn't think so, either. Dobbs was a long, straight street that had been closed down to car traffic entirely. There were no houses here. No apartments. Between their idling car and the burning hills in the distance were hundreds of patchwork tents and cardboard lean-tos set up in the middle of the road. People milled among the tents, and they didn't look anything like Cam. They were ragged, down on their luck, many of them strung out.

"Maybe the database is wrong," Luis said, pulling out his phone.

"Let's go check it out," Lilith said, and opened the passenger door.

Luis and Jean followed her to the edge of the tent city, stepping over broken bottles and moldy cardboard boxes. It was strangely cold here, and the wind was sharp. Lilith didn't know what she was looking for; she was no longer expecting to find Cam here.

The smell was overwhelming, like a sweaty landfill that someone had doused with gasoline. Lilith breathed through her mouth as she tried to make sense of this scene. At first, it looked like total chaos: Scrawny children running everywhere, men bickering over the contents of shopping carts, fires raging in trash cans. But the longer Lilith studied the world of Dobbs Street, the more it started to make sense. It was its own little community, with its own rules.

"I saw them first," a woman Lilith's mother's age said to another, younger woman, yanking a pair of canvas shoes out of her hand.

"But they're my size," the second woman argued. She had blond dreadlocks and wore a gray midriff tank top. Lilith could see her ribs. "You couldn't even get your big toe in them."

Lilith looked down at her own falling-apart combat boots, with the laces she kept having to knot together when they snapped. They were the only pair of shoes she'd had for years. She tried to imagine not having even them.

"Maybe we should take off," Jean said, looking antsy. "We can talk to Cam tomorrow at school."

"There," Lilith said, pointing ahead at a boy with a messenger bag slung over his shoulder exiting a dark green tent.

Cam paused for a moment and gazed up at the sky, as if he could read something there that the rest of them could not.

Against this backdrop, in the fading dusk light, Cam seemed like somebody else entirely. He looked older, tired. Had he always looked like that? She felt bad for him. She wondered how much of a front Cam had to put up at school to appear so confident and mysterious.

Was this really his home? Lilith had never known people lived like this in Crossroads. She'd never imagined anyone worse off than her own family.

He was walking their way, but he hadn't seen them yet. Lilith tugged Jean and Luis's shirtsleeves to pull them out of his line of vision.

Cam nodded as he passed two older guys. One of them raised a fist for him to bump.

"Hey, brother."

"How are you, August?" she heard Cam say.

"Can't complain. Just the toothache."

"I'm pulling for you," Cam said with a smile. He put a hand on the guy's shoulder and looked him deep in the eyes. The man seemed to relax, transfixed by Cam's gaze.

Lilith was transfixed, too. The people here shared a hungry, nervous look in their eyes. But not Cam. Beneath his exhaustion, he radiated a serenity that suggested nothing in this place could touch him. Maybe nothing in this world could touch him. It was one of the most beautiful things she'd ever seen. She wanted to be that way, too: at peace with herself, autonomous, free.

"I kind of get the feeling he does live here," Jean said.

"If you can call this living," Luis said, and started walking toward him. "He doesn't have to be here. We've got two extra bedrooms at my house. I'm sure my parents would let him crash."

"Wait." Lilith held him back. "It might embarrass him that we tracked him down here." Lilith knew it would embarrass her if the situation were reversed. "Let's talk to him tomorrow."

She watched as Cam strolled over to a burning trash can where a father was cooking two hot dogs for four small children over a metal grate. He cut each dog in two and turned them over on the grill, but when Cam paused before him, the man started to cut one of the hot dogs into smaller pieces.

"Hungry?" he said, and offered Cam a quarter of a dog.

"No," Cam said. "Thank you. Actually . . ." He reached inside his messenger bag and pulled out a foil-wrapped parcel. "You guys should have this."

The man unwrapped it and found a giant deli sandwich. He blinked at Cam and took a huge bite, then divided the rest between his children. As they ate, he hugged Cam in gratitude.

When they'd finished eating, the oldest boy—he looked about Bruce's age—held out a beat-up guitar. Cam tousled the boy's hair, then took a seat among them. He tried tuning it, but Lilith could hear it was hopeless. Two of the strings were broken. Still, Cam didn't give up, and soon the guitar sounded a little better than it had before.

"Any requests?" he said.

"A lullaby," the youngest boy said with a yawn.

Cam thought a moment. "I learned this one from a talented musician," he said, "named Lilith."

When Cam broke into the first bars of "Exile," Lilith sucked in her breath. Cam sang her song beautifully, slowly and with great emotion, bringing to it a depth she'd never imagined possible. He sang it twice. By the time he finished, the children in the group were nodding into sleep. Behind them, their father applauded Cam softly.

"Whoa," Jean whispered.

"Yeah," Lilith said. She was shaking, near tears, so moved that she could say no more.

"We should go," Luis said.

Hours earlier, Lilith had been certain she'd written Cam off for the last time. Now she followed her friends to Jean's car feeling dizzy, as if the world around her were shifting with each step.

The only thing she was sure of was how wrong she'd been about Cam.

TWELVE

SPELLBOUND

CAM

Six Days

Cam woke in a green tent on Dobbs Street with a stiff back and a stray dog at his feet. He'd slept here a couple times since he arrived in Crossroads. It was less lonesome than the roof of the Trumbull gym.

He nudged the dog off and peeked outside at the pale pink sunrise. Mornings started early here. Everyone was hungry, bleary from a rough night. The soup kitchen opened at seven, and Cam had volunteered to work the breakfast shift before he went to school.

He meandered down the street, passing families

getting ready for the day, unzipping their tents, stretching their limbs, rocking fussy babies. At the abandoned office building that had been repurposed as a soup kitchen, he pushed open the glass door.

"Morning." A gaunt older man named Jax welcomed Cam inside. "You can start right there." He nodded toward the dented steel counter where a giant box of Bisquick sat beside a mixing bowl.

Not a lot of small talk—which was fine by Cam. He added the milk and eggs and started mixing up the pancake batter, knowing that the Ballard boys, who loved his music, would be among the first in line. Half a hot dog and a few bites of sandwich was no kind of dinner for a growing kid. In a short time, Cam had come to care about the families that lived on Dobbs Street. He was addicted to mortal lives, and not just Lilith's. Humans fascinated him. All those little flames, forever lighting and going out.

"You okay there, Cam?" Jax asked from the range, where he was grilling slices of Spam. "You don't look so good."

Cam put down the bowl of pancake batter and walked toward the tinted window to look at his reflection. His green eyes were recessed behind dark purple sockets. Since when did he have jowls? And now even his hands looked ancient, mottled and wrinkly.

"I'm okay," he said, but his voice faltered. He looked—and felt—awful.

"Get yourself some breakfast before school," Jax said kindly, patting Cam on the back, as if a plate of pancakes would make every problem the devil was serving him simply fade away.

⁂

"Cam—"

Lilith found him at his locker before homeroom. He'd flown from Dobbs Street to campus so he could squeeze in a shower before the locker room filled up with track-team kids. He had thought a shower would make him look a little bit better, but when he'd dressed for school, the mirror in the locker room had been just as unkind as the soup-kitchen window.

Even his feet were changing now, turning black and cloven, like the hooves of the damned. He could no longer fit into his own boots. He'd had to steal a pair from a motorcycle shop downtown.

"Hey." Cam couldn't help but stare at Lilith's lovely face.

"How are you?" she asked softly.

"Been better." It wasn't the kind of thing he wanted to admit, but the truth slipped out before he could censor it.

Kids streamed past them through the hall. Everyone was talking about prom. Someone kicked a soccer ball at Cam's head. He ducked just in time.

"Anything I can do to help?" Lilith said, leaning against his locker and offering him a slight smile. She was wearing a Four Horsemen T-shirt tied in a knot at her narrow waist. Her hair was still wet from her shower, and it smelled like freesias. He couldn't help leaning in.

Remember me, he longed to say, because if she could remember Cam as he'd been when they first fell in love, she wouldn't only see him as the withering shell he was today.

"I thought you were mad at me," he said.

To his amazement, Lilith reached for his hand. Her fingers were cool and strong, calloused at the tips where she strummed her guitar. "There are more important things to worry about," she said.

Cam seized his chance and stepped closer, yearning to move his hand to her hair. He knew how it would feel: damp and gloriously soft, just as it had been in Canaan when she lay in his arms by the riverbank after a swim, her hair splayed against his bare chest.

"What could be more important than your trust?" he asked.

Lilith tilted her head toward Cam. A dreamy look came into her eyes, replacing the suspicion he'd grown accustomed to in this Hell. Her lips parted. Cam held his breath—

"So, kids . . ." Jean Rah appeared before them and raised his green plastic sunglasses. "Do we have a band, or what?"

Lilith stepped back and tugged down the hem of her shorts. She looked embarrassed, like someone coming out of hypnosis who couldn't remember what had happened a moment before.

Cam knew Jean meant well, but right at that moment he could have hit him.

"I assume that since you two are speaking," Jean continued, seeing the look in Cam's eyes, "you've made up and we can once again—"

"We were just working on that," Lilith said.

"Work faster," Jean said, and snapped his fingers. "We have an important matter to discuss *re* prom." He nudged Lilith. "Have you asked him yet?"

"Asked me what?" Cam said.

"To prom," Jean said.

Lilith's face started turning many shades of red as Cam's eyebrows shot up. He'd been waiting for a far more romantic moment to ask *her* to prom. Was she actually planning to ask *him*?

"Of course," he blurted out. "I'd love to."

Jean winced. "No, man, that was a joke. Sorry. I thought you'd laugh. Thought you'd both laugh—"

Cam gulped. "Hilarious."

"I don't need a date to play a song with my band," Lilith said. "So everybody just chill."

"Yeah, Prom King," Jean said, laughing. "Chill."

Cam shoved him into a locker. "Thanks, man."

"But I *was* wondering, Cam," Lilith said, twirling

a lock of her red hair, "if you'd consider rejoining the band." She glanced at Jean. "There. That's it. Okay?"

"Okay," Cam said, knowing better than to question what had made her change her mind. "Of course. I'd love to."

Jean placed one arm on Cam's shoulder, the other on Lilith's. "Now that *that's* settled, we can get down to business," he said. "Meet me in the parking lot right after school. We're going on a field trip."

"Destination where?" Cam asked. Whatever Jean's plans involved, Cam liked the idea of getting off Trumbull's campus with Lilith.

"Shopping for prom, the Battle of the Bands, aka our debut performance." Jean tapped the face of his watch. "It's six days away and we have no look."

"Jean, I sit next to Kimi in poetry," Lilith said. "I know about the cranberry satin cummerbund you special ordered to match her prom dress."

Cam burst out laughing.

"You shut up, and you shut up," Jean said, pointing at each of them. "Yes, I will be wearing a cranberry satin cummerbund for a portion of prom." He shook his head ruefully. "But not when Revenge performs. For that, we need to pull out all the stops."

Lilith looked down at her jean shorts. "I was just gonna wear—"

"We cannot wear our everyday clothes onstage!" Jean

said, more serious than Cam had ever seen him. "We don't want our audience to look at us like they do now."

Cam cleared his throat and glanced down at his boots. Was Jean suggesting he *not* wear them onstage? Unfortunately, he didn't have much choice. He looked around the hall at the kids hurrying to class. "I'm not sure they see us at all."

Jean rolled his eyes. "You know what I mean. You don't want that guy Luc to see you onstage and think of you sitting in detention, do you?"

"Probably not," Cam admitted, though he knew no costume would disguise him from Lucifer.

"He needs to think you're from another world," Jean continued.

"We're only playing one song," Lilith said. "Seems like a waste for aliens to come all the way from outer space just to play one song."

"Rock is about waste," Jean said. "Wasted time, wasted youth, wasted talent, wasted money."

Cam wondered where Lilith's apprehension about the new look was coming from; then he realized: She probably couldn't afford anything new. But that shouldn't stop her from finding something special. He would figure out a way to help her.

"Jean's right," Cam said to Lilith. "We need a unified look. Just not a pricey one. I can't afford a lot at the moment."

"No worries," Jean said, and Cam watched Lilith breathe a sigh of relief. "I can work with a budget. So we'll meet at three-forty-five and head to the Salvation Army."

Cam scratched his head. His leather jacket had been handmade in 1509 in Florence by Bartolomeo himself. He'd taken his last pair of boots from a dead American infantryman in a Rhineland field in 1945. His jeans were from the first batch made in 1873 by Levi Strauss. He'd brought them directly to Savile Row to be altered.

Oh, how times had changed.

"I'm in," Lilith said, just before the bell rang. "Meet you after school. By the way, Cam, I like your new boots."

※

"You, come with me, right now." Tarkenton grabbed Cam by the collar during lunch, when he was hoping to slink off to Rattlesnake Creek. He'd managed to swipe a cool black satin guitar strap at a music shop yesterday, and he wanted to leave it as a gift for Lilith on the antique desk.

"What am I being charged with?" Cam asked as Tarkenton dragged him back inside the cafeteria.

"Failure to fulfill your duties as a member of the prom court. Miss King informs me that you've skipped five of the meetings already, and you're not skipping another on my watch."

Cam groaned. "Isn't there some waiver I can sign to

opt out? There's gotta be some other kid who actually wants my spot."

Tarkenton steered Cam to a table in the center of the cafeteria, where Chloe King was sitting with the other girls in her band and three guys Cam had thus far successfully avoided knowing. They were sharing a pizza, all leaning in together and whispering. Everyone stopped talking as soon as they saw Cam.

"Sit down," Tarkenton ordered, "shape up, and start brainstorming colors for the balloon banner like a normal teenager." The principal motioned Cam toward the last empty seat.

"If I sit, will you go away?" Cam muttered as Tarkenton finally disappeared. Immediately, Chloe slid the box of pizza to the center of the table, out of Cam's reach.

"Don't give me that look," she said. "I'm *helping*. I'm sure you want to shed some pre-prom pounds. Trust me, you don't need this pizza."

"Don't be mean, Chloe," joked a square-headed boy named Dean. "Let the fatty have his fix."

The whole table started laughing. Cam couldn't care less what these kids thought of him. He only cared about the time they were sucking from him. He should have been either with Lilith or doing something special for her.

Just then, a folded piece of paper dropped onto the table in front of him. Cam looked up and saw Lilith passing by, carrying her lunch tray. She nodded at the note.

Cam's name was written on the outside in black. He unfolded it.

HANG IN THERE. . . . ONLY THREE HOURS TILL OUR FIELD TRIP.

Buoyed with happiness, he turned back to watch Lilith. She had taken a seat at the far end of the cafeteria, next to Jean and Luis. She was eating a bright red apple and laughing. She seemed to feel Cam's gaze on her and looked over, all the way across the cafeteria, to offer him a dazzling, sympathetic smile.

Chloe could take that pizza and shove it. Lilith's smile was all the nourishment Cam needed.

※

After school, Jean's Honda squealed into the Salvation Army parking lot and shuddered to a stop, straddling two spaces. Cam's fingers touched Lilith's as he pulled himself out of the back. When he looked up, she was smiling. It was the same smile she'd given him in the cafeteria, the smile that had helped Cam survive the thirty-five minutes of the prom planning meeting.

Cam had no opinion on where the photo booth should be placed at prom, or whether the DJ should wear a tux or something more casual, or if they needed flowers to decorate the table where the memory books would be signed.

But he did have a strong opinion on getting Lilith to be his date.

Things were going well today, and there was no new sign of Luc meddling, so Cam was feeling optimistic. But he still had work to do. He needed this trip to the Salvation Army to feel as romantic as a trip to the top of the Eiffel Tower.

"Divide and conquer," Jean said, beckoning them into the thrift store. The place smelled like mothballs spritzed with cat urine, mixed with a whiff of stale vanilla perfume. "Experiment. Have fun."

"But remember," Luis added, holding the door open for Lilith, "we're looking for costumes that elevate our stage presence."

Cam glanced at the freshman and laughed. "Whoa. What got into you?"

"I got a prom date," Luis said, doing a little dance. "No biggie."

"You finally asked her?" Jean asked, then grinned at Cam. "He's been drooling over Karen Walker all semester."

"Way to go, Luis," Lilith said, and high-fived the drummer, but as she started down an aisle overflowing with hats, Cam wondered if he'd heard a hint of envy in her voice. Even Luis had a prom date now.

Cam followed Lilith to a high wall of lime-green shelves, impressed that she'd sought out the most interesting section of the store so quickly. Cam had shopped at, donated to, and even worked in at least a hundred vintage stores over the years. He could step inside any one and know where the shoes and light fixtures were and how to find the really cool old suits.

Lilith seemed to have the same gift. She rose onto her toes to slide a three-piece navy pin-striped suit down from the shelf. She held the pants up to Cam, nodding approval. "Thoughts?"

"Dynamite." He took the suit, then picked through the rest, pausing at a glen-plaid one that was smaller than the others and looked spotless. Cam knew the jacket would plunge enticingly on Lilith, and that the pants would hug her just right.

"Oh, I *love* this," she said as he handed it to her. "Do you think I can pull it off?"

"I don't know if this town can handle how good you will look in that suit," he said.

"Really?" She examined it, looking for stains. "I'll try it on."

Cam flagged a tall lady wearing a name tag. "Would you mind showing us to your changing rooms?"

"In the back," the woman said, leading Cam and Lilith to a corner sectioned off by a yellow flannel curtain.

"In you go, kid," Cam said.

The dressing room was a mess, with old frocks and ponchos and fedoras and pajamas sharing hangers and wall pegs. It looked like anything that had been tried on and discarded in the past decade had just been left there in a heap.

"Come on in," Lilith said, and tugged the curtain closed behind them both.

Inside, the light was different; the incandescent bulbs mellowed to a softer, almost romantic glow through their dusty shades.

"Turn around while I put this on," she said.

"You don't want me to wait outside?" Cam asked.

"I told you what I want," Lilith said. "Turn around."

Cam followed her instructions. He listened to the sounds she made when she moved, the soft breaths she took, the plunk of her backpack dropping to the floor, the snap of the elastic band when she threw her hair up in a ponytail. Something brushed his shoulder, and he realized Lilith was undressing. With all the clothes heaped back here, there wasn't much space to move in the dressing room, so as Lilith shimmied out of her jeans, her bare hip bumped against Cam. His wings burned with the urge to let loose.

"You gonna try on your clothes, or what?" Lilith said.

It was a thrilling feeling, knowing there was something dangerously sexy going on behind him but not being able to see any of it, any of her. Cam felt like he and Lilith had a secret, a moment that was just theirs.

"Right." He pulled off his jacket.

Soon, they were standing bare back to bare back. The touch of Lilith's skin in the quiet curtained space was transporting. They could have been right back at the Jordan River. His body could recognize each curve of hers unseen.

Did Lilith recognize his, too? Thanks to Lucifer, Cam's body was nothing like it had been in Canaan, but still, he longed to know if being close like this jogged her memories.

"Yo!" Jean called from outside. "Opinions are required."

"Just a minute," Lilith called as she and Cam hurried into their outfits.

Cam zipped up the pin-striped pants, and a moment later, felt her fingertips on his shoulders, swiveling him to face her.

Only Lilith wasn't wearing the glen-plaid suit. Instead, she'd slipped into a light blue dress, with clean, simple lines. The neck was low but not plunging. Its hemline danced against the middle of her thigh. She must have just found it in the dressing-room pile, but it looked as if it had been sewn especially for her.

"You look beautiful," he said.

"Thanks," Lilith said. She eyed his suit, which felt like it had been made for the old Cam—not his current body. "It looked promising on the rack," she said politely. "But it's kind of giving you a used-car-salesman vibe."

"That's perfect," he said, "because you look like a sexpot fifties housewife in the market for a secondhand Cadillac."

"Ew," Lilith shrieked, but she was laughing. "Take that off immediately before its seediness rubs off on you permanently."

"What should I put on instead?" Cam asked, laughing too.

"Anything else!" Lilith grabbed a gray wool poncho with yellow and orange flowers from a peg on the wall at the back of the dressing room. It looked like it had once belonged to a Mexican desperado. "Here!"

Cam reached behind a voluminous green bathrobe and pulled out a pink, satiny Hawaiian hula dress. "Only if you try this on."

"I accept your challenge," Lilith said playfully and took the dress. She motioned with her pointer finger for Cam to turn around.

They were back-to-back again, Cam standing very still whenever he felt Lilith's bare skin brush his. He closed his eyes and imagined the Hawaiian dress sliding down the curve of her hips.

When she turned around, Cam was delighted to find that she'd plucked a white silk orchid blossom from a selection of fake plants in the corner of the dressing room. It was tucked behind her ear. "Aloha," she said, batting her lashes.

"Aloha yourself," Cam said.

"Boy knows how to work a poncho," she said, looking him up and down, approving.

Cam put on his cleanest Mexico City accent and took Lilith by the hand. "I know we come from different worlds, señorita, but now that I have laid eyes on you, I *must* take you back to my rancho."

"But my father will never allow it," Lilith said, pulling out an impressively convincing Hawaiian-priestess voice. "He'll kill you before he lets you take me away!"

Cam kissed her hand. "For you, I would risk anything, even the eternal flames of Hell."

"Hello!?" Luis shouted from outside the curtain. "What's going on in there? Have you guys found your look yet?"

Lilith giggled and pulled back the curtain, doing a little hula dance.

They found Jean wearing a black fedora and a tan trench coat. Meanwhile, Luis had found a football uniform, complete with pads, and somehow pulled it on over his clothes. "Mess with me now, jerks!" he shouted to the ceiling.

"Great." Jean glanced at each of them and shook his head. "We're going to look like the Village People."

"We aren't done, man," Luis said. "We just got here!"

"Well, so far, we look pathetic," Jean said. "Except for you, Lilith. Now, come on, let's try a little harder."

"Says the guy who picked a *fedora*," Luis said as they both disappeared into an ocean of corduroy.

"What now?" Cam said as he and Lilith returned to the dressing room. "We might get in trouble with Jean if we keep fooling around."

"Sounds dangerous," Lilith teased. She glanced around the dressing room, sifting through the hangers. "Let's surprise each other."

Again, they turned back-to-back. Again, Cam felt the dress slide over Lilith's head and fall to the floor at his feet. Again, he shivered with barely checked desire.

He eyed the clothing rack in front of him, reaching at last for a long, beige Indian caftan. He pulled it over his head and tied it at the neck.

"What do you think of this one?" Lilith asked a few moments later.

He turned to face her.

Lilith was wearing a gauzy white floor-length gown embroidered with deep-green leaves. "I couldn't help noticing you at the village well the other day . . . ," she said in a slow, husky voice.

She was still playing, but Cam could hardly breathe. He hadn't seen that dress since . . .

"Where did you find that?"

Lilith gestured at the heap of clothes piled against the back wall, but Cam couldn't take his eyes off her. He blinked and saw his bride-to-be, sunlight dappling her shoulders as she stood beside him at the Jordan River three thousand years ago. He remembered precisely the way that feather-light fabric had felt between his fingers when he wrapped his arms around her. He remembered the way its train had trailed as she left him.

It couldn't be. The fabric would have deteriorated long ago. But in this gown, Lilith looked exactly like the girl he'd lost.

Cam leaned against the rack of clothes, feeling faint.

"What?" Lilith asked.

"What *what*?" Cam replied.

"I look bad in this, obviously."

"I didn't say that."

"But you were thinking it."

"If you could read my mind, you'd apologize for that comment."

Lilith stared down at the dress. "It was supposed to be a joke." She paused. "It's stupid, I know, but, for some reason, I . . . wanted you to like the way I looked in it."

She left the dressing room to stand before the mirror outside. Cam followed, watching her finger the embroidery at her waist. He watched the skirt swish as she swiveled her hips a little. A change came over her expression. Her eyes turned dreamy again. He took a step closer.

Was it possible? Was she remembering something from their past?

"You are the most remarkable creature I have ever seen—" he said before he knew what he was doing.

"We *must* marry in the temple," she said sharply.

"What?" Cam blinked, but then the answer came to him. They had spoken these same words to one another before, on the riverbank in Canaan, the last time she wore this dress.

Lilith met his gaze in the mirror. Suddenly, anger flooded her eyes, contorting her features. She spun to face him, full of fury. The past she couldn't remember was rippling forward into the present. He could see that Lilith was confused by *why* she felt so angry but absolutely certain that it had everything to do with Cam.

"Lilith," he said. He wanted to tell her the whole truth. It gutted him to understand what she was feeling better than she could.

But before he could say anything more, Lilith burst out laughing. The sound was forced, not her natural melodic laugh. "What was *that*?" she said. "Sorry. I feel like an idiot."

Cam attempted a laugh. "Were you joking?"

"Maybe." Lilith tugged at the buttons at the back of her neck like the dress was choking her. "But my anger feels so real. Like I want to rip your face from your skull with my fingernails."

"Whoa," Cam managed to say.

"But the weirdest part of it," Lilith continued, studying him, "is that you're acting like you deserve it. I'm furious with you, and I have no idea why. But it's almost like *you* do." She pressed her fists against her temples. "Am I going crazy?"

He studied the embroidered vine climbing her torso. He had to get her out of that dress.

"I liked the other one better," he lied, returning to the dressing room and picking the modern blue dress up from the floor. It looked cheap and forgettable next to Lilith's wedding gown. "Here, let me help you out of this old thing. It smells like mothballs."

But Lilith brushed Cam's hand away from the buttons near her neck.

"I should buy this one." Her voice was faraway. "It makes me feel more like . . . myself." She called to the sales clerk, "How much for this dress?"

"I've never seen that one before," came the woman's response a moment later. "Either it just came in, or it's been in that pile in the dressing room for ages."

Cam knew it was the former—and he also knew who had brought it there.

"What's your best price?" Lilith said, and Cam heard her unzipping her backpack and fumbling through her wallet. "I've got . . . two dollars and fifty . . . three cents."

Cam went after her. "Maybe you shouldn't—"

"Well," the saleswoman said. "Dresses are half-off on Fridays, and most people around here have kind of a different style than . . . whatever that is. I'll take your two fifty-three at the register."

"Wait—" Cam started to say.

"Great," Lilith said, swishing away from him down the aisle, still wearing the dress.

As Cam changed back into his clothes, he spotted a tiny carved-wood gargoyle sitting atop a shelf of knick-knacks, looking out over the changing room. Cam and Lilith were finally getting along. But Lucifer couldn't have that. In order to win the bet, he needed Lilith to stay trapped—even clothed—in her rage. And she had never been angrier at Cam than on the last day she'd worn this dress.

Now, three millennia later, she would wear it again, and feel that fury again—on prom night, when Cam would need her forgiveness most.

THIRTEEN

MY IMMORTAL

LILITH

Five Days

"Can I take this thing off yet?" Bruce asked on Saturday, tugging at the T-shirt Lilith had knotted around his head as a blindfold.

"You can take it off when I say you can take it off," Lilith told him. From her seat on the Crossroads public bus, she pressed the yellow Exit button to signal the driver to make the next stop. Aside from the elderly couple sharing a Twix at the front of the bus, Lilith and Bruce were the only passengers.

"It's itchy," Bruce whined. "And it smells."

"But it's going to be *so* worth it." Lilith clamped her hand over her little brother's eyes, because if she were him, she'd definitely be peeking. "Now, come on."

Lilith's stomach knotted as the bus hit a series of potholes. She was nervous. She wanted this to be special, something Bruce would remember. She couldn't wait to see his face when she unveiled the surprise.

When the bus pulled over, Lilith guided Bruce down the steps and across an intersection, then paused before a storefront, patting her pocket to make sure she still had the cash her mom had given her.

When her mom had discovered all the groceries stocking their fridge a couple of days ago, she'd grilled Lilith on where she'd gotten them. Lilith had lied—no way was she going into the story of Cam with her mom—saying she was giving guitar lessons to a kid from school for a little extra cash. Her mom had looked at Lilith with genuine surprise, then she'd done something unprecedented: she had hugged her daughter.

Lilith was so surprised that she'd let the hug linger.

And then last night, when her mom got home from work, she'd knocked on Lilith's door. Lilith had been staring into her closet, but she'd quickly shut its door, concealing the strange white gown hanging inside. She'd already tried it on twice since she got back from the thrift store. It made her feel hungry for something she couldn't put into words. It was so not rock and roll, but it fit Lilith better than anything she'd ever worn. She couldn't stop thinking about the look Cam had given her when she turned to him in the dressing room.

"Hey, Mom," she said casually, opening her door.

Her mother held out a twenty-dollar bill.

"What's this?"

"I think they call it an allowance," her mom said with a smile. "Had a little extra this week, since you took care of the groceries." She paused. "That was really generous of you, Lilith."

"Sure," Lilith said. "No big deal."

"It is to me." She nodded at the money in Lilith's hand. "Have some fun. Take Bruce with you."

So she did.

"Where are we?" Bruce whined, scratching his forehead where the blindfold was tight.

Taking his hand, Lilith pushed through the tinted door into Lanes, Crossroads's only bowling alley. She was hit by the blast of air-conditioning; the smell of cheap, oregano-heavy pizza and pungent nacho cheese; the flashing lights above the lanes; the sugar-fueled shrieks of a hundred kids.

And then, rising above everything else: the crackle of a bowling ball knocking down ten pins.

"*Striiiike!*" Bruce shouted, still blindfolded, fists raised in the air.

Lilith yanked off the blindfold. "How did you know?"

Her brother's eyes widened. He staggered forward, then froze, resting his elbows on a ball-polishing machine. "I didn't," he finally said. "I was pretending."

Then the wind was knocked out of her as Bruce slammed into her with a full-body hug.

"I've wanted to come here my whole life!" he shouted. "I've begged Mom to take me here every day! And she always said—"

"I know," Lilith said.

" 'If you ever get well, son,' " Lilith and Bruce said together, imitating their mother's tired voice.

Since Bruce's last trip to the hospital, their mother had had moments of brightness, even kindness, like the night before. But this morning, when Lilith had invited her to join them at Lanes, she'd snapped at Lilith for not remembering she had agreed to pick up a shift at the night school.

"Now I'm better." Bruce laughed as if he still couldn't believe it. "And so we're here! Thank you!"

"My pleasure. Mom's pleasure, actually," Lilith said, showing Bruce the cash.

"This is amazing!"

Lilith blinked back happy tears as she watched her brother take it all in. He was mesmerized by the sight of a girl his age staggering under the weight of a glittering bowling ball, by the kids chewing pizza, waiting for their turn to bowl. He got to be a normal kid too rarely.

She glanced around the bowling alley and was surprised

to spot Karen Walker from her bio class bowling in a lane on the far side of the room. She was with a few girls Lilith recognized from school, all of whom cheered for Karen as she celebrated a strike.

Karen was shy, but she'd never been rude to Lilith, and she was going to prom with Luis, which earned her points in Lilith's book. Plus, she had to be a little interested in music, because she'd agreed to be Chloe King's guitar tech. Lilith had never considered that she might be friends with Karen, but now it seemed silly not to go over and say hello.

"I'll get us some shoes," Lilith said.

"I don't want to bowl," Bruce said, shaking his head.

Lilith gaped at him. "You don't?"

"Duh." His eyes lit up as he pointed at a dark doorway past the vending machines. Red, yellow, and green lights blinked above its cavelike entrance. "The arcade."

Lilith smiled. She looked toward Karen Walker's lane again, but this was Bruce's day. Maybe she'd talk to Karen tomorrow.

"Lead the way," she told her brother.

She followed Bruce into the game room, surprised at how comforting it was. There were no windows or overhead lights. No one looked anyone else in the eye. Everyone was free to focus on his or her own fantasy, be it blood-soaked or checker-flagged.

Bruce examined each of the games, spending a long

time looking at a frightening green demon painted on the side of a game called *Deathspike*. Soon they were standing before an air-hockey table. Bruce picked up one of the glow-in-the-dark paddles and slid it around, making slashing noises.

"Come on," he told Lilith, sliding the other paddle her way. "Let's play."

She slid quarters into the slots beneath the air-hockey table. Bruce squealed as the cool air rushed from the tiny holes.

"Are you ready to get your butt handed to you on a plate?"

"You did not just ask me that," Lilith said, snatching up the other paddle and taking her position behind the goal. Bruce was so excited; Lilith found the feeling was contagious.

"I'm not sick anymore," her brother said, "so none of this letting-Brucey-win crap, okay?"

"Now you're asking for it," Lilith said.

Neither of them had ever played air hockey before, but there seemed to be two methods of serving the puck: dead straight or banked off the side. Bank the puck and your opponent had to lunge and jerk like a fool. Shoot straight and humiliate him when the puck slapped the back of the goal.

Bruce was a banker. He tried three times to score off his serve, then switched to shadier tactics. He kept the puck in his corner an uncomfortably long time, then pointed over her shoulder and called, "Hey, what's that over there?" just before striking the puck her way.

"Nice try," Lilith said as she sent a straight shot into his goal.

She dominated the first half of the game, but Bruce never flagged. He seemed to be having the time of his life.

When the score was tied five-five, "Bye Bye Love" by the Everly Brothers came through the speakers. Lilith began singing along, not realizing what she was doing until Bruce started singing with her. They hadn't done this in years. Her brother had a dazzling voice, staying in tune even as he whacked the hockey puck with all his might.

Then, from the darkness behind Lilith, a third voice began to harmonize with theirs. She turned to see Cam leaning against Ms. Pac-Man, watching them, and she gave up an important goal.

"Yesssss!" Bruce cheered. "Thanks, Cam!"

"What are you doing here?" Lilith asked.

"Don't stop playing—or singing—on my account," Cam said. He was wearing a black knit hat and black sunglasses, his motorcycle jacket zipped up. Lilith liked the way he looked. "Your voices hang together like a sailor's knot."

"What does that mean?" Bruce asked.

"Your bond is strong," Cam said. "There's no music more beautiful than sibling harmony."

"Do you have siblings?" Lilith asked. He never talked about his family or his past. She thought about her trip to Dobbs Street and the green tent she'd seen him step out of. Was that really where he lived? Did he share it with anyone else? The more time she spent with Cam, the stranger it felt to know so little about him.

"More importantly," Bruce said, taking advantage of Lilith's distraction and somehow sliding in the final goal. "Do you want to play the winner?"

"You know, I have never had that honor," Cam said, and smiled at Lilith.

She held out her paddle. "Be my guest."

Cam took off his sunglasses and left them on a cocktail table with his phone. He took the paddle from Lilith, and this time, when their fingers touched, Lilith was the one who stayed still to let it last a little longer. Cam noticed— she could tell from the way he smiled at her as he stepped into position, and the way his gaze stayed on her even though he was about to play. Lilith blushed as she slipped in another batch of quarters and the game began.

Bruce smoked Cam with his first serve. Cam tried to bank the puck but hit it directly into Bruce's corner. Bruce pried the puck free and slapped it into Cam's goal in a flash.

"Yes!" Bruce shouted.

"Earthly objects should not travel at such speeds," Cam said.

Charmed by how seriously he played with her brother, Lilith pulled a black stool from under the cocktail table and sat down.

Cam was a lunger; his body moved wildly back and forth as he swung his paddle. But he didn't move fast enough, whether or not he was letting Lilith's brother dominate on purpose. Bruce seemed to get better with each goal he scored.

This was good. The two of them, bonding. Since their dad skipped town, Bruce hadn't had many guys to look up to, but he clicked with Cam right away. Lilith knew why. Cam was fun, unpredictable. It was exciting to be around him.

A flashing light drew Lilith's attention, and she peered down at Cam's phone. A brief glance told her he'd just received an email. A longer, less innocent stare told her the subject: *Somebody's Other Blues" by Lilith Foscor.*

"How did you score another goal? I didn't even see the puck!" Cam shouted at Bruce.

Lilith's fingers inched toward the phone to light the screen again. This time she saw the sender's name: Ike Ligon.

"What in the world?" she whispered.

She was not proud of what happened next.

She glanced once more at Cam's back as he met Bruce's serve. Then her finger slid across the touch screen to open the email.

Dear Lilith,

I read your lyrics. I could tell right away that you've got the songwriting bug pretty bad. You've got talent. Real talent. I know King Media has plans for announcing the winner of the contest, but I wanted to reach out, too. You win, kid. You killed it. Congrats. I can't wait to meet you and shake your hand.

Lilith let the phone go black.

Ike Ligon liked her song?

Her face scrunched up. It didn't seem possible. Out of everyone at school, she had won?

Even after she'd gotten over being mad at Cam for sending in the lyrics, Lilith had never expected to win. Chloe King was supposed to win, because Chloe King won everything, and that was the way the world worked. So what was up with this email?

Must be a joke.

But then she stopped herself. What a depressing first instinct. What if it wasn't a joke? Why couldn't she be happy like every other girl at school? Why couldn't she accept that Ike Ligon liked her song, that he thought she had real talent, instead of suspecting that someone was playing a trick on her? Why did Lilith distrust every good thing that came her way?

A tear landed on the screen of Cam's cell phone,

bringing her back to the arcade. Lilith turned away and stared down at the gum-encrusted carpet.

Bruce came up beside her. "Are you okay?"

When she lifted her head, Cam was watching her. "What is it?"

She held out the phone. "Ike Ligon just sent you an email."

He scratched his chin. It was a sore subject, Cam sending in her lyrics, and Lilith could tell he still felt guilty.

Lilith swallowed. "He likes my song."

"There was never any question that he would," Cam said.

"I won." She didn't know what else to say. Before Cam, music had been an escape, passion a daydream, love an impossibility. Since his arrival, all three of those things felt connected, like she had to *use* them to become a different kind of person.

It scared her.

Cam tossed Bruce a quarter and pointed at the arcade game on the other side of the air-hockey table. When the boy had scurried off, Cam stepped closer to Lilith. "This is a big deal."

"I know," said Lilith. "The Battle of the Bands—"

"It's bigger than the Battle of the Bands."

"Please don't say it's bigger than prom," she said, teasing a little.

"Of course not. Nothing is bigger than prom." Cam

laughed, but then his face grew serious. "You can have anything you want in life. You know that, right?"

Lilith blinked. What did he mean? She was poor, she was unpopular. Yes, she'd made a few friends recently, and yes, she had her music, but overall, her life still sucked.

"Not exactly," she said.

Cam leaned in close. "You just have to want it badly enough."

Lilith's heart was racing. The arcade suddenly felt like it was a thousand degrees. "I don't even know what 'it' is."

Cam thought for a moment. "Adventure. Freedom." He took a breath. "Love."

"Love?" she asked.

"Yeah, love." He smiled again. "It is possible, you know."

"Maybe where you come from," she said.

"Or maybe"—Cam patted his chest—"right here."

They were so close now that their faces were practically touching. So close that the tips of their noses nearly met, and their lips were almost . . .

"What are you guys talking about?" Bruce asked, not looking up from his arcade game as he fired another hundred rounds into an army of monsters.

Lilith cleared her throat and stepped away from Cam, embarrassed. "The Battle of the Bands," she and Cam said at the same time.

Cam reached for Lilith's hand, then Bruce's hand. "Come on, let's go celebrate."

He led them to the snack bar back in the main room of the bowling alley. He hoisted Bruce onto a red pleather stool and flagged down a waitress with poufy blond hair.

"A pitcher of your finest root beer," Cam said. Root beer was Lilith's favorite. Had she ever told him that? "And a gigantic bucket of popcorn, extra butter for this guy." He jerked his thumb at Bruce, who pumped his fists.

Cam pulled out his phone and started typing something quickly.

"What are you doing?" Lilith asked.

"Spreading the good news to Jean and Luis." A few seconds later he showed her a text he'd just gotten back from Jean. It was all emojis—fireworks exploding, bouquets of flowers, guitars, treble clefs, and, inexplicably, a samurai sword.

Lilith grinned. Her friend was truly happy for her.

"What are the odds?" a familiar voice said behind them. Lilith turned to see Luis with his scrawny arms spread wide, waiting for a hug. Lilith slid off her stool and into his arms. She squeezed him tight.

"Hey, don't make my lady jealous," Luis said, stepping aside to let Karen Walker and a couple of their friends into the circle.

"Luis just told us your good news, Lilith," Karen said, and smiled.

"So lucky that I came to meet Karen and could be here to toast you," Luis said.

"Is that what we're doing?" Lilith laughed, blushing.

"Of course," Luis said.

"You deserve it," one of Karen's friends added. Lilith didn't even know her name, but she recognized her from Mr. Davidson's open mic. Before this moment, she would have assumed the girl hated her, like she assumed the rest of the school hated her. "Your music's really good."

"Thanks," Lilith said. She was overwhelmed with happy shock. "You guys want some popcorn?"

Cam had already poured root beer into enough cups for everyone. He raised his and smiled at Lilith. "To Lilith," he said. "And 'Somebody's Other Blues.'"

"I'll drink to that," Bruce said, and chugged his drink.

As Lilith sipped her root beer, surrounded by surprise friends and her brother and Cam, she thought about the lyrics to her song. She'd written them in a grim and lonely state. They'd poured out of her as a kind of purge, the only therapy she could afford. She'd never dream those sad words might lead to something as happy as this.

And they never would have if Cam hadn't believed in her. This moment was proof that Lilith should believe in herself.

Maybe Cam was a little forward. Maybe he pushed her buttons . . . frequently. Maybe he'd done some things he shouldn't have done. But who hadn't? He wasn't like anyone she'd ever met. He surprised her. He made her laugh. He cared about her brother. When he stood next to her, he made her stomach churn—in a good way. He was here with her, celebrating, now. And all of that together made Lilith sway where she was standing. She gripped the barstool to steady herself and realized:

This was what it felt like to fall in love with someone. Lilith was falling for Cam.

INTERLUDE

STRANGER

TRIBE OF DAN, NORTHERN CANAAN

Approximately 1000 BCE

The sun didn't rise over Lilith anymore. Moonlight no longer spilled into her dreams. She drifted through her days, still wearing the embroidered wedding gown, now soiled with sweat and dirt, collecting nervous glances from others in her tribe.

Without Cam, her world was bleak.

In the gray and misty dawn, Lilith was meandering near the river when a hand touched her shoulder. It was Dani. She had not seen him since the day Cam left, and it hurt to see him now, for he was part of the world she associated with being in love. Dani did not belong in this emptiness.

"It's like looking into a mirror," Dani said, his gray eyes brimming with concern. "I never knew it could hurt this much for someone else."

Lilith had always liked Dani, but he could be a little vain. "They said you had returned to your tribe," she said.

He nodded. "I'm only passing through."

"From where? Have you—"

Dani frowned. "I don't know where he is, Lilith."

She closed her eyes, unable to pretend that that was not what she'd intended to ask.

"I wish I could tell you it gets easier," Dani went on, "but when you truly love someone, I'm not sure it ever does."

Lilith squinted at the blond boy before her, seeing the pain in his eyes. Liat had been gone only one month longer than Cam, yet Dani spoke as if he'd had centuries of heartbreak.

"Goodbye, Dani," she said. "I wish you happier days."

"Goodbye, Lilith."

Still wearing her dress, she dove into the river. The chill of the water reminded her that she was alive. She rose up, then floated on her back and watched a pair of starlings cross the sky. Before she knew it, the current had carried her around a bend, and Lilith found herself before a familiar bank of wildflowers.

This was where she'd first held hands with Cam, first felt his touch.

She waded to the bank and climbed out of the river, wringing water from her hair, feeling the sodden dress weigh down her steps. The carob tree's branches stretched toward her, familiar as an old lover.

This had been her place before it had been hers and Cam's. She pressed her hands against the tree's rough bark and felt around for the recess where she'd stowed her lyre. It was still there.

She left it where it was.

Thunder rumbled, and the sky grew ominous. A sharp, cold rain began to fall. She closed her eyes and let the pain of missing him swell within her.

"Take my love with you when you go."

Lilith opened her eyes, startled by the way the song had snuck up on her, like it had been borne in the rain.

The song was raw and haunted, just like she was.

She sang the words aloud, changing a few notes of the melody. Applause came from above her. Lilith shot to her feet and looked up at a boy about her age sitting on a branch.

"You scared me," she said, pressing her hand to her chest.

"My apologies," the boy replied. He had a square face, wavy amber hair, and brown eyes. He wore a camel-skin cloak, like most of the men in her tribe, but beneath it

Lilith noticed strange, coarse, blue pants that were tight around his ankles, and bright white slippers tied in an elaborate crisscrossing fashion by thin, white ropes. He must have traveled from a village very far away.

He swung down to a lower branch, watching her. Rain shone in his hair. "Are you a writer of songs?" he asked her.

Tucked behind her lyre was the parchment book her father had given her as a harvest gift. It contained all of Lilith's songs. "I used to be," she said. "Not anymore."

"Ah." The boy leapt down from his branch. "You are suffering."

Lilith was unsure how this boy seemed to know what she was feeling.

"I can see it in your eyes," he continued. "All great makers of music have one thing in common: heartbreak. It is where they draw their inspiration from." He leaned forward. "Perhaps someday you'll thank Cam for the inspiration."

Lilith's pulse quickened. "What do you know about Cam?"

The boy smiled. "I know that you still long for him. Am I right?"

In the distance, Lilith could see glimmers of her peaceful village. She could hear her sisters' voices.

"I believe my heartbreak to be very deep," she said. "I hope it *is* the deepest, for I would not wish this pain on anyone."

Lilith closed her eyes and thought of Cam. He had been everything to her. Now everything was gone.

"You deserve an explanation," the boy said as though he could read her mind.

"Yes," Lilith found herself saying.

"You want to see him."

"Desperately."

"You want to convince him that he's been a fool, made the universe's greatest mistake, that he'll never find love like yours again?" His hazel eyes glimmered. "I know where he is."

She stood, aching. "Where?"

"I can take you to him, but I must warn you: The journey will be long and dangerous. And there is another thing. I will not be passing back this way."

He waited a moment as his meaning sank in. She looked toward her tribe once more and imagined never again hearing the rustle of the grain harvest, the tinkle of well water, her sisters' laughter. Was it worth it to see Cam again?

"When can we leave?" she asked.

"Shall I spell out my proposal?" the boy said.

Lilith was confused. "Your proposal?"

"I shall take you to see Cam." The boy brushed his hands together. "If the two of you reconcile, then you shall stay together. But if your true love denies you . . ." At this, he took a menacing step forward. "You will stay with me."

"With you?"

"My world could use a touch of beauty, a little inspiration—your voice, your poetry, your soul." The boy twirled his finger through the chain around his neck. "I can show you places you have never seen before."

Lilith wasn't interested in seeing the world. She was interested in seeing Cam. She wanted to reconcile, to revive their love, and then, later, when it made sense again, marriage, a family—just as they'd planned.

She glanced at the boy before her. She didn't even know his name. Something about him made her uneasy. And yet, if he could lead her to Cam . . .

She reached into the carob tree for her lyre and her book. Would this be the last time she would stow her music in her favorite tree, the last time she would look upon the glittering water at this bend of the Jordan? What about her family and her friends?

But if she stayed here, she would never know what might have been.

She closed her eyes and said, "I'm ready."

The boy took her hand and said in a low voice, "You have yourself what will someday be known as a 'deal.'"

FOURTEEN

THE NEW ZERO

CAM

Four Days

The morning after he met Lilith and Bruce at the arcade, Cam sat next to Lucifer atop a splintery wooden scoreboard. They gazed down at the football field and, beyond it, the ever-burning hills.

The air was damp and cloaked with smoke. At seven a.m., the school was even quieter than the cemetery at Sword & Cross had been back before Cam had discovered that Lilith lived on in endless Hells, when all he had to worry about was playing games with Luce and Daniel. He wished he'd appreciated how charmingly simple his life had been back then.

Four days remained in his wager with the devil, and Cam had no idea how it would end. There had been moments—like when Lilith tried on her wedding dress—when Cam had known she could almost glimpse their shattered past. And while he hoped with all his heart that she was close to loving him, she had not yet said the words.

They hadn't even kissed.

Lucifer reached into a paper bag and handed Cam a steaming Styrofoam cup. He was in the guise of Luc, but when he and Cam were alone, the devil let his true, terrifying growl come out. "If you lived another sixteen trillion years," he said, "you'd never stop being naïve."

"I'd rather be naïve than cynical," Cam said, and sipped his coffee. "Besides, how do you account for what's happened? She's changed. Once you set a ball rolling, you can't tell where it will go."

"That's the beauty of being number two." Lucifer smiled, and Cam glimpsed the maggots running through the gaps in his teeth. "No one expects you to succeed. Behold!"

Beneath them the wooden scoreboard lit up, the words *Home* and *Away* glittering in the morning light. The devil released his tarnished wings and swooped down to the bleachers, beckoning for Cam to join him.

Putting down his coffee, Cam sighed, glanced around to be sure they were alone, then let out his wings. He'd wanted to release them every time he was with Lilith, but he couldn't show her his true self, not yet. Maybe not ever.

Cam felt his wings extend behind him, then saw Lucifer's eyes trolling over them.

"What's going on there?" the devil asked with narrowed eyes.

Cam tried not to look surprised at the sight of his brindled wings, which were now equal parts white and gold. "You tell me," he said as he swooped from the top of the scoreboard to hover next to Lucifer. It felt good to be in the air, to feel weightless, the wind surrounding him. "My hair, my waist, my wings. You're the brilliant stylist, right?"

The bleachers creaked underneath Cam and Lucifer's feet, and from somewhere, Cam heard a rustling, a whisper of fabric. Or maybe that was just the sound of Lucifer's scaly wings folding back in upon themselves. Cam also drew his wings back, lest a pair of mortal eyes fall upon them.

"We are now in what I'll call the third quarter," Lucifer said, exhaling a cloud of black smoke. It spiraled through the air until it was hovering over the scoreboard, then it disappeared. The box designating football quarters lit up with the number three. "Let's see how our teams are stacking up."

Lucifer's mouth twitched, and Cam realized the devil wasn't sure how their game would play out, either. He'd brought Cam here to gauge the Away team's confidence. Cam couldn't allow Lucifer to see any weakness—any crack the devil spotted in his façade would immediately become a target.

"Your first move was a strong one, I'll admit," Lucifer said. "Starting a band with Lilith: one point!" A numeral 1 appeared under the *Away* box on the scoreboard. Then he laughed. "Stealing her journal, followed by distributing those song lyrics? Definitely a point for *moi.*"

When the numeral 100 appeared under *Home,* Luc zipped out his wings, flew forward, and slapped the scoreboard a few times. "What's wrong with this thing?"

He swooped back to the bleachers, and Cam watched his wings recede into his shoulders, noting the way they glittered darkly in the morning light.

"I cured her brother," Cam said. "That's worth more than anything you've tried to undo."

"I will allow you that," Luc said. Under *Away,* the number 1 became a 2. "But you also got old and flabby and bald, which everyone can agree is a big *fat* point for me." The figure 200 appeared on the *Home* scoreboard.

Cam rolled his eyes. "If you haven't noticed, Lilith doesn't care how you manipulate my appearance."

"It's not that she doesn't care!" Luc spat. "For some reason, she doesn't see how your body is changing."

Cam was confused. "You mean I'm ugly to everyone *but* Lilith?"

"Ding ding ding." The scoreboard lit up a 3 under *Away.* Luc looked directly into the sun without squinting. "I don't get it, either. I was sure that altering the way you look would disgust her, but—"

"It's Lilith," Cam said, realizing something for the first time. "She sees what's inside of me, and even you can't taint that." He gazed down at himself, feeling more confident than he had in days. "I don't know why it took losing my looks for me to realize that." He nudged the devil. "You should give yourself an extra point for that."

"Don't mind if I do." Lucifer turned toward the scoreboard, which now read, *Home: 300; Away: 3.* Then he narrowed his eyes at Cam. "I can't imagine why you're so confident. You're losing."

"How do you figure?" Cam asked.

"For the first time in any of her lifetimes, Lilith is learning to enjoy her Hell," Lucifer said. "She's quit comparing her dreams to her reality."

"She's adapting, learning to survive," Cam agreed. "She's almost . . ."

He paused, thinking about the way Lilith had smiled at him the other day from across the cafeteria, and the sound of her voice yesterday when she'd sang along with Bruce at the arcade, and the look in her eyes when they'd toasted her winning lyrics with warm cups of root beer.

". . . happy," Cam finished.

"But a happy girl doesn't need saving by someone like

you," Lucifer said with a snarl. "Face it, Cam: You need her to hate her life so that she can love you. Or else you lose the bet—and her." *Home* rang up 2,000 on the scoreboard. The sound of the numbers changing so rapidly pinged like rain on a tin roof. "Yes, a Prom-night defeat is certain," Lucifer said. "But then, it always was."

"You're wrong," Cam said.

"Tell you what I'll do." Lucifer leaned close. The devil smelled like anise mixed with burning coal. Cam's stomach turned. "I'll let you off the hook."

"What do you mean?" Cam asked.

"I'll call off the bet. You can go back to moping around the middle reaches of the universe, never realizing your potential. I'll go back to keeping everyone confused."

In the devil's red-rimmed eyes, Cam recognized something desperate.

"You think you're going to lose," Cam found himself saying.

Lucifer let out a burst of laughter that seemed to shake the ground beneath them.

"Why else would you offer to cancel our wager?" Cam asked.

His laughter ended abruptly. "Maybe what happened with Luce and Daniel changed me, too," Lucifer growled. "Maybe I'm showing mercy to you. Disgusting as that sounds."

"You're bluffing," Cam said. It didn't matter what the

devil said. There was no chance of Cam backing out of their deal. "I won't abandon Lilith. I can't go on without her."

"I applaud your perseverance," Lucifer said as the numeral 4 lit up under the *Away* side of the scoreboard. "But you don't know what you're talking about. Do you even know *why* Lilith is one of my subjects?"

Cam swallowed. The question had haunted him since before he got here, since Annabelle had told him where to find her.

"Suicide," Lucifer said, slowly, enunciating each syllable.

"She wouldn't—" Cam whispered.

"You think you know her? You don't. And you don't have a chance." Lucifer glanced down at the desolate campus he had created. "And everyone—even all those silly kids down there—knows it but you."

"Tell me what happened," Cam said, hearing the tremor in his own voice. "When did she take her life? Why?"

"You have till the end of the day to forfeit," Lucifer said, his eyes a wilderness of evil. "Otherwise? Things are about to get dirty."

"For a change?" Cam asked.

The devil flashed him a dangerous look. "You'll see."

Cam paced the parking lot, waiting for the buses to arrive, for another day at Trumbull to begin. The devil's warning had put him on edge.

He needed to see Lilith. He closed his eyes and tried to picture her walking to school, but all he could focus on was the suicide Lucifer had mentioned. When had she done it? Where?

Could Cam have been responsible?

From the moment he'd met Lilith, Cam had known there would be no way to disentangle her existence from his own. She was his one true love. If Cam had learned anything from Luce and Daniel, it was this: When you find that soul you cherished above all others, you do *not* let it go.

The high-pitched squeal of brakes announced the arrival of the school buses. When the yellow fleet had filled the circular drive, kids marched down their steps and flowed toward the school, just as they did every day. But something was different this morning. Something dark was in the air.

The students spoke in whispers, and when their eyes fell on Cam, they stiffened, they recoiled, they turned quickly away.

A girl he'd never seen spit as she walked past him. "How do you sleep at night, pig?!"

As more and more suspicious gazes fell on him, Cam's wings began to burn within his shoulders. Lucifer had warned him that things would get ugly, but what exactly had the devil done?

He made it to homeroom a few minutes before the bell. There were only a few kids in the classroom, but all of them turned their backs toward him when Cam walked into the room.

A girl with long black hair and freckles glanced over her shoulder and scowled. "I can't believe that monster was nominated for prom court!"

Cam ignored everyone, sat down, and waited for Lilith.

She walked in as the bell rang. Her hair was still wet, her clothes were wrinkled, and she was clutching a half-eaten apple. She wouldn't look at Cam.

He waited fifty torturous minutes, then pulled her aside right after class.

"What?" he said. "What's wrong?"

"It's not my business who you were with before you knew me," Lilith said, her eyes wet with tears. "But that girl *killed* herself."

"*What* girl?" Cam asked.

"Why do I have to explain this to you?" Lilith said. "Have you been with more than one girl who killed herself?"

"Where are you getting this from?" Cam asked, though, of course, he didn't have to ask. Lucifer must have whispered some trumped-up story into one kid's ear, and now Cam was the school pariah.

"Everyone on my bus was talking about it this morning." Lilith noted the glares aimed at Cam. "Seems like the whole school knows."

"They don't know anything," Cam said. "But you do. You know me."

"Tell me it isn't true," Lilith said. Cam could hear the pleading in her voice. "Tell me she didn't kill herself because of what you did."

Cam looked down at his boots. Lilith was in Crossroads because she'd killed herself, but had she killed herself because of Cam?

"It's true," he said, in agony. "She took her life."

Lilith's eyes widened, and she backed away. Cam understood that she hadn't actually been expecting the truth.

"Is he harassing you again, Lilith?"

Cam turned to find Luc, his hair slicked back and perfectly coiffed. The devil took Lilith's arm, flexing his bicep. "Shall we, gorgeous?"

"I'll make it on my own." Lilith pushed away from Luc, but she was looking at Cam as she spoke.

"Meaning," Luc murmured as she turned away, "don't follow her, Cam."

Cam clenched his fists.

"Last chance to fold," Lucifer said.

Cam shook his head in silent rage. As he watched Lilith walk away, he feared he'd finally lost her for good.

"It's not *all* bad," Luc said, and pulled a folded note from his back pocket. He handed it to Cam. "The principal will see you now."

※

The secretary's desk outside Tarkenton's office was empty, and the principal's door was closed. Cam straightened the APPETITE FOR DESTRUCTION T-shirt he'd picked up at the thrift store, finger-combed his hair, and knocked.

The door swung open.

He stepped in hesitantly, seeing no one.

"Mr. Tarkenton? Sir? You wanted to see me?"

"*Arrrrrrrrrggggghhhh!!!*" Roland and Arriane jumped out from behind the door and doubled over with laughter. Arriane slammed the door behind Cam and locked it.

"*Sir!?!* You wanted to see me?" she said in her best Cam voice.

"That is the funniest shit I've seen in centuries, *sir,*" Roland said.

"Yeah, yeah, laugh it up," Cam said. "Forgive me for trying to blend in here."

He found himself hugging Roland, then Arriane. They were the last people he had ever expected to turn up here, but Cam had never been more grateful to see friends.

"You are *going* for it, man," Arriane said, wiping her eyes. She'd shaved her head and was dressed all in black.

The only color on her was the bright orange fringe of her false eyelashes. "And I love that. But, uh"—she grimaced, glancing at Cam's midsection—"what's up with the wheat belly?"

"Lucifer's idea of fun," Cam said. "He thought it would be a turnoff, but Lilith can't even see the difference—at least she *couldn't* see it, back when she liked me. I don't know about now." He looked at his friends, overwhelmed with emotion. "How did you guys get in here, anyway?"

"Also Lucifer's idea of fun," Roland explained. He looked exquisite in a tailored pin-striped suit and a lavender French-cuffed shirt, and he smelled like expensive cologne.

"Right," Cam said, understanding instantly. "He knows he's going to lose, so he wants you two to talk me out of going through with the bet."

"Could be, brother," Roland said, "but we're in agreement with him on that."

"In other words," said Arriane, "what are you doing, Cam?"

"If I'm not mistaken," Cam said, "the last time I saw you, you suggested I fix my mistakes. Remember?"

"Not like this!" Arriane shoved Cam. "After Luce and Daniel earned your sorry soul a second chance . . . I just—I mean—*dude*."

Back at Sword & Cross, Arriane and Roland had spoken of Luce and Daniel as if the angelic lovers were a model of love the rest of them should follow. But the way Cam saw things, Luce and Daniel had really only ever cared about each other, and that was fine with Cam. They had never intended to start a revolution.

And yet, somehow, they had. Because of Luce and Daniel's choice to risk everything for love, Cam was here in Crossroads.

"I'm not seeking advice," Cam said.

"That hasn't stopped Arriane yet." Roland leaned against Tarkenton's desk. "Why throw your eternal future away on a rigged bet with the devil? And then, when he makes an offer to let you out of that bet, why refuse?"

Cam could see it looked impossible from the outside: fifteen days to get a girl to love him—a girl whose hatred of him had been forged by three thousand years in Hell. But Cam didn't care what it looked like. In his heart, there was no question that he had to save Lilith. It wasn't a choice. It was a measure of his love for her.

Arriane took Cam's shoulders and pushed him into Tarkenton's leather swivel chair. She balanced the principal's bronze hog in her palm. "Look, Cam. You've always been self-destructive. We get that, and we love you for it, but it's time to stop playing games with Lucifer."

"He never loses," Roland said. "Maybe once in a violet moon."

"I can't do it," Cam said. "Don't you see? This is how I honor Luce and Daniel's choice to give up their immortality. I have to save Lilith. It's the only way I can save myself." He leaned forward in his chair. "The person I love is being abused. What happened to your sense of duty? The Roland and Arriane I know would never forgive me if I didn't try to get Lilith out of here."

"We had a sense of duty when it came to Lucinda's fate," Arriane said. "But Lilith is so much less important than Luce. A blip on the radar."

Cam blinked. "Maybe to you."

"To everyone," she said. "That's why we all spent six thousand years following Luce around. She faced a choice with cosmic implications."

"Lilith matters, too," Cam said. "She deserves better than this."

"Are you at least taking her to prom?" Arriane asked, and sighed. "I've always wanted to go to prom."

"I haven't asked her yet," Cam admitted. "The moment hasn't been right."

"You are so off your game!" Arriane said. "Maybe Ro and I can help in that department. After all that practice with Luce and Daniel, we're masterminds of the romantic setting. Think about it?"

The door flew open. "Is there some way I can be of service to you?" Tarkenton asked.

Arriane carefully set Tarkenton's paperweight hog back on his desk. She patted its head. "This is a real nice pig. I'll give you a quarter for him."

"GET OUT OF MY CHAIR!" Tarkenton thundered at Cam. He turned to Arriane and Roland. "Who are you delinquents?"

"We're fallen angels," Roland said.

"Don't insult my religion!" Tarkenton commanded, his face twisted. "I could have you arrested for breaking and entering. And you, Mr. Briel, you're suspended for the rest of the day and all of tomorrow. Leave campus before I have you removed."

"Please don't suspend me, sir," Cam said. "I need to be here."

Roland squinted at Cam. "Are you kidding me, dude? You *care*?"

Cam cared. The days were long and lonesome when the girl you loved was in school and you were not. His bet with Lucifer ended in four days. If he was going to free Lilith from this hell, he needed every moment he could get with her.

FIFTEEN

~ ‡ ~

QUEEN OF HEARTS

LILITH

Three Days

At lunch the next day, Lilith, Jean, and Luis met in the band room.

It was finally free, since the Perceived Slights were all busy at a prom court meeting. Lilith had walked by their table in the center of the cafeteria after grabbing a sandwich and had noticed the empty seat where Cam was supposed to sit. He hadn't been in homeroom or poetry that morning either, and Lilith was trying not to wonder why.

"Hey, Luis." She mustered a smile for the drummer in his blue tank top and fingerless leather gloves.

"Hola," Luis said, playing a tight drumroll. He was getting better. He was almost good.

"That sounded fly," Lilith said.

Luis grinned. "Fly's my middle name."

The battle was three nights away. They were down one guitar player—again—and far from having their act together, but Lilith was determined not to give up. She would figure out a way to pull this performance off.

"I take it we're not waiting for Cam?" Jean asked, giving her a sympathetic look. He had taken off the top of the Moog synthesizer and was tightening the screws inside.

"Nope." Lilith sighed. "Just us."

She was rusty and exhausted. She'd been nauseated since yesterday when she'd boarded the bus and felt every kid's eyes on her. At first, she'd been stupid enough to think that people were suddenly noticing her because they'd heard she'd won the lyrics contest. But not one person said anything to Lilith about the Four Horsemen playing her song at prom.

Instead, Cam's horrible news eclipsed Lilith's good news entirely. By now the whole school had become a buzzing hive of students spreading the same ugly story: The last girl Cam had dated, a girl who'd been in love with him, had killed herself when they broke up.

Lilith knew Cam had known other girls. But this latest story . . .

Suicide.

"It sucks," Jean said. "I mean, Revenge will be great, but without Cam . . ."

Lilith knew what he was thinking. Cam was a great musician. He was charismatic onstage. He brought a needed edge to the band. Revenge would be lesser without him.

Plus, he really wanted to be in the band. She knew that because he'd called her home phone seven times the night before.

"Don't answer it—" she'd said to Bruce a second too late.

"Hello?" Bruce had said, then held out the phone to Lilith, mouthing, "It's Cam."

Lilith had quickly scribbled a note and held it out to Bruce.

"Sorry, Cam," Bruce said. "She says you have the wrong number."

Lilith had mouthed for Bruce to hang up the phone quickly and groaned once he did. *"Thanks."*

"Why don't you want to talk to Cam?" Bruce asked. "What happened?"

"It's a long story," Lilith told her brother. "I'll tell you when you're older."

"But I like him," Bruce said.

Lilith frowned. "I know. Just don't pick up the phone again."

It was possible Cam had called more than seven times,

but seven had been her mom's limit. After that, she'd disconnected the phone. And in the silence that followed, Lilith's heart began to ache. She hadn't meant to let him get close enough to hurt her, but here she was, hurt and bewildered and longing for him to make things right.

She would have to go back to looking out for herself, expecting nothing from anyone, guarding herself against pain.

Now Jean put down his screwdriver, rubbed his jaw, and studied Lilith. "You don't mean you believe those rumors? Cam's a good guy. You know he is."

"I don't want to talk about it." Lilith sat down against the wall between two giant xylophones. She took out her notebook and riffled through the pages.

"What are you doing?" Jean asked.

"Making an edit to the chorus of 'Somebody's Other Blues' before we practice," Lilith said.

"Wait, does that mean we're not breaking up?" Luis let out an audible sigh of relief.

"Course not," Lilith said, standing up and grabbing her guitar.

It wasn't just the band Lilith needed to hold together. It was her friendships with Jean and Luis. Unlike Cam, these boys weren't complicated. They hadn't taken hold of her heart in dangerous ways. But what they had done— showing her a place where she belonged—mattered to Lilith, and she wasn't going to give it up. "Let's do it."

"*That's* what I'm talking about," Jean said, and powered up his synth.

"Hell yeah!" Luis said, readying his drumsticks.

"Two, three, four," Lilith counted off, a new confidence stirring inside her as Revenge began to play.

⚜

"There you are." Mrs. Richards flagged Lilith down as she was leaving her locker after school. "I need a favor." Her glasses were smudged, and she looked frazzled. Lilith knew the teacher had been working overtime with the prom committee, ensuring they were making "green" choices for the dance.

"Sure," Lilith said. Since she'd apologized to Mrs. Richards and taken her advice about Bruce's diet, the two of them had been getting along much better.

"Chloe King went home sick this afternoon," Mrs. Richards said. "I need a student to deliver her homework to her house."

"I'm not friends with Chloe," Lilith said. "I don't even know where she lives. Can't June or Teresa or the other one do it?"

Mrs. Richards smiled wistfully. "Last-minute prom court meeting! Besides, I thought you were turning over a new leaf." She pressed a stack of folders into Lilith's hands. Chloe's home address was written on a green sticky note on top. "It would really help me out. I hate to see a bright student fall behind."

So Lilith boarded the bus for the rich kids, which was mostly empty because the upperclassmen who lived in Chloe's neighborhood all had their own cars.

She watched the street signs as the bus meandered through the fancy neighborhood, dropping kids off at big new houses tucked away behind huge, well-manicured lawns. She watched one freshman boy walk into a house with a For Sale sign planted in its lawn and wondered where his family was moving.

Lilith imagined them packing up their belongings, climbing into a luxury car, and speeding down the open highway, fleeing Crossroads. The fantasy was enough to make her envious. Escape was never far from Lilith's mind.

Soon they turned onto Maple Lane, and Lilith double-checked Chloe's address. She rose to get off the bus when it stopped in front of a huge white faux-Tudor McMansion girded by a moat filled with koi.

Of course Chloe lived in a house that looked like this.

When Lilith rang the doorbell, someone buzzed her in and lowered an electric drawbridge over the koi moat.

Across the moat, a housekeeper opened the door to a gleaming marble foyer.

"Can I help you?" she asked.

"I'm here to drop off Chloe's assignments," Lilith said, surprised by the way her voice bounced off the walls; the foyer had crazy acoustics. She handed the folders to the housekeeper, eager to jog back to campus, where she was supposed to meet Jean and Luis.

"Is that *Lilith*?" Chloe's voice called from somewhere upstairs. "Send her up."

Before Lilith could argue, the housekeeper ushered her inside and closed the door.

"Shoes," the housekeeper said, pointing at Lilith's combat boots and the white marble shoe rack next to the door.

Lilith sighed and unlaced her boots, then kicked them off.

The house smelled like lemons. All the furniture was massive, and everything was decorated in shades of white. A huge white baby grand piano sat on a white alpaca rug in the center of the living room, playing automated Bach.

The housekeeper led Lilith up the white marble stairs. When she deposited Lilith at Chloe's white bedroom door and handed her back the folders, she raised her eyebrows as if to say, *Good luck; she's in rare form today.*

Lilith knocked on the door.

"Come in," a voice said.

Lilith peered inside the room. Chloe lay on her side, her back to Lilith, facing a white-curtained window. Her bedroom was nothing like Lilith would have expected. In fact, it looked just like the living room: an oversized white four-poster bed, white cashmere throws draped over the bed and the chairs by the window, an expensive crystal chandelier hanging from the ceiling.

Chloe's bedroom made Lilith think of her own room more fondly, with its old twin bed and thrift-store desk, the mismatched lamps her mother had found at a garage sale. She had three Four Horsemen posters, one from each of their most recent albums. She used the space above her desk to tack up lyrics she wanted to find melodies for and quotes by her favorite musicians.

The only thing on Chloe's wall was a platinum record in a white frame with a plaque that read AWARDED TO THE PERCEIVED SLIGHTS FOR FUTURE SALES. MERRY CHRISTMAS. LOVE, DADDY.

Lilith knew Chloe had a lot of passions—not just her band but also the prom court, the bingo team, her student-government campaigns. It was weird that there was no sign of them in the place she spent the most time. It was like her interests had been whitewashed by an expensive interior designer. It made Lilith feel a little bit sorry for Chloe King.

Chloe sniffed and reached for a box of tissues on her nightstand.

"Sorry you're sick," Lilith said. She placed the folders on Lilith's white dresser. "I brought your homework. You think you'll be better by prom?"

"I'm not sick," Chloe said. "I took a mental health day." She rolled over to face Lilith, her face splotchy from crying. "I didn't think I'd ever want to see you again after what you did to me today, but now that you're here, you might as well entertain me."

"What are you talking about, what *I* did today?" Lilith said, leaning against the doorway. "I didn't even see you."

"I heard your band practicing at lunch," Chloe said. "I was just walking by after the prom court meeting, but then I heard you guys through the door and I couldn't help listening." A sob shook her shoulders. "You weren't supposed to be competition."

"Oh," Lilith said, taking a step closer to Chloe. "So my band offended you by being good?"

"Do you know how much pressure I'm under to win?" Chloe wailed, sitting up in bed. "Everyone thinks I'm perfect. I can't let them down." She forced herself to take a few deep breaths. "Besides, my dad is sponsoring the whole deal, so it's extra embarrassing if I don't win."

"Look," Lilith said, "I've never heard your songs. But, like, a hundred people show up every time you have a gig. I always hear kids talking about it the next day."

"That's because they're scared of me," she blurted out, then looked shocked by what she'd said. She pulled the covers over her face. "Even my own band is scared of me."

"For what it's worth, not many people at Trumbull like me, either," Lilith said, even though Chloe, who had spent years publicly highlighting Lilith's flaws, knew this better than anyone.

"Yeah," Chloe acknowledged, peeking out from under her duvet. "But it doesn't bother you, does it? I mean, you have so much else going on. You're too focused on your music to care about popularity. Do you know how much free time I'd have if I didn't have to constantly manage my social status?"

Lilith used to lament her lack of friends, but being a loner for so long had made her a really strong songwriter. Now that she had a group of friends, Lilith had the best of both worlds.

Suddenly she felt even worse for Chloe.

"'Managing My Social Status' is a great title for a song," Lilith said, and noticed Chloe's guitar stashed in her closet. She walked over and picked it up. "We could write it together, now."

"I don't need to be reminded of your superior song-writing skills," Chloe huffed. "Give me that guitar."

Lilith did, and Chloe smiled gratefully. Somehow, sitting down on Chloe's bed seemed like the right thing to do next. Lilith sank into the mattress, amazed by how luxuriously soft it was.

"Listen to this," Chloe said, and started strumming. Soon, she broke into song. *"Rich bitch, rich bitch . . ."* When she had finished, she looked up at Lilith. "That's what we're playing at prom. It sucks, doesn't it?"

"No way," Lilith said. "It's just . . ." She thought for a moment. "You're singing it from the perspective of someone else looking at your life and being envious. What if you sang it from your own perspective, and put all your own feelings into it? Like how it hurts to feel like the rest of the world doesn't know you."

"It does hurt," Chloe said quietly. "That's actually not a totally stupid idea."

"Try it again."

Chloe did. She strummed the guitar, closed her eyes, and sang the song so differently, with so much emotion, that she was crying again by the time she finished. Lilith was shocked to find tears welling in her own eyes, too.

When she played the last chord, Lilith applauded with genuine enthusiasm. "Yes! That was amazing."

"Yeah," Chloe agreed. "It was." She set her guitar aside on her bed, then reached for her lip gloss, dabbed it on, and offered Lilith some. "We're doing a show tomorrow night at Alfie's. You should come."

Chloe had never invited Lilith to anything before. It was one thing to have this weird, private breakthrough in Chloe's room. But to show up in public and not act like they hated each other?

"You're not worried anymore about me being 'influenced by your sound'?"

"Oh, shut up." Chloe swung a pillow at Lilith's head. "And thank you."

"For what?" Lilith asked.

"Helping me with my song. I wouldn't have done the

same thing for you," Chloe said, with a surprising amount of honesty. "But I really appreciate it."

Lilith waited a few seconds for the other shoe to drop, for Chloe to say that she was kidding and reveal the webcam she'd been using to punk Lilith, but it never happened. Chloe just went on acting like a regular person, and Lilith realized, to her surprise, that it wasn't a total drag to hang out with her.

"Maybe I'll see you there," Lilith said, then made her way toward the bedroom door. Out of the corner of her eye, she could see Chloe smiling.

"Wait," Chloe said. "There's one more thing."

"Yeah?" Lilith asked from the doorway.

"Yesterday morning, I was meeting Dean under the bleachers."

Dean . . . Dean . . . Lilith racked her brain to remember who that was, then recalled that it was the name of Chloe's jock boyfriend.

"Don't look at me like that; it was totally innocent," Chloe said. "We were practicing our moves for the first dance at prom."

"Sure." Lilith smirked. Nobody hung out under the bleachers to practice anything but making out.

"Anyway," Chloe said, "I heard voices. It was Cam talking to my dad's intern, Luc. They were arguing. About *you*."

Lilith tried to control her face so the shock wouldn't show. "Me? What about me?"

"I didn't catch all the details," Chloe said. "Dean was taking up a lot of my attention, but I heard them mention . . . a bet."

Just then, Chloe's mom poked her head into the room. "Chloe, you need your rest."

"We're almost done, Mom," Chloe said, smiling brightly until her mother disappeared, without so much as glancing Lilith's way.

"What kind of bet?" Lilith asked.

Chloe leaned forward in her bed. "I didn't get it exactly, but basically Cam said he bet he could get you to run away with him after prom. And get this: If he can't, he becomes Luc's bitch. Forever."

Lilith laughed nervously. "That sounds a little farfetched."

Chloe shrugged. "Don't shoot the messenger."

"Luc's bitch?" Lilith repeated. "How would that even work?"

"There's clearly a lot about those two freaks we don't know," Chloe said, making a sour face.

Lilith tried to think why Luc and Cam would be hanging out in the first place, let alone making some bet about her. They hated each other. Was Chloe lying? That would normally be Lilith's first assumption, but Chloe seemed more open and less scheming than Lilith had ever known her.

She almost seemed to be telling the truth.

"We must be missing some information," Lilith said, trying to pretend she didn't suddenly feel anxious. "Maybe Cam owes Luc money or something."

"I don't think so," Chloe said. "Those guys were talking as if money was no object. They didn't even seem to care about life or death." She stared at Lilith. "All they cared about was you."

SIXTEEN

DANGEROUS DAYS

CAM

Two Days

In poetry class the next day, Cam tried to lock eyes with Lilith. Because of his suspension, he hadn't seen her in almost two days. The sight of her now, scribbling in her notebook, immersed in another world, drove him mad with desire. He ached to unwind the black scarf from her neck and kiss the pale skin underneath.

He tried passing her a note, begging her to meet him after class. When she pushed it off her desk unopened, he tried passing another, not even bothering to fold this one, his message exposed for anyone to see. *Please just talk to me.* But Lilith refused to read it.

A boy named Ryan Bang finished reading his experimental sestina and Mr. Davidson started clapping.

"Now, *that's* the kind of poem the *New Yorker* wants to publish!" the teacher said with gusto.

Cam was hardly paying attention, though. He wished he could have denied the rumor Luc had spread, but he couldn't lie to Lilith. The problem was he didn't know how to tell her the truth.

At the front of the room, Mr. Davidson looked down at his notes. "Cameron, you're next."

"Next at what?" Cam asked, refocusing.

"The assignment? Choosing a poem that clearly expresses a theme? Earth to Cameron." Mr. Davidson must have registered the blank stare in Cam's eyes. "I imagine you will choose something about death, as usual? Come stand before the class and state your theme."

Cam didn't have anything prepared, but he had been around for long enough to encounter some of the world's most brilliant poets, and right now one sprang easily to mind.

Cam made sure to walk past Lilith as he went to the head of the class. He wanted to brush his hand against her as he passed, but she would hate that. So instead, he simply rapped his fingers on her desk, hoping to get her attention.

It worked. She looked up as he stood before the class and announced, "My theme is love."

The class groaned, but he paid them no mind. When

Cam had fallen in love with Lilith in Canaan, Solomon had not yet been king of the Israelites. He'd been a boy of eighteen, newly in love himself with a girl from a neighboring village. Cam and Solomon had met in a Bedouin tent one night, both of them traveling in different directions. They'd shared only one meal together, but Solomon had recited to Cam the lovely words that would later become famous as the *Song of Songs*. Now, Cam gazed at Lilith and started reciting the poem by heart. When he got to his favorite part, he slipped out of English and into the poem's original language, ancient Hebrew.

"'Rise up, my love, my beautiful one, and come away,'" he said.

At her desk, Lilith dropped her pen. She stared at him, her mouth open, her face ghostly pale. He wished he could know what she was feeling. Did she remember anything?

By the time Cam reached the end of the poem, the bell was ringing. The classroom grew chaotic as students leapt up from their seats.

"Did you hear that?" a girl with rosy cheeks and a huge red backpack giggled to her friend as she walked past. "He switched to gibberish when he forgot a line."

Her friend snorted. "He does look old enough to have Alzheimer's."

"Nice job," Mr. Davidson said. "That's one of my all-time favorites. And you know the Hebrew!"

"Yeah, thanks," Cam said, pushing out of the room and racing after Lilith. He spotted her at the end of the hall, talking to Jean and Luis. They were looking at a poster taped to a classroom door.

"Lilith! Jean! Luis! Wait up," he called, but by the time he had fought through the crush of students to reach the end of the hall, Lilith and the boys had turned the corner and disappeared.

Cam sighed. He couldn't catch a break. And now he might not see her again all day.

He stared at the poster she'd been reading.

ARE YOU READY TO ROCK?!

He'd seen it before. It was advertising the same gig he'd tried to invite Lilith to his first day at school. The Perceived Slights were opening for a local band called Ho Hum. It was taking place that night at a fancy coffee shop a couple of miles away.

Was Lilith planning on going now? She hated Chloe King. So did Cam, for that matter. But on the off chance that Lilith did go to scope out the competition, Cam would be there.

❄❄

As the sun went down that evening, Roland, Cam, and Arriane crunched through the grass to cross High Meadow Road, forcing cars to swerve around them. Cam was deep in thought. He barely noticed the screeching tires and blaring horns.

"I don't know how we stuck around Sword & Cross as long as we did," Roland said as a motorist flipped him off. "I can't get kicked out of these atrocious mortal high schools fast enough."

"Get out of the road!" a woman shrieked over her horn.

"Did you know that almost all car horns are tuned to F-sharp minor?" Arriane asked. "That's why you should always listen to music in the key of A when you're driving in a city. Or sing a song in A."

"*She's a kind-hearted woman, she studies evil all the time,*" Roland sang.

"Where are we going again?" Arriane asked.

"A coffee shop called Alfie's," Cam said, distracted. He had Lilith on his mind. He had to make up with her tonight in order for his plan to work.

"And why is that again?" Arriane patted Cam's stomach. "Cammy's hungry? Wants some crumb cake? You might want to watch your carb intake. Do they even make tuxes your size? Which reminds me, have you asked Lilith to prom yet?"

"Not yet," Cam said. "Not yet. I'm going to need your help tonight," he told his friends as they rounded the corner to the front of the café. "Don't forget the plan."

"Yes, right, the secret plan!" Arriane said, stopping to

touch up her lipstick. "I love secrets. Almost as much as I love plans. Put us to work, boss."

Cam walked into the coffee shop and held the door open for his friends. The entrance was crammed with shelves of knickknacks and trinkets, little metal trees meant for holding jewelry, coffee mugs painted with cheesy slogans for sale—all to make room for a small stage that had been set up at the back of the café.

The walls were mirrored, so Cam tried to avoid looking almost everywhere. He couldn't stand to see the way he looked now. He was indisputably ugly.

"Come on, I need a mocha," Arriane said, taking Cam's hand and squeezing them through a narrow space between two bookshelves so they could join the audience.

There were probably a hundred kids there, most of whom Cam recognized from Trumbull. It was the popular crowd and some of the second tier—and most of their necks swiveled when the fallen angels entered the scene. Cam and Roland were the only guys not wearing khaki shorts and polos. Arriane was the only girl who didn't look like every other girl. Cam watched a dozen high school guys scope her out.

"Jeez, fellas," she said. "Leave my drawers on, will ya?" Then she leaned in close to Cam and whispered, "I'm not wearing any drawers!"

Roland scooted off to get some drinks while Cam

and Arriane grabbed seats at one of the high tables by the window.

"This is dreadful," Arriane said, looking around at the snobby group of students. "I can't believe you've suffered through two weeks here. All for Lilith. It's almost like you like her or something."

"Or something." Then Cam spotted her. "There." He pointed across the room.

Lilith was sitting in the third row with Jean Rah; his girlfriend, Kimi; and Luis. Karen Walker joined them after she finished tuning Chloe's guitar.

Lilith was all dressed up. She had on glossy lipstick, and her short velvet dress was black as coal, setting off her fire-red hair in thrilling contrast.

"I think I'm starting to understand your dedication," Arriane said, and whistled. "Girl is *fine*."

Cam agreed, of course, Lilith looked beautiful, but she didn't look radiant the way she had at the bowling alley. That was the day Cam had felt closest to her, just before Lucifer spread the word about the suicide. Tonight, sadness softened Lilith's edges, and Cam knew it was because of him.

"What are we talking about?" Roland said, plunking coffee cups before Cam and Arriane.

"Hottie alert," Arriane said, and nodded in Lilith's direction.

"She's still got it, even after all these years." Roland turned to Cam. "What's your strategy, man?"

"I don't have one yet," Cam admitted, watching Luis crack a joke to Lilith that he yearned to hear. "I'm hoping one will come to me."

"Basically," Arriane said, and swigged her drink, "he's screwed."

Then the audience started cheering, and Cam watched as Chloe King and her band took the stage. They wore short black leather skirts, corseted tops, and big hoop earrings. The whole band was wearing silver lipstick, but Chloe was the only one who could pull it off.

"Sup, y'all," Chloe said as she picked up her guitar and the rest of the girls grabbed their instruments. "We're the Perceived Slights, but you already know that."

"Give it to us, Chloe!" one guy yelled out.

"Show me how bad you want it," Chloe said.

The audience went wild.

Chloe grinned. "This is a special preview of the song we'll be playing at prom," she said into the mic, and winked at the audience. "Only the cool kids will be able to sing along tomorrow night."

Cam watched as Chloe scanned the audience and her gaze fell on Lilith. He readied himself to lunge if Chloe fired off some nasty insult about Lilith being there, but then, to his amazement, Chloe nodded subtly at Lilith and smiled.

"Two, three, four," she shouted as her band began to play a song called "Rich Bitch." It wasn't anything like Cam had expected—no pop, all melancholy, leaning heavily on the recorded backbeat, with Chloe's guitar screaming feedback the whole time.

Chloe's band members had all obviously had years of expensive lessons. They played their instruments well enough, their voices never strained, and they looked good. But they had none of Lilith's glittering rawness. Even sitting down in a crowd, Lilith made these girls look boring.

Chloe's face was red and she was out of breath when she released the final note. Lilith was the first to rise from her seat and cheer, whooping and clapping her hands.

Cam had assumed Lilith came tonight to scope out the competition, but clearly something deeper was going on. He hated feeling so distant from her that he couldn't even guess what she was thinking. He sat through three more songs of the Chloe show before the first set was over and the band took five.

"Can we flee yet?" Arriane whined.

Roland raised an eyebrow. "Cam?"

"Give me a minute," Cam said. As the audience went to grab more coffee or hit the bathroom, he made a bee-line for Lilith. She was heading toward the coffee bar. He swooped in right behind her and touched her shoulder.

"Hi, Lilith."

She spun around immediately. The sight of Cam seemed to drain her of energy. "Why are you here?"

"I wanted to see you." Cam stared at her lips. They

should never go this long without being kissed. "What can I do to make things right?"

"Did you make a bet with Luc that you could get me to fall in love with you?"

Cam opened his mouth. He rubbed his jaw. How did she know that? This was not a conversation to have in public. "Can we step outside?" he asked.

"Does that explain the band, and your interest in me in general?" She paused, swallowed. "The bet, Cam. Did you make it?"

"No," he said. "Yes."

Just then the girl taking coffee orders leaned over the counter and raised her voice. "Next? Hey, redhead. You want something or not?"

Lilith stepped out of line. "I just lost my appetite."

"Lilith, wait," Cam said.

"What are you trying to do, Cam? Drive me to suicide like that other girl?"

He reached for her. Everyone was staring at them now. "It's not what you think."

"I'm done being played." She shoved him away and headed for the door.

A bunch of kids from school *ooh*ed in Lilith's wake. Cam closed his eyes and tried to tune them out. He sensed Arriane and Roland at his side.

"That did not look good," Arriane said.

"You're cutting it close, Cam," Roland said. "I know

you like to live dangerously, but you've got one more day. I don't see this ending well."

The café door swung open, and in swanned Luc. "Hello, old friends." He shot them all an incredibly fake smile. "Talking about my favorite subject, Cam's inevitable doom?"

Cam couldn't stop himself: Without thinking, he pitched his coffee cup in the devil's face. The plastic top popped off, and the sizzling brown liquid splashed across Luc's skin. Cam heard the students' gasps, but he was more concerned about Lucifer's reaction. That had certainly been a very dumb thing to do.

The devil took out a handkerchief and wiped his face, then leaned in close to Cam, his face strained with rage.

"I gave you an out," Luc said. "You should have taken it."

He spoke to Cam in his true voice, quietly enough for the kids around them not to hear it, though they certainly felt the rumbling of the earth beneath their feet.

"And *you two*." The devil turned to Arriane and Roland. "You were allowed in for one reason and one reason alone. Do your job. Talk some sense into your senseless friend. Or face me."

"We're working on it, sir," Roland said. "You know how stubborn Cam can be."

"This is between me and Lucifer," Cam said. "And it's not over yet."

"It was over before it began," Lucifer said, motioning to the door Lilith had fled through. "You've managed to make her hate you even more now than she did before you got here." He let out a low laugh. "Yes, it is definitely over."

The devil stepped closer, until he and Cam were inches apart. Cam could smell the rot of Lucifer's breath, the stench emanating from his skin. "By the end of the day tomorrow," Lucifer said, "you'll be mine. Forever."

INTERLUDE

SACRIFICE

ISLE OF LESBOS, GREECE

Approximately 1000 BCE

Cam sat on the deck of a wooden boat anchored in a small marina.

He was shirtless, with his ankles crossed, gazing out at a low moon. For the past two hours, he'd been trying to teach himself to play the lyre he'd stolen from a man selling saffron at the market. Surely if he could conquer Lilith's instrument, he could conquer the Lilith-shaped hole inside him.

So far, it wasn't going well.

"Cam," a sultry voice purred, "put that thing down and come over here."

He turned to the young, olive-skinned girl behind him. She was propped on an elbow, her long legs folded behind her. Her golden hair undulated in the breeze.

"I'll be there in a moment," Cam said.

Since he'd left Lilith, Cam had surrounded himself with a series of girls, hoping in vain that they would distract his broken heart.

When he'd fled Canaan on his wedding day, he had sought out Lucifer in the clouds. Since the Fall, Cam had had little to say to the devil. Every century or so, Lucifer proposed a deal—Cam's allegiance for a dominion within the underworld—but Cam was never interested.

That time, though, when Cam turned up, Lucifer smiled knowingly and said, "I've been waiting for you."

Now, a second golden-haired girl interrupted Cam's memory as she walked the plank from the marina to the boat. "I thought I'd find you here," she called.

"What are *you* doing here, Xenia?" the first girl demanded. She looked at Cam. "Did you invite her?"

"Korinna?" Xenia exclaimed. "Why are *you* on Cam's ship?"

Cam set down his lyre, glad of the distraction. "I see no introductions are required."

Hands on hips, the two girls glared at him and each other.

He took a breath and forced a smile. "You're two beautiful girls on a beautiful moonlit night. Unless you prefer fighting, why don't we have a little fun?"

He dove into the sea. When he surfaced, he floated on his back, looking toward the boat. Maybe they'd join him. Maybe they wouldn't.

He didn't care either way.

"Still want to go through with this?" the boy asked from the helm of a cedar rowboat anchored at the edge of the marina. Lilith had discovered his name was Luc, but otherwise had learned very little about her companion.

Lilith listened to the splashing and the laughter from the water near Cam's boat. She swallowed, a lump in her throat.

She had come all this way to find him. It hadn't occurred to her that he might already have moved on to the next girl, and the next. She ached inside, but she would not leave Lesbos without trying to know his heart once more.

Soon, Lilith spotted Cam crossing the marina, walking along the shore. His wet hair shone in the starlight.

"This is your moment," Luc said. "Take it."

Lilith dove into the sea and swam toward Cam, her white gown billowing around her as she kicked.

Behind her, Luc looked on from his boat with a smile.

Near midnight, Cam was climbing a steep slope, lyre in hand, seeking a new kind of distraction. A voice warbled in the distance, accompanied by rich notes from a lyre. He saw a scrubby desert bush marking the entrance to a cave and angled himself toward it.

Inside the cave, in a narrow space between two tall rocks, an old man was playing an intricate song. His beard hung to his navel, and his hair stood out in filthy strands. His eyes were shut, and a flagon of wine sat at his feet. He seemed unaware of Cam's presence.

"You're very good," Cam said when the man's song ended. "Will you teach me to play?"

The man slowly opened his eyes. *"No."*

Cam tilted his head. Ever since he had aligned himself with Lucifer, he had discovered a new layer of persuasion in his voice. He was learning how to use it to his advantage.

"I will take you flying, far above the clouds, if you will teach me. You can bring your wine and drink among the stars."

The man's eyes widened; he was clearly affected. "Begin," he said, and strummed a chord.

Cam quickly brought his lyre into playing position.

The man kicked the instrument to the ground. "Piece of driftwood shit," he said. "Sing."

Unprepared to improvise, Cam found that Lilith's song, the first one he'd ever heard her sing, rose to his lips. She'd stolen his heart, he reasoned. Now he would steal her song.

"Where love spurs me I must turn
my rhymes, my rhymes . . ."

The man squinted at Cam, impressed. The melody he played on his lyre complemented Lilith's lyrics perfectly. He handed the flagon to Cam.

"I will teach you, and you will stay with me." He wrapped his arm around Cam. "Now," the man said, leading Cam toward the entrance of his cave, "can you really fly?"

Cam stepped back into the night. He was just about to release his wings when a shadow moved behind the desert bush.

Lilith? Was he dreaming?

She was still wearing her wedding gown. It was filthy by now, green with moss and dripping with seawater. It clung tightly to her body. Her hair was wild and wet, trailing halfway down her back, and her skin looked pale and bright in the moonlight. She looked into his eyes, then at his bare chest, then at his hands, as if she could see how much they ached to hold her.

But Cam and Lilith did not embrace. They faced each other like strangers.

"Hello, Cam," she said.

Cam shrank back. "Why are you here?"

Lilith scowled at the question. She took a breath and tried to form the words she had come so far to say. When she spoke, she looked at the sky so she wouldn't have to see the way his eyes clouded over at the sight of her.

"The night you left, I dreamt I taught a flock of nightingales a love song, so they could find you and sing you home to me. Now I am the nightingale who has traveled all this way. I still love you, Cam. Come back to me."

"No."

She gazed into his eyes. "Did you ever love me, or were you only passing through?"

"You rejected me."

"What?"

"You refused to marry me!"

"I refused to marry *at the river*," Lilith insisted. "I never refused to marry you!"

Since he'd last seen Lilith, Cam had joined Lucifer's ranks. If he had been afraid to show Lilith his true self before, it was impossible to do it now. No. There was no past. There was no Lilith.

There was only his future alone.

"You destroyed our love," Cam told her. "Now I'm left to live in its ruins."

There was a sense of urgency in Lilith's eyes that Cam didn't understand. She was nervous, trembling. "Cam, please—"

The backs of Cam's shoulders were burning, itching to release his wings. For weeks he'd hidden them from Lilith. To protect her, he had told himself.

He could not bring himself to look at her, to see how much she was hurting. He was a demon. He was dangerous to Lilith. Any kindness he showed her would draw her deeper into darkness.

"This is the last you'll see of me," he said. "You will never know who I truly am."

"I know who you are," she cried. "You are the one I love."

"You're wrong."

"Do you still love me?"

"Goodbye, Lilith."

"Don't!" she begged, sobs choking her voice. "I still love you. If you go—"

"I'm already gone," Cam said, and turned and ran down the mountain, out of her sight. He threw his head back and released his blinding, golden wings. He watched the shimmering light they cast around him. He would fly until his heart no longer ached. He would fly forever if he had to.

He flew fast and never looked back, so he never saw Lucifer step from the shadows and take Lilith's hand.

Lilith stared at the pale, freckled hand in hers. Her breath came shallowly. "He's gone," she gasped. "I left everything. For nothing."

"Come along," the devil said. "I kept my end of the bargain. It is time for you to keep yours."

SEVENTEEN

A FOREST

LILITH

Twenty-Three Hours

Lilith's headphones were blaring.

She lay on her stomach on her bedspread, scribbling lyrics in her journal for a new song called "Famous for a Broken Heart." It was one in the morning. She was tired, but she knew she'd never sleep. She kept replaying the conversation she'd had with Cam at the café.

He'd made a bet that he could make her fall in love with him. Like she had no free will, like she was just a coin to be tossed.

Had Cam almost won that bet? She had felt something

deep and strong for him. Was it love? Maybe, but she could never love a guy who treated her like a game to be won.

Suddenly, Lilith heard a sound that wasn't part of the Four Horsemen song in her headphones. It was coming from outside. Someone was knocking at her window. She turned her music off and raised the blinds.

Cam's leather jacket was zipped up, and he was wearing that knit hat she liked. Beneath its brim, his green eyes pleaded as he motioned for her to open the window.

She slid the pane up and stuck her head out. "My mom will kill you if she finds out you trampled her weeds."

"I'll take my chances," he said. "I've got to talk to you."

"Otherwise you'll lose the bet, right?" she said. "Remind me how many hours I have to fall madly in love with you?"

She looked past her lawn to the street, where a vintage black Honda motorcycle was parked, two helmets dangling from its handlebars. The bike looked expensive. Lilith studied Cam, remembering him strolling among the tents on Dobbs Street. How could he afford a motorcycle? He was a walking contradiction, but Lilith wasn't going to let it drive her crazy anymore.

"It's late," she said. "I'm tired. And you're the last person I want to see right now."

"I know," Cam said. "Lilith, I need you—"

"You don't need me." She didn't like when he said things like that. If she wasn't careful, she'd believe him.

Cam glanced down at his boots and sighed. When he looked up a moment later, his green eyes had taken on an intensity that made Lilith hold her breath. "I will always need you, Lilith. For many reasons. Right now, I need you to come with me."

"Why would I go anywhere with you?"

"So I can tell you the truth."

She'd been tricked before. "Tell me right here," Lilith said, standing her ground.

"So I can *show* you the truth," Cam corrected himself. "Please," he said softly, "give me one more chance to show you that my feelings for you are real—then, if you don't believe me, you'll never have to see me again. Fair?"

She studied his face and realized how familiar his features had become over the past two weeks. The first time she'd seen him at Rattlesnake Creek, he had been so different from anyone she'd ever met; he'd seemed more like a figment of her imagination than a real guy. But now she knew him. She knew he licked his lips when he was thinking, and the way his eyes twinkled when he was listening really closely. She knew the way his hands felt in hers and how smooth his skin was just above the collar of his T-shirt.

"One more chance," she said.

A dark gloom hung over Rattlesnake Creek.

Lilith's heart raced as Cam guided her deep into the forest, toward her favorite spot. She'd never been here so late, and it was eerily exciting.

Branches cracked as she stepped along the familiar path and turned into the clearing where her carob tree stood. For a moment, she didn't recognize it. Her tree had been decorated with strands of soft, twinkling red and yellow lights.

Beneath it, a boy with dreadlocks was arranging a bouquet of irises on the antique desk Cam had given her. Lilith thought she recognized him.

When a thin girl with a shaved head and orange false eyelashes ran to Lilith and stuck out her hand, Lilith knew where she'd seen them both before. The café, with Cam, earlier that night.

"I'm Arriane," the girl said. "That's Roland. Glad you could make it."

"What's going on?" Lilith asked Cam.

"First?" Cam said. "A toast."

Roland knelt by the bank of the creek and fished out a bottle of champagne. He reached beneath the desk and produced two champagne flutes, then opened the bottle with a pop. He filled the glasses with the fizzy liquid and handed one to Lilith. *"Salud."*

"To second chances," Cam said, and raised his glass.

"We're on at least fifth or sixth chances by now," Lilith said, but she clinked his glass anyway.

"Saucy!" Arriane called. "I like it."

"I suspected when I saw Lilith that Cam had met his match," Roland said.

Lilith chuckled. She felt oddly comfortable with these unexpected companions. They seemed more interesting than anyone she'd ever known, except maybe Cam.

"Don't mind my friends," Cam said. "We've known each other a long time."

"So, first is a toast," she said to Cam, glancing around the creek. "What's second?"

"A favor," Cam said.

"I'm not letting you back in the band yet—"

"That's not what I was going to ask," Cam said, though the word *yet* made him smile. "The favor is this. Cast aside all that you've heard about me from others, and spend an hour with me, here under the stars. Just us. Well, and Arriane and Roland, but you know what I mean."

"We're good at camouflage," Arriane said.

"Okay?" Cam said.

"Okay," Lilith replied, letting him take her hand and lead her toward the desk, which was set with crystal glasses, mismatched golden cutlery, white napkins folded in the shape of swans, and two gleaming Russian samovars.

Behind them, Roland began strumming a 1930s Martin guitar in a soft, syncopated blues rhythm. It was a very cool-looking instrument, different from any guitar Lilith had ever seen, and she wondered where it had come from. Arriane whipped the napkins off the desk and unfurled them onto Cam and Lilith's laps.

"Please allow me," she said when Lilith moved to lift the silver lid. Inside, a steaming cast-iron skillet was filled to the brim with a fragrant red casserole, on top of which swam two over-easy eggs garnished with lush green sprigs of parsley.

"Shakshuka," Lilith said, inhaling deeply.

"Don't let her fool you," Cam said. "Shakshuka is the only dish Arriane knows how to make."

Lilith frowned at her plate. "I've never even heard of it. The word just rose up in me."

"It's an old Israeli dish," Cam said. "Very light."

"I'm starving," Lilith said, and raised her fork. "How do you guys know each other?"

"It's a long story," Cam said. "Oh, maître d', you forgot to open my samovar."

"Open it yourself, jerko," Arriane called from the creek bank, where she was skipping rocks and mimicking Cam. "*The only dish Arriane knows how to make.*'"

Lilith laughed, scooping up a bright orange egg yolk. She savored her first delicious bite, then washed it down with a sip of champagne. "Wow, this is good, too."

"It should be," Arriane called from the bank. "It's older than your grandma."

Lilith put her fork down and turned to Roland, who was still sitting in the shadows, strumming his guitar. "Is that my song?"

He was concentrating on the neck of his guitar, playing an intricate melody.

"Roland's a fan," Cam said.

"What's this about, Cam?" Lilith asked, glancing from Roland to Arriane to the transformed tree. No one had ever gone to so much trouble to impress her before. "It's nice and all, but—"

"But it seems like an elaborate lead-up to a promposal?" he asked.

Lilith's head swiveled to gape at Cam.

"Don't worry," he said quickly. "I'm not going to ask you to prom."

"Good," she said, surprised to feel a little disappointed.

He leaned in close enough to kiss her and took her hands. "You told me you didn't need a date to play your music at the battle, and I respect that. It doesn't mean I wouldn't love to go with you, to buy you a corsage and have your mom take our picture and stand in line with you for punch and donuts, all the stuff that I would never want to do if I didn't get to do it with you." He smiled a smile that lit up his entire face. "But I can still respect your wishes. So instead, I brought the prom to you." He glanced around the forest. "See, prom's just like this, only with a few hundred more people. And a photo booth. And balloon arches."

"Hmm . . . it's not as bad as I imagined," Lilith said playfully. "It's actually kinda nice."

"Thank you," Cam said. "It took a lot of not-prom-court meetings to pull it off." He laughed, but then his face grew serious. He lowered his voice. "Whatever Chloe thinks she overheard, all Luc and I were talking about was how much I like you. He was convinced I didn't have a chance, and it brought out my competitive side. Because there's nothing I want more than to have a chance with you."

Lilith studied Cam's full lips, and found herself leaning closer to him. Suddenly, she didn't care about any of the rumors. She wanted to kiss him, badly. That was real. Everything else could fall away. Why hadn't she seen things so clearly before?

"Care to dance?" he asked.

"I care," Lilith said.

"I think she said yes," Arriane whispered loudly to Roland, who celebrated with a joyful riff on his guitar.

Cam gently pulled Lilith to her feet. Their shoes sank in the mulchy leaves, and Lilith was a little dizzy from the champagne. She looked up through the carob branches, amazed by how bright the stars were over Rattlesnake Creek. In her backyard you could maybe see one star through the smoky sky, but here there must have been a trillion shining down on them.

"Beautiful," she murmured.

Cam looked up. "Trust me, those stars have nothing on you."

"Pardon me!" Arriane said, coming between them. "If I could make one sartorial suggestion." A moment later she pressed something soft into Lilith's hands. Lilith held it up to the light. It was the gown she'd bought at the thrift store.

"How did you . . ."

"You should really start locking your bedroom window," Arriane said, and chuckled. "There are some real ding-dongs out there who might have stolen your dress before I did."

Lilith blinked. "You were in my room?"

"No big deal," Arriane said. "While you were busy breaking up or making up or whatever it is you're doing with Cam, I made a few updates to represent your evolving style."

Lilith looked more closely at the dress and noticed the hemline had been significantly shortened in front—to miniskirt length—while it stayed long in the back. A black lace panel had been sewn into either side of the bodice, making the waistline look even smaller than it was. The neckline had been lowered to a sweetheart cut, trimmed with black lace.

"Wow," Lilith said.

"Turn it over," Arriane said. "There's more."

She did, and saw new cutouts in the center of the gown's back, in the shape of wings. It was the same dress, yet it was totally different. Lilith didn't understand how this girl had made such swift and savvy alterations, but she knew she would wear this dress proudly at the Battle of the Bands.

In fact, she wanted to wear it right now.

"Thank you," she said to Arriane. "May I . . . ?"

Arriane read Lilith's mind. "No peeking," she told the boys, then nodded at Lilith.

Lilith turned her back to the creek, then slipped her T-shirt over her head and tossed it on the ground. She pulled on the dress and shimmied out of her jeans. Arriane's hands found Lilith's side and did up what must have been fifty tiny buttons.

"In a word," Arriane said, "stunning."

Lilith stared down at herself, at the dress illuminated by the stars in the sky and all of the twinkling lights Cam and his friends had strung. She felt beautiful . . . and strange, the way she had in the thrift-store dressing room. She couldn't explain it. She realized Cam was looking at her, and she could tell he felt it, too.

"I'm ready," Lilith said.

She stepped into his arms and they began to move in time, their eyes locked on one another. Cam knew how to lead. He was careful not to go too fast and never came close to stepping on her toes. Every dip and turn felt instinctive, and his body felt so right against hers, as if they were two puzzle pieces snapping into place.

"I still don't understand how we got here," Lilith whispered, arching back so her red hair reached the ground.

"We took the bike," Cam joked. "Remember? The wind in your hair?"

"You know what I mean," Lilith said. "You. Me. Us."

"*Us.*" Cam repeated the word slowly. "You know, that has a nice ring to it. We make a really good 'us.'"

Lilith thought for a moment. He was right. They did. And suddenly Lilith didn't want prom to end at Rattlesnake Creek. For the first time, she wanted to do more than just play her song at the battle and duck out. She wanted to experience the whole thing, with her friends and, especially, with Cam.

"Cam," she said, her heart picking up pace as they swayed to the music, "will you be my date to the Battle of the Bands?"

Lilith thought she had seen Cam happy, but now his face lit up with something new. He twirled her around in a grand circle. "Yes!"

"I think he said 'yes'!" Arriane hissed at Roland.

"We knew *he* was going to say yes!" Roland replied.

"Oh yeah. Sorry. Don't mind us," Arriane said.

Lilith giggled as the girl returned to washing their dishes in the creek.

"There's one condition," she said, turning back to Cam. "You have to rejoin the band and play our song. Think you can handle that?"

"Lilith," Cam said, "I would play music with you forever. Or at least until you kick me out again."

"Then it's settled," she said. "Tomorrow night, me and you. And all of Trumbull."

"Technically," Cam said, checking his watch, "prom is *tonight*."

Roland's guitar playing modulated to something foreign and familiar. It sounded Middle Eastern, but Lilith could have sworn she'd heard it a million times before.

"Now close your eyes," Cam said. "Let me show you how it really feels to dance."

Lilith closed her eyes and let Cam lead her, their footwork becoming more and more intricate as the song progressed. She'd had no idea dancing could feel so effortless. His hands grasped her waist and lifted her until she could have sworn that his feet had come off the ground, too; that they were floating up above the creek, above the trees, above the burning hillside, into the dense tangle of stars, about to kiss the moon.

"Can I open my eyes?" she asked.

"Not yet," Cam said.

Then he kissed her deeply, his mouth firm and warm on hers—and Lilith kissed him back. A warm tingle spread through her as Cam pulled her closer, kissed her harder. She'd never done this before. Not even close.

His lips seemed made for hers. Why had it taken them so long to get here? They could have been kissing just like this all along. They should stay kissing, just like this, until—

"Lilith," he whispered as their lips parted. "Lilith, Lilith, Lilith."

"Cam," she replied. She felt light-headed. A cool breeze whipped around them, tossing her hair, and before she knew it Lilith felt the ground beneath her feet.

"*Now* you can open your eyes," he said, and she did. Up close, Cam's were flecked with gold and ringed by an even deeper green. She couldn't stop staring at them.

"Was that dancing?" she asked breathlessly. "Or flying?"

Cam wrapped both arms around her waist. "When it's done right," he said, touching his forehead against hers, "there isn't any difference."

EIGHTEEN

LOVE'S SECRET DOMAIN

CAM

Four Hours

Cam climbed out of the backseat of the old stretch limousine Roland had mysteriously scrounged up for the evening. He mounted the concrete steps to Lilith's front door and listened to the locusts zap against the porch light. His heart drummed as he reached to ring her bell.

Self-doubt had never been Cam's style. It clashed with his leather jacket, his original Levi's, his cool green eyes. But now, as the sun sulked behind the burning hills and a cold wind claimed the streets, he wondered: Had he done enough?

A few band practices. A few arguments. One exquisite kiss. To Cam, every moment had brimmed with passion. But would Lilith recognize it as *love*?

Because if she didn't . . .

She would. She had to. Tonight.

Arriane flung open the door, fists on her hips, her fine eyebrows arched. "She's ready!" she sang. "Her updo will be the stuff of legend, but I'm *most* pleased with my alterations to her dress. Hey, they don't call me Arriane Alter for nothin'." She looked over her shoulder. "Bruce, bring out the babe."

A moment later, Lilith's brother rounded the hallway corner wearing his dinosaur-print pajamas. On his arm was Lilith, all dressed up. Cam held his breath as she walked toward him with slow, measured steps, meeting his eyes the whole time. That dress, and the dreamy look in her eyes, took him right back to the wedding they'd never had.

She was luminous. Her red hair had been braided a dozen ways, all swirled together in a high shaggy twist. Her eyelids were shimmering green, her lips crimson and matte. She wore black vintage ankle-high motorcycle boots. She was lethal.

She let go of Bruce's hand and spun in a slow, sexy circle. "How do I look?"

When she stopped in front of him, Cam took her hands. She had the softest skin he'd ever known. "You look so good, it ought to be illegal."

"No costume for you?" Lilith asked, smoothing the lapel of Cam's leather jacket. "Jean's going to be pissed, but I think you look smokin'."

"Smokin'?" he laughed. When Lilith looked at him that way, Cam could forget that his muscles had lost their definition, that his skin was paper-thin, that his hair was falling out and his hooves made it hard for him to walk. Lilith saw him differently than the rest of her world did, because she cared for him, and hers was the only opinion that mattered.

"Cam, do you mind if . . . ," Lilith said nervously. "Would it be okay if I properly introduced you to my mom? She's kind of old-fashioned, and it would mean a lot—"

"No problem. Moms love me," Cam lied. Mothers of teenage girls could usually smell the bad boy in Cam right away. But for Lilith, he would do anything.

"Mom?" Lilith called, and a moment later her mother appeared in the hall. She wore a pink terry-cloth bathrobe that was stained and worn thin. Her hair was pulled back messily with a plastic clip. She touched it fretfully, teasing out a little strand.

"Mrs. Foscor." Cam extended his hand. "I'm Cameron Briel. We met once before, when you were taking Bruce to the hospital, but I'm glad to see you again. I want to thank you."

"For what?" Lilith's mother asked.

"For raising a remarkable daughter," he said.

"Anything you like in her is probably just her rebelling against me," her mother said, and then, to Cam's amazement, she laughed. "She does look beautiful, though, doesn't she?"

"The stuff of love songs," Cam said.

When he glanced at Lilith, her eyes were damp; Cam understood how rare praise from her mother must have been.

"Thank you," Lilith said, embracing her mom, then her brother. "We won't be out too late."

"Don't you want to come see Lilith perform?" Cam asked Lilith's mom.

"I'm sure we'd only embarrass her," her mother said.

"No," Lilith said. "Please come." She glanced at Cam. "I don't know, do you think they let non-students into prom?"

"Don't worry about that," Arriane chimed in, pulling at the neck of her black V-neck shirt. "I know a guy who knows a guy who can get us all front-row seats."

"That's very generous," Lilith's mom said. "I'll go get dressed. You too, Bruce."

When her family had disappeared into their rooms, Cam turned to Lilith. "Shall we?"

"Wait," she said. "I forgot my guitar."

"You might need that," Cam said. "I'll wait outside."

He stepped onto the porch, Arriane following behind him. She patted his cheek. "I'm proud of you, Cam. And inspired by you. Ain't that right, Ro?"

"Right on." Roland called from the open window of the limousine. He was wearing a sharp-looking tuxedo with a navy bow tie.

"Thank you, guys," Cam said.

"Regardless of what happens tonight," Arriane added.

"You still have no faith that I can win?" Cam asked.

Arriane scampered to catch up with him. "It's just, on the off chance that you don't—"

"What she means is," Roland said, getting out of the car and coming up behind Cam, "we'd miss you, man." He leaned against Lilith's front porch's rusty railing and gazed up at the sky. "Won't you miss her?"

"Because if you lose," Arriane said, "she'll be back to snow-globe Purgatory, and you . . ." Arriane shuddered. "I don't even want to think about what Lucifer will have you doing."

"Don't worry about it," Cam said. "Because I'm not going to lose."

Arriane sank onto the hood of the limo, and Roland climbed back into the driver's seat. The front door opened, and Lilith stepped out, bathed in moonlight, holding her guitar.

"Can you handle one more accessory?" Cam asked, pulling a small white box from his pocket.

Lilith opened it and smiled when she saw the blue and yellow irises pinned to the small elastic band.

Gently, Cam slipped the flower onto Lilith's wrist. Their fingers intertwined.

"No one's ever given me a corsage," Arriane said longingly.

Then something landed at her feet with a thump. Arriane jumped back in alarm, then looked down and saw a small white box identical to the one Cam had given Lilith. She smiled.

"You're welcome," Roland called from the driver's seat. "Now get in, kids; you're wasting valuable prom time."

⚜

At the edge of Trumbull's campus, Cam helped Lilith climb out of the limo. Small groups of done-up kids hung out on the hoods of cars in the parking lot, dressed in their finest dresses and suits, but most of the action seemed to be coming from the football field, where Luc had constructed the replica Colosseum.

Like its Roman model, it was open to the elements, with three tiers of tall arches around the exterior. As Cam studied it, he realized there was something slapdash about the structure. Instead of being made of limestone, it was formed entirely of packed ash from the fires of Lilith's Hell, like cheap concrete. It drove home to Cam how temporary this was—the evening; the school; the small, sad world of Crossroads.

Lilith gazed at the venue before them, and Cam knew

she saw none of the things that worried Cam. To Lilith, it was just another ugly building in her ugly town.

Bass thumped through the walls. "It's no Rattlesnake Creek," Lilith said, "but I guess we'll make do."

"We can do better than that," Cam said. "We can rock this place so hard its walls come tumbling down. It'll be the fall of Rome all over again."

"My, you're ambitious," Lilith teased, taking his arm.

"Thanks for the lift, Roland." Cam turned to the demon, who closed the limo door behind him.

"Break a leg, brother," Roland called to his friend.

Cam and Lilith entered the faux Colosseum through a long arch made of gold and silver balloons. On the other side they found the party in full swing. Students clustered around candlelit cocktail tables, laughing, flirting, snacking on cheese cubes, and sipping punch. Others danced to fast pop songs on a big parquet dance floor that was open to the stars.

Cam's gaze was drawn to the back of the Colosseum, where a grand stage had been erected, rising twenty feet above the rest of prom. Red velvet curtains created a backstage area where the other bands could wait before they played. Off to one side was a small judges' table over which hung a banner: TRUMBULL PREP WELCOMES THE FOUR HORSEMEN.

Lilith nudged Cam and pointed at the dance floor. "Check out Luis."

Cam followed her finger to find their drummer, wearing a white tuxedo and strutting like a chicken around Karen Walker, who was burying her face in her hands.

"Work it, Luis!" Lilith called out.

"What?" Luis shouted at her over the music. "This is my jam. I need to move my feet."

Just then, Dean Miller walked up to Lilith and Cam. He wore a dark tux with a thin black tie that ran like a stripe down his chest. "Tarkenton's been looking for you all night." He handed Cam a folded blue cloth. "Prom court. You have to wear it. You'd know that if you'd bothered to show up to our last meeting."

Lilith buried a laugh in the crook of her elbow as Cam held up a pastel-blue satin sash with his name printed across it in white block letters. Dean wore a matching sash over his tux that read *Dean Miller.*

"Great." Cam raised the sash. "Good luck tonight, man."

"Thanks, but unlike you, I don't need it," Dean said with a smirk as Chloe King came up and slipped her arm through his.

"Dean, I need you for a photo—"

"Chloe," Lilith said. "Hi."

Chloe looked at Lilith's dress, clearly impressed. "Did you hire a stylist or something? Because you actually look nice."

"Thanks, I guess," Lilith said. "You look nice, too."

Chloe turned to Cam and narrowed her eyes. "You'd better treat her right," she said before leading Dean away.

"Since when are you and Chloe King friends?" Cam asked.

"I don't know if I'd say *friends*," Lilith said, "but we hashed some stuff out the other day. She's not so bad. And she's right." Lilith raised an eyebrow. "You'd better treat me right."

"I know," Cam said. It was the thing he felt most committed to in the universe.

Lilith took his blue prom-court sash and pitched it into a nearby trash can. "Now that that's settled, let's make a plan." She glanced at her watch. "The battle starts in twenty minutes. I think we have time for a dance before we have to get ready."

"You're the boss," Cam said, drawing Lilith close and moving toward the dance floor.

Luckily the next song was a slow one, the kind that seemed to make everyone want to wrap their arms around someone. Soon, Lilith and Cam were surrounded by couples, the dance floor bright with jewel-colored dresses and elegantly contrasting tuxedos. Kids Cam had passed a dozen times in the forgettable halls of Trumbull now looked extraordinary under the starlight, smiling as they swayed to the music. It tormented Cam that everyone here felt like they were on the brink of everything, when in fact they were only on the brink of the end.

He drew Lilith close. He focused on her only. He loved the light touch of her fingers on his shoulders. He loved the way her iris corsage smelled against her skin and the heat of her against him. He closed his eyes and let the rest of Crossroads disappear, imagining they were alone together.

They had only danced together once before last night at Rattlesnake Creek, in Canaan, by the river, right after Cam had proposed. He remembered how Lilith had seemed featherlight that first time they had danced, rising off the ground with the slightest sway of Cam's body.

She felt the same right now. Her feet skimmed the dance floor, and she looked up at Cam with pure delight in her eyes. She was happy. He could feel it. He was, too. He closed his eyes and let his memory take them back to Canaan, where they'd once been so open and free.

"I love you," he whispered before he could stop himself.

"What'd you say?" Lilith shouted, her voice barely louder than the music. "You're looking for the bathroom?" She pulled away and glanced around, looking for signs for the men's room.

"No, no," Cam said, drawing her back into his arms, wishing he hadn't spoiled the mood. "I said"—but he couldn't, not now, not yet—"I said *nice moves*."

"Enjoy 'em while they last," she shouted. "We gotta get backstage."

The song ended, and everyone turned toward the stage as Tarkenton strode up the steps. He wore a navy tuxedo with a red rose pinned to his lapel. He tweaked his mustache and nervously cleared his throat as he approached the microphone.

"All contestants in tonight's Battle of the Bands should now have reported backstage," he said, casting his gaze around the prom. "This is the last call for all contestants in the Battle of the Bands. Please use the door at stage left."

"We're cutting it close," Lilith said, grabbing Cam's hand and pulling him through the throng of students, closer to the stage.

"Don't I know it," Cam muttered to himself.

They cut left, scooting around a girl and boy who were kissing as if they were the only ones in the room, then finding the black door at stage left where the contestants were supposed to check in.

Cam held it open for Lilith. On the other side was a dimly lit, narrow hallway.

"This way." Lilith took his hand, gesturing to a poster with an arrow. They took a left and then a right, then found the row of dressing rooms with labeled doors: Love and Idleness, Death of the Author, the Perceived Slights, the Four Horsemen, and, at the end of the hall, Revenge. Lilith turned the knob.

Inside, Luis sat in a director's chair, shoveling peanut M&M's into his mouth, his feet up on a vanity. He had changed into a black cowboy shirt and white slacks, with a black fedora tilted low. His eyes were closed, and he was rehearing the backup harmonies to "Somebody's Other Blues" under his breath.

On a couch in the corner, Jean was making out with his girlfriend Kimi, who looked great in her long cranberry satin dress. He broke away from their kiss for a moment to look up and give Cam and Lilith a peace sign.

"Ready to rock, man?" he said, adjusting the tan leather fringed vest he'd found at the Salvation Army.

Behind them, Cam's guitar was propped against Jean's synth, next to Jean and Luis's tuxedos, which had been removed and hung up carefully—clearly by Jean's girlfriend.

Kimi stood up and straightened her dress. "Time for me to scoot," she said. From the dressing-room door, she blew Jean a kiss. "Make me proud."

Jean reached up to catch the air kiss, which made Cam and Lilith burst out laughing.

"It's our thing," Jean said. "Do I make fun of you guys for getting into fights every fifteen minutes? I do not, because that's *your* thing."

Cam glanced at Lilith. "We haven't fought in at least half an hour."

"We're overdue," Lilith agreed. Then she put her hand on Jean's shoulder. "Hey, thanks for putting up with all of our drama."

"Nah," Jean said. "You should see how Kimi gets when I don't return her texts in under sixty seconds."

"It's prom!" Luis said. "When in the history of the world has the lead-up to prom not inspired major drama?" He pulled his drumsticks from his back pocket and practiced a drum roll on his thighs.

"Two minutes to show," a voice called from the hallway. Cam leaned his head out to find Luc idling outside with a clipboard and a headset. He flashed Cam a lupine grin and lowered his voice to its true pitch. "You ready for this, Cambriel?"

"Born ready," Cam said. Of course, that wasn't true. He hadn't even felt close to ready to win the wager against Lucifer until he'd held Lilith in his arms last night.

The devil laughed, popping a few of the lightbulbs in the ceiling with a cackle so grating it was inaudible to everyone but Cam. His voice went back to its fake smoothness when he announced, "All bands, report to your positions in the wings."

Cam came back into the dressing room and closed the door, hoping the others couldn't tell he was riled. He glanced at Luis in the mirror. The drummer's complexion had turned sallow.

"You okay?" Cam asked.

"I think I'm going to be sick," Luis said.

"I told you not to eat all those M&M's," Jean said, shaking his head.

"It's not that." Luis was breathing shallowly, resting his palms on the vanity. "None of you guys get stage fright?"

"I do," Lilith said, and Cam looked over to find her

trembling. "Two weeks ago I would never have thought I'd be standing here. Now that I am, I want to be great. I don't want to screw up because I'm nervous. I don't want to throw it all away."

"The thing about performing music no one's heard before," Jean said, tucking his Moog under his arm, "is no one knows if you screw up."

"But *I* would know," Lilith said.

Cam sat down on the vanity, facing Lilith. He touched her chin and said softly, "We just go out there and do our best."

"What if my best isn't good enough?" Lilith asked, looking down. "What if this was all a mistake?"

Cam put his hands on her shoulders. "The measure of this band is not a three-minute performance at prom. The measure of this band is all the steps it took us to get here. You writing those songs. Us learning to play them together. All our practices. Our trip to the Salvation Army. The lyrics contest you won."

He looked from Lilith to Jean to Luis and found them hanging on his words, so he kept going. "It's the fact that we all actually like each other now. And every time you threw me out of the band. And every time you graciously let me back in. *That's* Revenge. As long as we remember that, nothing can stop us." He took a deep breath, hoping the others didn't notice the tremor in his voice. "And if we don't succeed, at least we'll have had this time together.

Even if this *is* the end, it was worth it to get to play with you for a little while."

Lilith tilted her head at Cam and gazed deep into his eyes. She mouthed something Cam didn't quite catch. His heart soared as he leaned close to her lips.

"What did you say?"

"I said *thank you*. I feel better now. I'm ready."

Well, that was something. But would it be enough?

Cam lifted his guitar off its stand. "Let's go."

The four members of Revenge gathered in a corner of the wings, instruments tucked under their arms. They were all supposed to enter from stage left, and there were no curtains separating the various acts, so the performers just huddled in little cliques. There was a certain electricity backstage, made of nerves and anticipation and hair spray. Everyone could feel it.

From behind the curtain, Cam peeked out at the crowd on the dance floor. With the stage lights off, he could see them clearly. They were restless but excited, jostling each other, flirting, giggling over nothing, one boy bodysurfing through the mass of kids. Even the faculty hovering at the edges of the crowd seemed cheerful. Cam knew a band was lucky to have an audience in this mood. They wanted something from the show, something that matched their own energy that night, which was supercharged.

At the judges' table to the right of the stage, Tarkenton was trying to converse with four punk-rock boys. Cam had almost forgotten that Ike Ligon was judging this thing, and he was amused to see what passed for a "rock star" in Lilith's Hell. The lead singer of the band was pouty enough, with spiky blond hair and long, lean limbs, but the other three looked like they had about two brain cells between them. Cam reminded himself that this was Lilith's favorite band and told himself that maybe they looked better onstage.

A flash of movement behind the judges' table caught Cam's attention. Arriane and Roland were there, setting up folding chairs for Lilith's mother and brother. Arriane caught Cam's eye and pointed: *Look up.* He glanced overhead and was cheered to see that she had somehow hung the disco ball from the rafters above the stage.

He looked back to Arriane and gestured his applause. *Nice,* he mouthed. Cam thought of all that his friends had done for him last night at Rattlesnake Creek, and wondered if he could have gotten this far with Lilith without them.

Roland looked up at the stars, worry straining his smooth brow. Cam's gaze followed his friend's. The starlight, which seemed strangely bright tonight, wasn't starlight at all. Instead, Lucifer's demons had gathered high in the firmament above. It was their eyes that shone like stars through the wildfire smoke. Cam bristled, knowing they were here to see what would become of him. The Trumbull kids weren't the only ones eager for a big performance tonight.

The houselights went out.

The crowd fell silent as a spotlight found Luc. He had changed into a blue pin-striped suit, wing-tip shoes, and a fuchsia pocket square. He held a gold-plated microphone and smiled at a teleprompter.

"Welcome to the Trumbull prom," his voice boomed. Whoops rose from the audience until Luc waved one hand and silenced the crowd. "I am honored to play a role in this momentous occasion. I know you're all eager to know who will be crowned prom king and queen. Coach Burroughs is backstage now, tallying your votes. First, we will commence with the much-anticipated Battle of the Bands."

"We love you, Chloe!" a few kids screamed from the front row.

"Some of the bands you'll hear are fan favorites," Luc said. "Some are relative unknowns, even to their relatives . . ." He waited for laughter, but instead, a half-full can of soda landed at his feet.

"Some," Luc continued, his voice darkening, "have never stood a chance." He turned and winked at Cam. "Here to fire the first shot, Love and Idleness!"

The audience sounded its approval as two sophomore girls dragged stools onto the stage. They looked like sisters, with dark skin, freckles, and pale blue eyes. One had white-blond curls and the other had a dyed black bob. They raised their ukuleles.

Cam was impressed to recognize the opening chords of an obscure folk song that had been passed down through time in dark speakeasies. It was called "Silver Dagger," and the first time he'd heard it had been a couple of hundred years ago, aboard a boat being tossed around a high sea in heavy blackness.

"She's badass," Jean said.

"Which one?" Luis said.

"Both of 'em," Jean said.

"You have a girlfriend," Luis said.

"Shhh," Jean said.

Cam tried to catch Lilith's eye, but she was locked in on the performance.

Love and Idleness was good and seemed to know it. But they would never know how well they had chosen their song, or that they were singing to ten thousand pairs of immortal ears that had been present when the song was first performed off the Barbary Coast. Cam knew some of the demons would be chanting along from above.

He stood behind Lilith, wrapped his arms around her waist, and swayed, singing softly in her ear.

"My daddy is a handsome devil . . ."

"You know this song?" Lilith asked, turning her head slightly so her cheek brushed Cam's lips. "It's catchy."

"Lilith," he said, "there's something I've been wanting to tell you."

Now she turned fully, as if she could hear the intensity in his voice.

"I don't know if it's the right time, but I have to let you know that—"

"Hey," a voice interrupted Cam, and a moment later Luc shoved Cam aside to stand in front of Lilith. "Have you kids signed the waiver yet? Every performer has to sign the waiver."

Lilith glanced at the densely printed document. "What's it say? It's hard to read in here."

"Just that you won't sue King Media, and that we can use your image for promotional materials after the show."

"Really, Luc?" Cam said. "We have to do this right now?"

"Can't go onstage unless you do."

Cam speed-read the document to make sure he wasn't locking himself into any darker deal with Lucifer. It seemed, though, that it was nothing but a way to interrupt the moment. Cam dashed out his signature. "It's fine," he told Lilith, and watched as she signed, too.

Cam shoved the documents back at Lucifer, who slipped them in his pocket and grinned. By then, the performance was over and the applause for Love and Idleness had diminished.

Luc strode back onto the stage. "Provocative." He smirked. "Without further ado, our next band: Death of the Author!"

The crowd cheered weakly as a short kid named Jerry and his three friends strutted onto the stage. Cam cringed as Jerry tried to adjust the shared drum kit to fit his small stature. After a few painful moments, Lilith nudged Cam.

"We should help them," she said.

Cam was surprised, but of course Lilith was right. She really was different from the angry loner girl she'd been two weeks ago.

"Good idea," Cam said as they hurried onstage to help adjust the height of the drums.

When the instruments were tuned and the band was counting off, Lilith and Cam slipped back to the wings. Lilith didn't seem to care how bad Death of the Author was. She was simply happy to have helped a fellow musician. But she was the only one who was happy. Jean squirmed miserably as Jerry belted out the lyrics to a song called "Amalgamator."

"He doesn't even know what an amalgamator is," Jean said, shaking his head.

"Yeah," Luis said. "Totally. Um . . . what *is* an amalgamator?"

The audience was bored before the first verse ended.

People booed and drifted away to buy sodas, but Death of the Author didn't notice. At the end of the song, Jerry embraced the mic, nearly falling over with adrenaline. "We love you, Crossroads!"

As Jerry and his band left the stage, Luc returned to it. "Our next act is already well-known throughout town," he said into the mic. "I give you the lovely and talented Perceived Slights!"

Applause echoed throughout the Colosseum as the crowd went wild.

Cam and Lilith peeked through the curtain to see the popular crowd from Trumbull all but rushing the stage. They were screaming, girls hoisted up on their dates' shoulders, chanting Chloe's name. Cam took Lilith's hand. Even if she *had* smoothed some things over with Chloe, it must be hard for her not to envy the reception the Perceived Slights were getting.

"You okay?" Cam asked, but the crowd was too loud for Lilith to hear him.

Luis gave Karen Walker a pat on the butt as she dashed out from behind the curtain to check the Perceived Slights' amp connections. Fog from a few buckets full of dry ice filled the stage, and a few moments later Chloe King and her band emerged from the wings.

They were pros. They beamed and waved into the stage lights, finding their places at their mics as if they'd played a thousand shows bigger than this. They wore matching white stilettos and leather minidresses in a variety of colors, their pastel pink prom-court sashes draped over their dresses. Chloe's dress was buttercup yellow, to match her solid-gold glittery eye shadow.

"The feeling is mutual, Trumbull!" Chloe shouted.

The crowd roared.

Chloe pouted and leaned seductively into the mic. The crowd was mesmerized, but all Cam could do was watch Lilith. She was leaning forward, chewing her nails. He knew she was comparing herself to Chloe—not just to the way the audience responded, but to the way Chloe grabbed the mic with the flick of a wrist, the way her voice filled the Colosseum, the passion she brought to her guitar.

If he could hold Lilith one more time before they played, Cam was convinced that he could make her see that this performance wasn't about competing with Chloe. It was about what she and Cam had together. He could say the three words that had been burning in him for fifteen days, and her response would tell him whether they had a chance.

Three little words. Would she say them? They would determine both Cam and Lilith's fate.

But before he had a chance to reach for her, Cam felt Jean come stand on his left, then Luis stand on his right. Cam felt the energy coming off of them and realized Chloe's song was over and the crowd was cheering and Lilith was tilting her head toward the sky, maybe praying for good luck. Because Revenge was about to go on, and it was all about their music now.

The Colosseum went dark except for the pinhole spotlight on Luc's eyes as he stood in the center of the stage. When he spoke, his voice was barely a whisper.

"Are you ready for *Revenge?*"

NINETEEN

END OF THE DREAM

LILITH

Two Hours

Center stage.

Deep darkness.

Lilith cupped the cold mic in her hands. Then a blinding spotlight shone on her, and the audience disappeared.

She glanced up at the twinkling disco ball suspended from the rafters. If it hadn't been for Cam, Lilith would have been alone tonight, writing songs in her bedroom. She wouldn't be at prom, facing a packed dance floor, nodding at her bandmates, about to rock.

She ignored her quaking knees, her pounding heart.

She took a long breath and felt the weight of her guitar across her chest, the light fabric of her gown. "Two, three, four," she counted off into the mic.

She heard the drums, sudden as a downpour. Her fingers caressed her guitar strings in a slow, sad riff, then exploded into the song.

Cam's guitar found hers in the maelstrom, and they played as if it were their last night on earth, as if the fate of the universe depended on how they sounded together. This was the moment she'd been waiting for. She wasn't afraid anymore. She was living her dream. She closed her eyes and sang.

> "I dreamed life was a dream
> Someone was having in my eyes . . ."

Her song sounded the way she'd always hoped it might someday. She opened her eyes and turned back to Jean Rah and Luis. Both of them were completely absorbed in the music. She nodded at Cam across the stage, strumming his guitar skillfully, keeping his eyes on her. He was smiling. She'd never realized how much she loved the way he smiled at her.

When she turned back to the audience to play the second verse, she caught a quick glimpse of her brother and her mother. They were standing apart from the crowd, but they were dancing with abandon.

Lilith could hardly hear herself above the audience's cheers. She spun away from the microphone to jam, arching her back, letting her fingers fly across the strings. This was joy. There was nothing but Lilith, her band, and their music.

After the bridge she reached for the microphone again, and on the last verse Cam joined her, finding harmonies they'd never even practiced.

Lilith lifted her arm and stopped playing, pausing before the final couplet of the song. Jean, Luis, and Cam stopped, too.

The audience screamed louder.

When her arm came down on the final chord, the band fell in with her, right on time, and every voice in the audience screamed.

There was only one thing to do when the song was over. She rushed toward Cam and grabbed his hand. She wanted to be with him when they bowed. Because without him, she wouldn't be here. None of this would have happened.

He reached for her. He smiled. They held hands and moved downstage.

Hold on, Lilith found herself saying to Cam's hand. *Hold on to me, just like this. Don't let go.*

"Lilith rules!" A voice rose over the applause. Lilith thought it sounded like Arriane.

"Long live the queen!" called another voice that might have belonged to Roland.

"Take a bow, rock star," Cam murmured into her ear. "Take it with me."

Elation swept through Lilith as she and Cam bent forward. The motion felt natural, as if she and Cam had been touring forever, bowing to rapt audiences all their lives. Maybe this was reverse déjà vu, and she was experiencing what the future held.

She hoped so. She wanted to play again with Cam, and soon.

She turned to him. He turned to her.

Before she knew it their lips almost—

"Save it for the after-party," Luc's voice boomed as he hurried onto the stage to stand between them, pushing them apart.

The stage lights dimmed, and Lilith could see the audience again. They were all still cheering. Arriane, Roland, Bruce, and her mother had moved to the front row and were hooting like Lilith was an actual rock star. She felt like one.

Security guards held kids back as they tried to rush the stage. Even Principal Tarkenton was clapping. Lilith saw the empty seats next to him and realized that the Four Horsemen must be backstage right now, preparing to close out the night.

The battle had already been so epic, it seemed insane that Lilith was now about to see her favorite band.

"Quite a night, eh?" Luc asked the audience. "And there's more to come!"

Two ponytailed guys in crew T-shirts guided the other competing bands back onto the stage. Chloe bounded over to Lilith and slung an arm around her waist.

"Nice job," she said. "Even if I was better."

"Thanks." Lilith laughed. "The Slights were great, too."

Chloe nodded. "That's how we roll."

"Settle down," Luc said, motioning for quiet. "Winners and losers must be determined."

Lilith fidgeted between Chloe and Cam. Tarkenton was mounting the stairs to the stage, carrying an envelope and a trophy topped with a golden guitar.

"Have the esteemed judges reached a decision?" Luc asked.

Tarkenton tapped the mic. He seemed as stunned by the performances as Lilith. "The winner of the Battle of the Bands, sponsored by King Media, is—"

A synthesized drumroll blared through the stadium speakers. A sudden competitive surge filled Lilith. Their band had killed it tonight. They knew it. The audience knew it. Even Chloe King knew it. If there was any justice in this world—

Luc grabbed the envelope from Tarkenton. "The Perceived Slights!"

Then Chloe's band was screaming, crying, pushing everyone else out of the spotlight.

"Next stop, prom queen," Chloe squealed, and hugged her friends.

Lilith's ears were ringing as Chloe accepted the trophy. Only moments before she had been having the night of her life. Now she felt brutally defeated.

"Sucks," Jean Rah said.

Luis kicked a stage marker. "We were better."

Lilith knew Cam was watching her, but she was too dumbfounded to meet his gaze. She'd felt like their song had changed the world.

It hadn't.

She felt ridiculous that she'd let herself believe otherwise.

"Hey," Cam's voice was in her ear. "You okay?"

"Sure." Tears stung her eyes. "We should have won. Right? I mean, we were good—"

"We did win," Cam said. "We won something better."

"What?" Lilith asked.

Cam glanced toward Luc. "You'll see."

"Contestants, please exit stage left," the crew boy said.

The Slights were escorted to a card table that had been set up next to the judges' table. On it sat a folded paper placard that read Reserved for Winners. The other bands squeezed into the wings. Cam took Lilith's hand. "Come with me. I know a place where we can watch the Four Horsemen."

"Not so fast," Luc said as he took Lilith's other hand.

She was caught onstage between the two of them,

wanting to go with Cam, wondering what Luc wanted. She looked out at the audience, surprised to feel as nervous as she'd been before her performance. On the school's Jumbotron, the huge clock read *11:45*. Lilith's usual curfew was midnight, but since her mother and Bruce were in the audience, Lilith could probably get away with staying out later.

"So it comes to pass," Luc said into his microphone, "that Love and Idleness, Death of the Author, and Revenge are not the only losers tonight. All those who entered tonight's lyrics contest . . . are also losers. All of you except for one."

Lilith's breath caught in her chest. She had nearly forgotten the email from Ike Ligon. The Four Horsemen were about to cover her song.

Her disappointment waned. Winning the Battle of the Bands would have been great, but the music she made onstage with Cam, Jean, and Luis was what mattered. Everything else was gravy.

"I've asked Lilith to stay onstage," Luc said to the audience, "because I think she knows the song the Four Horsemen are about to play."

A curtain rose at the back of the stage, and behind it were the Four Horsemen. Rod, the beefy dark-haired bass player, gave the audience a wave. Joe, the eccentric blond drummer, held his drumsticks aloft with a bemused expression. Matt, the keyboard player, was glancing at his set list. And in the center of the stage, Ike Ligon, Lilith's musical idol, looked at her and grinned.

She couldn't help it. Lilith screamed, along with every other girl and three quarters of the boys in the audience.

"This is so cool," she said to Cam.

He just smiled and gave her hand a squeeze. There was no one Lilith would rather be here with than Cam. This moment was perfect.

Ike locked eyes with her and said, "This one's for Lilith. It's called 'Vows.'"

Lilith blinked. She'd never written a song called "Vows." Her heart started racing, and she didn't know what to do. Should she tell someone there'd been a mistake? Maybe Ike had simply gotten the title wrong?

But by then it was too late. The band began to play.

"I give my arms to you
I give my eyes to you
I give my scars to you
And all my lies to you
What will you give
To me?"

The song was beautiful, but Lilith hadn't written it. And yet, as she listened, chords began to jump out to her in the fraction of a second before the band played them, as if she could anticipate where the song was going.

Before she realized what she was doing, the words were in her mouth and she was singing, too—because somehow she knew "Vows" was meant to be a duet:

"I give my heart to you
I give the sky to you
But if I give my speed to you
I cannot fly to you
What will you give
To me?"

A boy's voice filled her ears, singing along to this song she somehow knew from deep within her soul. Only it wasn't Ike.

It was Cam. There were tears in his eyes as he sang, his gaze locked on Lilith.

"I give a heart to you
I give a soul to you
I give a start to you
Do you know what to do?"

Why did it feel like they had sung this song together before?

They couldn't have. But when she closed her eyes, a vision came to her: the two of them seated before a body of water. It was not the fading trickle of Rattlesnake

Creek but a swelling, crystal river somewhere far away and long ago.

She'd just written the song, for him. She wanted him to like it. She could see in his eyes that he did. She could feel it in his kiss when he bent down and graced her lips with his. There was no strain between them, no resentment, and no fear. Wherever, whenever they were, she had loved him deeply, and they had been practicing for something—a wedding.

Their wedding.

Somewhere, long ago, Cam and Lilith had been engaged.

Lilith opened her eyes.

The Four Horsemen were just finishing the song. The guitar cut out, and Ike sang the final line a cappella.

"What will you give to me?"

The crowd burst into applause. Lilith stood still.

Cam took a step toward her. "Lilith?"

Her body shook. Light exploded before Lilith's eyes, blinding her.

When she could see again, her gown looked different: whiter, and without Arriane's alterations. Lilith blinked, making out what looked like a dark cave at sunset, the sky fiery with streaks of red and orange. She was still facing Cam, just as she'd been facing him onstage.

She clutched her hands over her heart, not understanding why it hurt so much. She spoke words in a language that was new to her, but that she somehow understood.

"The night you left, I dreamt I taught a flock of nightingales a love song, so they could find you and sing you home to me. Now I am the nightingale who has traveled all this way. I still love you, Cam. *Come back to me.*"

"No."

His answer was so clean, like the slice of the sharpest knife, that Lilith doubled over in pain. She gasped and rubbed her eyes—and when she drew her hands away . . .

The cave was gone, the sunset gone. Cam was gone.

Lilith was in a dismal shack, leaning against the wall. She recognized the unmade bed, the wooden bucket full of rancid water and days-old dirty dishes in the corner. Flies the size of hummingbirds swarmed streaks of lard on the plates. Everything was familiar, though she didn't know why.

"I told you to clean the dishes," a woman's voice said in a slow drawl. "Ain't gon' tell you again."

Somehow, Lilith knew that on the other side of this wall, a metal wire had been strung between two nails. She knew that she could play that wire, could make it sound like a fine instrument of many strings. She yearned to be outside with it, to feel the sting of copper on her calloused fingers.

"I told you, you can't play that dumb wire until you clean the dishes," the woman said, picking up a knife. "I've had it with that wire."

"No, please!" Lilith shrieked as she raced outside after the woman.

Lilith wasn't fast enough, and the woman carelessly cut the wire in two. Lilith fell to her knees and wept.

She closed her eyes again, and when she opened them, she was straddling a horse bounding across a frozen road in a hilly countryside. She grasped the reins, holding on for her life. Her breath fogged before her, and her skin blazed, and she knew that she was dying from a fever. She was a gypsy, sick and starving, dressed in rags, expected to sing love songs in exchange for crumbs.

She blinked again, and again, and each time Lilith remembered another hellish experience. She was always a struggling musician, miserable and doomed. There was Opera Lilith, sleeping in an alley behind the theater. Orchestra Lilith, tormented by a cruel conductor. Troubadour Lilith, starving in a medieval city. In every existence, worse than her poverty, the loneliness, and the abuse was the rage darkening her heart. In every existence, she loathed the world she inhabited. She wanted revenge.

Come back to me, she'd begged Cam.

No.

"Why!" She shouted the question she'd been too hopeless to ask every other day of her life until now. "Why?"

"Because"—a deafening hiss filled her ears—"we made a deal."

"What deal?" she asked.

Lilith opened her eyes. She was back onstage in Crossroads. The audience was motionless, terrified. It was as if time had stopped. The Four Horsemen were gone, and in their place Luc was standing in the middle of the stage.

"Lilith!" she heard Cam scream. He rushed toward her, but Luc held him back and beckoned to Lilith to step toward him.

She looked around at all of the frozen faces in the audience. "What's happening?"

"Here," Luc said into the microphone. She stepped toward him, and he handed her a glass ball—a snow globe. "The missing piece."

Lilith held it up. Inside was a miniature cliff jutting out over a tumultuous ocean. A tiny figurine—a girl in a white wedding gown—stood at the cliff's edge. The ground beneath Lilith swayed, and then she *was* the girl in white, inside the snow globe. She scrambled backward, away from the edge. She could smell the churning ocean, and beyond it she could see the glass encasing everything.

"Take a good, hard look at your future, Lilith," a voice behind her said.

She turned to see Luc, reclining on a rock.

"Without Cam," he said, "what do you have to live for?"

"Nothing."

He nodded at the water. "Then it's time."

Luc looked the same as he did in Crossroads, but Lilith understood that he was more. The boy before her was the devil, and he'd made her an offer she'd been too lovesick to refuse.

"I brought you to him," he said, "and you did your best. But Cam didn't want you, did he?"

"No," she said miserably.

"You must hold up your end of our agreement."

"I'm scared," she said. "What happens after—"

"Leave that to me."

She gazed into the sea and knew she had no choice.

She didn't jump so much as lean forward—into the air, and then into the water. She let it take her. When the waves crashed over her, Lilith didn't try to rise above them. What was there left to try for? Her heart was heavy, like an anvil, and she sank.

Then she was at the bottom, in the filtered light, alone. Black water filled her nose and mouth, her stomach, her lungs.

Her soul.

⚜

Back onstage, Lilith faced Cam.

She could sense Jean Rah, Luis, and the other performers from the battle, all gathered around them. The audience was dumbstruck, waiting to see what Lilith would do. But she could focus only on Cam. There was a wild look in his eyes.

"What did you see?"

"I saw . . . *you.*" Her voice trembled. "And . . ."

It hit Lilith then that the rumors going around Trumbull about the girl Cam had driven to suicide had been true. "The girl who killed herself," she said, her voice echoing across the Colosseum, "was me."

"Oh, Lilith," Cam said, shutting his eyes.

"I took my life because I loved you," she said as the facts of her past began to resurface, "and you—"

"I loved you, too," he said. "I still—"

"No. I begged you. I bared my soul to you. And you told me 'no.' "

Cam winced. "I was trying to spare you."

"But you couldn't. I'd already made a deal." She turned and pointed a single, shaking finger at Luc. "With him."

The skin around Cam's eyes tightened. "I didn't know—"

"I was certain that if I could just find you, I could win you back."

Cam closed his eyes. "I was a fool."

"But I was wrong," Lilith said. "What I just saw . . . those other lives I've lived . . ."

Cam nodded. "Other Hells."

Other Hells? Lilith froze. Did he mean—

This life, *her* life, was not actually a life at all?

All the horrors she'd been forced to suffer, she had suffered because of Cam. Because long ago he had tricked her into falling in love with him. And she'd been stupid enough to fall into the same trap again.

Suddenly, Lilith was so furious she could barely stand.

"This whole time, I've been in Hell?" She stepped away from Cam, out of the spotlight and into darkness. "Because of *you*."

TWENTY

HEAVEN IS WAITING

CAM

Five Minutes

Cam stood onstage before Lilith, beneath the twirling lights from the disco ball, feeling the gaze of a thousand teenagers, and above them, the eyes of a million demons waiting in the sky.

He reached toward Lilith. "There's still hope."

She stepped away. "*You're* the reason I've suffered so much. *You're* the reason I've been so angry and sad. *You're* the reason I hate my life." Her eyes filled with tears.

She was right. It *was* Cam's fault. He'd rejected Lilith because he'd been too afraid to tell her the truth.

"I'm so stupid. I thought you showing up in Crossroads was the best thing that ever happened to me, but it was the worst thing happening to me all over again."

"Please," Cam begged. He held out his hands to her, but was shocked by what he saw: his fingers were gnarled, his nails thick and yellow. "You don't understand—"

"For the first time, I understand everything. I believed in our love, and you didn't, but I was the one who paid the ultimate price." She looked out over the walls of the Colosseum, where it opened up to the sky. Flames rose in the distance, licking the night. "Why did you come back? To taunt me? To delight in my suffering?" She flung her arms out, tears streaming down her face. "Are you satisfied?"

"I came because I love you." Cam's voice trembled. "I thought you were dead. I never knew you were in Hell. As soon as I learned, I came for you." His eyes began to burn. "I made a deal with Lucifer, and I've spent these past fifteen days falling in love with you all over again, hoping you could fall in love with me again, too."

"So that was the bet." Lilith looked at Cam with disgust. "You haven't changed at all. You're just as selfish as ever."

"She's right," a voice boomed from everywhere as a hot wind swirled across the stage. Cam spun around to find Luc stripped of his youthful mortal guise. The true Lucifer stood in his place, chest heaving, eyes red with evil. With each breath, Lucifer's body swelled; he grew larger and larger until he dwarfed the stage and eclipsed the moon.

The audience screamed and tried to flee, only to find that every exit had been locked and bolted. Some students tried scaling the walls, others huddled together, crying. Every effort, Cam knew, was futile in the face of the devil.

Lucifer's fingers sharpened into razor claws the size of butchers' knives. Reptilian black scales coated his body, and his features were jagged and devoid of mercy. He tipped his head back, closed his eyes, and released his tarnished green-gold wings.

"Lucifer," Lilith gasped in recognition.

"Yes, Lilith," Lucifer bellowed, his voice slithering into every crevice in Crossroads. "I am the maker of your misery."

The other student performers were long gone; they were now trembling somewhere in the audience, leaving the stage empty of everyone but Cam, Lilith, and Lucifer, and, he now realized, Jean and Luis. His two bandmates stood back, watching from the edge of the stage, their shoulders touching, their faces pale and horrified. Cam wished there was something he could do to console them, but he knew the horrors of the evening were only going to get worse.

The stars pulsed and swelled as Lucifer's legion of demons flew closer, growing discernible in the darkness, streaming in through the glassy firmament, swirling darkly, directly over Lilith.

"Even now," Lucifer said, "Cam lies to you, withholding his true nature from you. Behold!"

The devil pointed at Cam and suddenly an insuppressible urge came over him. His shoulders felt as if they were engulfed in flames as Lucifer forced open Cam's wings. They unfurled with a sound like tearing vinyl. For all eternity, Cam had known only the glorious beauty of his wings. Tonight, he looked back and gasped.

They were hideous, leathery, limp, and charred, like the wings of the lowest demons in hell. He felt the bones inside his body twisting painfully, his skin pulling and tightening. He screamed, then looked at his hands—which had now turned into scaly claws.

He touched his face, his chest, and knew his transformation was complete. Not even Lilith would be able to deny his monstrous appearance—

And suddenly, Cam was glad of that. He would hide nothing from her, ever again.

"Long ago," he said, feeling tears in the corners of his eyes, "I was afraid you wouldn't love me if you knew who I really was."

She studied his aging demon's face, his decrepit body, his repulsive wings. "You never even gave me the chance to love the real you," she said. "You didn't trust that I might have accepted you."

"You're right—"

"I *loved* you, Cam. I wanted to marry you, and that meant every part of you, the good and the bad, the known and the unknown."

"I wanted to marry you, too. But I couldn't do it in the temple as you wished—"

"Screw the temple," Lilith said. "Who cares about that?"

"You did," he said. "It mattered to you, but I dismissed it so that I wouldn't have to tell you what I am. I tried to make it your fault, but I was the one who backed out of our marriage."

She stared at him, her expression strained with hurt.

"I knew you could never forgive me," he said, "so I ran away. I thought I had lost you for good. But then I found this second chance, and I came here to redeem myself. This time with you has shown me that my love for you is bigger than my fear. My love for you is bigger than anything I know."

A tear rolled down his cheek. He closed his eyes. He had so much more to say and so little time for it to matter.

Lilith shrieked.

Something acrid singed Cam's nose, and he remembered what had happened in the library the last time he had cried. He wiped his cheeks, but it was too late. Beneath his feet he saw the hole his tear had made when it hit the stage. Black smoke billowed from it. Acid ate away at the stage, forming a crater that yawned and stretched until it spread like a canyon between Cam and Lilith.

"Say goodbye, Lilith," Lucifer said with a sneer.

Cam leapt into the air, spreading his poor, feeble wings. All he needed to do was close the distance between himself and Lilith. She shrieked and scrambled backward, toward Lucifer and away from the expanding crater.

Cam landed at her feet. The end was coming. He would lose. He had not convinced her to love him again, so there was only one thing left to do.

He fell to his knees before the devil and raised his hands in supplication. "Take me."

Lucifer smirked. "We shall be very busy."

Cam shook his head. "Not as your second in command."

Lucifer roared. "Our deal was clear."

"This is a *new* deal," Cam said, rising to shield Lilith as the stage shook beneath their feet and the lip of the crater approached his boots. It was nearly midnight. This was his last chance. "I stay down here in exile. I take her place in Hell, as your subject. And you set her free."

"No!" Lilith shouted. She grabbed Cam by his jacket collar. "Why would you do that—sacrifice yourself for me?"

"I'd do anything for you." Cam reached for her hand, amazed when she didn't pull away.

The crowd's screams grew deafening as the crater made by Cam's tear reached into the audience, swallowing students by the dozen. But Cam couldn't see them: The air had grown thick with smoke, and everything was cloudy and chaotic.

His heart raced. He had to hurry. "I'll do whatever you want, go wherever you want me to go, suffer any punishment you want me to," he said to Lucifer. "Only free Lilith from this Hell."

As he spoke, he noticed a change in Lilith's expression. Her features softened, and her eyes grew wide. Even when the walls around them stretched and twisted and started to cave in, Lilith didn't take her eyes off Cam.

"You *have* changed," Lilith said. "You have given me so much these past two weeks."

"I should have given you more." Cam reached for her, trying to find her hands through the thick, dark smoke.

"I'm not going to let you take my place here in Hell," Lilith said. "Wherever you are is where I want to be."

A well of tears fell from Cam's eyes, streaming down his cheeks and burning away the world around them. He couldn't have stopped them if he'd tried. "I love you, Lilith."

"I love you, Cam."

He embraced her as the crater grew and the stage disintegrated beneath them. Shrieks erupted from the audience as the thick walls of the new Colosseum shuddered and collapsed.

"What's happening?" Lilith gasped.

"Hold on to me," he said, gripping her tightly.

"Mom!" Lilith screamed in horror, gazing in the direction where the audience had been, though by then it was impossible to see her family, to see anything more than a few inches away. Her lungs filled with smoke, and she began to cough. "Bruce!"

Cam had no words for her loss. How could he explain that everyone Lilith knew was one of the devil's pawns, that her freedom came at the price of losing them? He cupped her head and held her close.

"No!" she screamed and wept against his chest.

The Colosseum and the school beside it disappeared behind great plumes of smoke, the structures curling like burning paper. Moments later, everything around Cam and Lilith had been consumed. The world became a heap of ash that fluttered, then blew away.

The parking lot, the school, the desolate stand of carob trees marking the entrance to Rattlesnake Creek, the roads leading nowhere, the night sky that had inspired so many songs—all of it was on fire. The flames in the hills had closed in, encircling Cam and Lilith. The flames of Hell.

He focused on holding her tightly, shielding her from the sight and from the demons who flew overhead in a frenzied mass of golden wings.

A flash of silver entered Cam's vision. Arriane swooped before him, her glamorous iridescent wings as bright as starlight.

"Arriane!" Cam called out. "I thought you'd gone."

"Abandon you in the final moments?" Arriane said. "Never."

"Glorious," Lilith whispered at the sight of Arriane's wings. "You're an angel."

"At your service." Arriane grinned and bowed. "Cambriel, you pulled it off. With a little help." She nudged Lilith. "You guys smoked it."

Cam held Lilith closer. "I let you go in Canaan. It was my biggest mistake, bigger than joining Lucifer's ranks. Losing your love is my only regret."

"And finding your love is my redemption," Lilith said. She touched his chest, his face. "I don't care what you look like. You're beautiful to me."

"Touching," Lucifer said, swooping above them, flames licking the backs of his wings. "Touching nonsense."

Cam shouted up at Lucifer. "We fulfilled your terms! She loves me. I love her. We have earned our freedom."

The devil was silent, and Cam noticed something strange: his wings looked thin, almost translucent. Through their fibers, Cam could see the twisting flames behind him.

"Lucifer," he hollered. "Let us go."

Lucifer threw his head back as his wings curled and singed at the edges. The devil's form grew paper-thin, caving in upon itself. His claws flexed toward Cam one moment, then curled and disintegrated the next. His mouth opened, and the wretched sound of mirthless laughter made Cam and Lilith wince.

Soon, his body shrank and faded, until he was nothing more than an infinitesimal black hole in the center of the ring of fire.

"Is he gone?" Lilith asked.

Cam stared at the sky in disbelief. "For now," he said.

Then an unholy din came from above. Lilith covered her ears. Cam looked up at a charge of demons, a stampede of fallen angels, black as the soul of midnight, rocketing through the sky. They headed for where the devil had just been, led by Roland's mottled black-and-gold wings. Cam had never seen such wild heedlessness as appeared on Roland's face.

"Which way did he go?" Roland said.

"Into darkness," Cam said. "Like he always does."

Arriane slung an arm around Roland. "Ro, will you marry me?" Then she blinked and shook her head quickly. "Don't answer that. It was the thrill of victory talking. Forget I said anything."

"What's this all about?" Cam asked Roland, pointing at the army behind him. "What are you doing?"

The demon raised a dark eyebrow. "I'm going after Lucifer."

"What?" Cam asked.

"The revolution has been a long time coming. You

know that better than anyone." He nodded at Lilith, then reached out to shake Cam's hand. "Hey, brother?"

"Yeah?"

"Check your wings."

Cam glanced to his left, then his right. His wings were thickening, spreading, leathery pieces of them sloughing away as strong new filaments grew in. The charred bits flaked and fell away.

And underneath, Cam's wings were white.

Only here and there at first, but it was spreading. He stretched out his arms, reaching for the stars, and beheld his transformation. Within moments, his wings had been restored. Not to the legendary golden glamour to which he had grown accustomed, but to their original incandescence. White. Strong. Brilliant.

Allied to nothing but love.

"Thank you," he whispered.

Cautiously, he touched his hair—thick and lustrous again. His body had returned to its lithe, muscular form, and his skin was smooth and pale once more.

He held his breath as Lilith touched his wings. She ran her fingers over their ridges, flattening her palms against them, her nails dancing up to the most sensitive tissue just behind his neck. He trembled with pleasure. Everything seemed limitless.

"Cam," she whispered.

"Lilith," he said. "I love you."

Suddenly, the whole world went white. Cam felt pressure around his body, and then his feet touched down on the ground.

He and Lilith were back in the food court where Cam had first made his deal with the devil. Someone had cleaned the place up, taken out the trash, restored the burned-out food-court signs. Lilith gazed around her. Cam could tell she recognized Aevum but wasn't exactly sure how.

"Am I dreaming?" she asked.

Cam shook his head, took her hand, and sat down next to her at the nearest table. There was a brown tray on its center. A snow globe sat on top. Both of them gazed into it and saw the burning ruins of Crossroads.

"I think you just woke up," Cam said.

His mind traveled to Lucinda and Daniel, and he thought he knew how they might have felt in their last moments as angels, after they had finally made their choice and before they started over.

"I always knew there was something special about you," Lilith said. "You're an angel."

"A fallen angel," Cam corrected her. "And I'm yours."

"Everything we knew is behind us." Her eyes were tinged with sorrow at the life she'd left behind, but her smile was full of hope. "What happens now?"

Cam leaned forward and kissed her softly. "Oh, Lilith. We haven't yet begun."

ACKNOWLEDGMENTS

With special thanks to Rod Bryan, Barry Poynter, Emma Angeline Branch, Alex Piazza, Brooks Tipton, Ben Hubbard, Jill Johnson, the Bass family, Madelyn Albright, and Chevy Impala.